TUBE

TUBE. Copyright © 2019 by Ksenia Anske. All rights reserved. Printed in the United States of America. No part of this book may be used or reproduced in any manner whatsoever without written permission except in the case of brief quotations embodied in critical articles and reviews.

Published by Ksenia Anske
www.kseniaanske.com

FIRST EDITION

Edited by Sarah Grace Liu (www.threefatesediting.com)
Proofread by Spencer Hamilton (www.nerdywordsmith.com)
Cover design by Vera Golosova (www.veragolosova.pro)
Formatted by Sandeep Likhar (www.likharpublishing.com)

Library of Congress Cataloging-in-Publication Data has been applied for.

ISBN 978-0-9861979-5-6 (paperback)
ISBN 978-0-9861979-6-3 (ebook)

To Little Olesya—
wherever you are.

TABLE OF CONTENTS

AUTHOR'S NOTE

Dear Reader,

What you're about to read is an unusual ghost story.

It began with a train.

In 2014 I won the Amtrak Residency Program. There were twenty-four of us winners. Twenty-four writers selected from over 16,000 applicants. As our prize, we got to ride the train and to write whatever we wanted.

In my application, I foolishly promised that if I won, I'd write a novel about a train. True to my word, I did exactly that. What I didn't know was that it'd take me five years, ten drafts, and over a million discarded words before it came to this: a short, spartan, and outright skeletal ghost story about a ghost toy train engine—TUBE—and a Russian ballerina caught up in its wake.

Not all is what it seems.

I went through periods of hating this story so much that I wanted to give up. I wanted to scrap the whole thing. I wanted to shelve it. It was only some quiet inner voice that kept me going. The voice of my personal toy ghost. You know what I mean. We all have those, from the dark corners of our childhood.

But most of all, this is a story of betrayal set in the cold Soviet winter of 1989, on the train from Moscow to

Simferopol and in the Black Sea resort town Alupka. The places that hold memories. Ghosts of memories. Ghosts of . . .

Well, you'll see.

Get your ticket ready. And beware. This is a ride not for the faint-hearted. If the dark, forgotten alleys of your mind scare you—if you're afraid to turn the key to them and step inside—best close this book now and read something else. Something happy. Something sunny. This is not a sweet bedtime story. It's not even a proper ghost story.

As I said, it's an unusual ghost story in that it's not a ghost story at all. It's real, but only as much as you'll allow it to be. Like those passing shapes behind the window of the moving train. What are they?

Do you really want to know?

Ksenia Anske
Seattle, Washington
September 2019

PS: The subject matter is very hard to talk about. I struggled with it. I struggled with putting it into words that would make it easy for you to digest—digest this bitter pill—until it was too late. You'll see that the writing is very much matter-of-fact. Over the five years of rewriting it, and rewriting it, and rewriting it *yet again*, I removed all meat and fat and left only bones. And even those I have polished to the point of being almost transparent. Immaterial. Ghostlike. I hope you enjoy this style. It's designed to let you finish this book in one reading. It is my hope you have no dreams after this. I'd worry that if you had any, you'd wake up screaming.

How strange it is, how inexpressibly strange, that behind this wall, behind this very wall, a man is sitting on the floor, stretching out his long legs in orange boots, an expression of malice on his face.

We need only drill a hole in the wall and look through it and immediately we would see this mean-spirited man sitting there.

But we shouldn't think about him. What is he anyway? Is he not after all a portion of death in life, materialized out of our own conception of emptiness?

— Daniil Kharms, *Russian Absurd: Selected Writings*

"He's the strongest man in the world."

"Man, yes," said Pippi, "but I am the strongest girl in the world, remember that."

— Astrid Lindgren, *Pippi Longstocking*

PROLOGUE

"Do you want to play TUBE?"

"Yes, Papa."

"You won't tell Mama?"

"No, Papa."

"That's my girl. That's my little ballerina. Come here. That's a good girl. Let's lay down the tracks. What's the matter, silly? Why are you crying?"

"I'm not."

"Come on. Papa loves you. You know Papa loves you, don't you?"

"Yes."

"Yes, what?"

"Yes, I know you love me."

"Never forget that."

"I won't."

"Good. Now, let's lay down the tracks."

LAYING DOWN THE TRACKS

MOSCOW-TULA
5 February 1989
10:27

Olesya Belaya sat in a train compartment, naked. Today, this hour, this minute, would be the last of her cursed virginity. Tomorrow she'd look at herself in the mirror and say, "Happy twenty-first. You're normal. You had sex."

The man she'd chosen to do it with was her Bolshoi Ballet partner and boyfriend of three months, Dima Rumyantsev. They'd attempted sex before—once in Olesya's apartment on her sofa, and twice on the squeaky bed in Dima's rented room. They got as far as getting undressed. Then Olesya would freeze into a porcelain doll that Dima said he was afraid to touch. In case she broke to bits. So they decided to give it a rest.

The very next day, their ballet mistress, Alla Borisovna Krysanova, strolled into the studio with an air of importance. The renowned Bolshoi prima was still graceful and sharp for her sixty-two years but was looking more and more like a rat. Old Bitch, they called her behind her back. She straightened her back and announced a *Swan Lake* tour to Simferopol in two weeks. To Simferopol, of all places! They'd be taking the train.

While the dancers grumbled, Olesya hatched a plan. As soloists, she and Natasha Ryzhik qualified for a luxe two-bunk compartment. She'd ask Natasha to hang out with the girls while she and Dima—

Well . . .

This snowy morning, when riding the metro to Kursky station, Olesya whispered to him, "Let's try one more time."

"You sure?"

"Yeah. A new place. You know . . . maybe it'll work."

Dima nodded.

But now that she was sitting here, naked, watching him unbutton his pants, an unexpected calamity wrecked her plans once more.

He took off his briefs and reached for her.

Olesya stared.

In the place of his erect penis, there was TUBE.

Olesya's mouth dried up.

TUBE was a toy train engine from the train set Papa had given her on her fifth birthday. It stuck out from Dima's crotch like it belonged there, its metal body painted bright red. And it pointed at her.

Olesya scooted back on the bunk until she hit the wall.

The round headlamp lit up, the whistle blared, the tiny wheels started spinning. TUBE rolled forward, pointing between her legs.

Olesya thought she'd die. Thought it'd skewer her. Kill her.

Her breath stopped in her throat, and her heart seemed to stop beating. She couldn't be seeing what she was seeing. Couldn't. It was long gone, lost, forgotten. Yet there it was, as if mocking her. Real.

There were two ways she could deal with it: close her eyes and pretend she never saw it, or grab it to make sure it was real. She grabbed it, jerked her hand away, then screamed.

"What's wrong?" Dima said.

"TUBE," she said. Her voice cracked.

He sat next to her.

She looked at his pale body, his straw-blond hair that contrasted with his slanted brown eyes. Those eyes, he had told her, were his father's favorite reason to beat his mother while she was alive. For cheating on him with some Tatar trash.

"TUBE?"

Olesya explained.

"My *what*?" He looked down at himself. "A . . . *what*? A toy train engine?"

"Well, it was," she said. "I mean, it's gone now. I don't know how it got there, but I saw it. I saw it, okay?" Her skin goosed, and she hugged herself.

Dima draped a blanket over her shoulders. "You cold?"

"No."

"What's wrong?"

She looked at him. "What's *wrong*?"

"Yeah."

She looked away.

"Olesya."

"Never mind."

"No, please. What just happened?"

She sighed. "Why do you ask?"

"I don't know." He shrugged. "You said something strange about—"

"Strange?"

"Yeah, strange."

"Of course. Strange. I get it."

"Come on, help me out here. What am I supposed to think?"

"What do you want from me?"

He recoiled. "I don't want anything. I just—"

"You just want to make me feel better."

"Sure. What's wrong with that?"

"Nothing." She turned away.

They sat in silence for some time.

The train wheels beat their tempo. The snow rolled behind the window. An occasional telephone pole passed by, then it was snow again. Cold. White.

Dima got up and started putting on his clothes.

Olesya looked at him, alarmed. "Where are you going?"

"Just getting dressed."

"Don't," she said.

"Don't what?"

"Don't go."

He looked at her.

She dropped her face in her hands. "Please. I want . . . I want to have sex with you."

"You want to have sex with me."

"Yes."

He sighed. "All right."

"Right now."

"All right, all right. I'm here." He sat back down.

"It's my birthday tomorrow."

"I know."

"I'm turning twenty-one."

"Yeah, I know."

"No, you don't understand. It's not that. It's just . . . I want to wake up and look in the mirror and say, 'Happy birthday, Olesya. You're no longer a virgin.' "

"Okay," he said.

Olesya said nothing.

"Can I ask why it's so important—"

Blood rushed to her face. "Go! Just go!" she shrieked. The force of her voice surprised her. Where did it come from? "I'm sorry, I—I don't know why I said, I really don't. Ignore it. Dima—"

He moved back, silent. Then he stood and stepped into his shoes.

"Dima, please."

He took hold of the door latch.

"Let's try it. One more time. Please." She lay down and spread her legs, waiting.

He looked at her and through her, motionless. His face lost color. "I need to get some fresh air. Be right back."

"No, you won't," she said.

He flashed her an angry look. "Why? Why did you just say that? Why do you always have to be so negative?"

"I'm not."

"I'm going."

"No. Please." She reached out to him.

He passed a hand through his hair and gazed at the floor. "Look, Olesya. The truth is . . . well, I can't. Do you hear what I'm saying?"

"What?"

"I can't, okay? Not like—I can't just . . . *fuck* you."

She winced.

"I want to make love to you. And I want you to make love to me back, not lie there like . . . I don't know."

She sat up and crossed her arms. "Say it. Go ahead."

He pulled at the latch.

"Like a doll. Is that what you were going to say?"

"I'm going."

"Dima." She jumped up, grabbed his arm. "Please. I need to tell you something . . ."

He waited.

Their eyes met.

She stood shivering, biting her lip.

"Can it wait?" he asked.

The train heaved, swung around a curve, and entered a tunnel.

Olesya stumbled and dropped on the bunk. The lights winked out for a few moments, to pitch-black.

When they came back on, Dima was gone.

Olesya sat still for what felt like a very long time. Then she got up, walked to the door, and banged her head against the mirror with methodical repetition until blood gushed out of her nose. She paused, but not to wipe it. Blood had never stopped her. What stopped her was what she saw by her feet.

TUBE.

11:09

The moment Olesya bent over to pick up TUBE, it vanished.

She looked and felt about the floor: nothing.

She folded up her bunk and inspected the storage bin. It contained her old backpack and her tattered dance bag.

She folded up Natasha's bunk. In the bin sat the two new suitcases her parents brought her from Bulgaria. Made from real leather, not like Olesya's cheap junk.

No TUBE.

"Shit," she muttered, folding the bunks back down. She stood still for some time, then got dressed, wiped her face with a towel, and sat by the window.

"There is no TUBE," she said. "You lost it, remember?"

She did, only too well.

Olesya pressed her cheek to the cold glass, thinking about her father, Grigory Vasilievich Bely, the way she remembered him before he was killed.

He worked as a car attendant and had a weakness for all things foreign. He knew a passenger who routinely smuggled in goods from America. Papa helped him hide them, and one day the passenger gave him a gift—for his little daughter. At least this was Mama's version of the story. How true it was,

Olesya didn't know, but the toy train Papa presented to her on her fifth birthday was true enough.

"This is a very special toy, Olesya," he said. "Every child's envy. In the Soviet Union we don't have toys like that."

Olesya didn't understand the word *envy*, but she was too afraid to ask. When Papa got excited, his eyes bulged out, and it was best to keep quiet.

"Feel the quality." He grabbed her hand and slid it over the smooth metal body. "Feel it. It's from America. It's called TUBE: Trans-Urban Blitz Express." He pointed to the letters stamped on the side. The engine was painted red, and it had a big headlamp like a mean blind eye.

Papa pressed it into her hand. "Say TUBE."

"TUBE."

"Trans-Urban—"

"Trans-Urban . . ."

"—Blitz Express."

". . . Blitz Express," Olesya dutifully repeated, taking care to pronounce it exactly as he said.

Papa smiled. "That's my girl. Want to play with it?"

Six years later he was killed in an accident.

It was an unusually cold winter, and his own train had stopped a few kilometers from Simferopol. He was hacking the ice off the wheels of the last car. The official explanation was that he didn't hear the freight train until it was too late. It slammed into the car, telescoped through it, and killed Papa and twelve more unfortunate passengers.

The real version? Who knew. They were never told.

A month after Papa's funeral, Mama collected all his things and threw them in the trash. And in August of that same year, Baba Zina—Papa's mother—died from a heart attack. Mama and Olesya took a train to Simferopol, and from there a taxi to Alupka.

At her funeral, people were saying that Baba Zina died from grief. Olesya asked Uncle Shurik how one could die from grief. He told her Baba Zina never felt grief once in her life. As her son, he knew it. People were just afraid to say what she really died from.

"What's that?" Olesya asked.

"Meanness," he said.

Three days later they returned to Moscow, and TUBE was missing.

Olesya peeled her cheek away from the glass and looked down at her hands.

The terror she felt when she saw Dima's penis as TUBE had already started to fade. She was good at forgetting. She'd forget this too. She'd talk to Natasha to distract herself. Better yet, she'd ask her how she did it. How did she sleep with all those men and have them run after her like dogs, tongues lolling out? And what an orgasm felt like anyway. How could she come ten times in a row?

"If I come, maybe Dima will love me. He doesn't love me right now. He doesn't even want me."

The train started slowing. The engineer announced a five-minute stop at Tula station.

Olesya put on her coat, grabbed her hat, and went out to go look for Natasha.

TULA STATION
11:31

The aisle rang with sharp, impatient voices. Passengers bundled up to their ears pushed their way through, dragging behind them fat suitcases and silent children. Olesya squeezed past them, hopped off the train, and pulled on her hat, scanning the snow-swept platform.

Local babushkas huddled by the station building, selling steaming food.

Passengers stood in a queue at the telephone booth.

But no Natasha.

Olesya walked along the platform.

She'll roll her eyes when she hears. She'll tell me it was my fault. And I'll tell her she's right. Then I'll ask her how to seduce him. She'll laugh, of course. So what. Let her. As long as—

An angry voice broke her from her thoughts.

"Hurry up, will you?"

An attendant woman ushered a man and a little girl into a car. The girl was no older than five, wearing a heavy coat. She tripped and fell.

Her father yanked her up by the arm. "Get up. Get *up*, I said! What a klutz."

Olesya's stomach shrunk.

The girl turned to look at her, tears rolling down her cheeks. Her father shoved her in the back, and they climbed inside.

A loudspeaker cracked to life. "Attention. The Moscow–Simferopol train is departing in three minutes. I repeat . . ."

Olesya rushed back toward her car.

"Olesya!" Natasha caught up with her. She sucked on a cigarette and blew smoke through her lips. Her fur coat was unbuttoned. Her auburn hair sparkled with snowflakes, her cheeks the perfect pink.

Olesya shivered. *How does she do it?*

No matter how cold it was, Natasha never wore hats. One day after ballet class—they were both thirteen—she had declared to Olesya that hair was a woman's sexiest feature. She'd read about it in a foreign magazine. A month later she had her first man, then her second, then her third.

She stopped hanging out with Olesya after that, and Olesya spent her evenings alone, dancing until her toes bled. Still, their friendship held. Natasha loved telling Olesya the details of her adventures, and Olesya loved to listen. Together they graduated from ballet school and got accepted into the Bolshoi Theatre troupe. They became soloists, went on tours. But while Olesya quietly worked, Natasha enjoyed what Olesya couldn't: Alla Borisovna's patronage, audience admiration, loving parents, and plenty of sex.

Then, in December, Dima Rumyantsev, a gifted dancer from Leningrad, joined Bolshoi, and for the first time in her life Natasha found her charms ignored.

"It's not *him* who doesn't want *me*," she told Olesya. "It's *me* who doesn't want *him*. Get it? He's just not my type."

A week later, Olesya and Dima were dating.

"Well?" Natasha asked.

Olesya watched her breath turn white. The words she had prepared evaporated. "Well, nothing."

"You're kidding me."

Olesya shook her head.

"You mean, you kicked me out of our compartment"—Natasha blew smoke in her face—"for *nothing*?"

Olesya looked down, cheeks burning. The pit of her stomach roiled. She froze, unable to think, to speak, to move. Whatever it was that made her feel this way could hold her in its grip for hours, sometimes for days. The only way out was to say something, anything, even if it didn't make sense. Even if it was stupid. Make a noise. Make her tongue move.

"How do you seduce a guy?" she blurted.

"What?"

"How do you seduce a guy?"

Natasha laughed. "What, Dima doesn't know where to stick it in?"

Olesya bit her lip. How could Natasha talk about sex so easily? And why couldn't she, Olesya, do the same? What was wrong with her?

"How do you seduce a guy?" she repeated. "Any guy. Not just Dima."

Natasha blew out smoke. "You're funny. You think I can give you instructions, and you can do it?"

"Sure. Why not? You do it all the time."

"All right. Here is how. You tell a guy you want to sleep with him. You go to his apartment. You take off your clothes, lie on the bed, spread your legs—"

"Natasha."

"What?"

"It's not funny."

"What did I tell you?"

Olesya sighed. "I don't like the taste of it."

"She doesn't like the taste of it. Jesus, devotchka. It's just vodka." Natasha took Olesya by the arm. "Fine. I'll do it for you. I'll sleep with him, and I'll tell you what he likes and what he doesn't like. Then you'll have your *instructions*."

Olesya stared at her.

"Attention," echoed the loudspeaker. "The Moscow–Simferopol train is departing from siding number one at eleven thirty-four—"

"Come on," Olesya said. "We'll be late."

"Relax, will you?" Natasha flicked her cigarette. "We've another minute."

"You can finish smoking once we're on. Please."

"They're not leaving without us."

"They will."

"Fine. Let them. They'll have to send a taxi to fetch us. Old Bitch will love this. It'll give her an excuse to fire someone important."

Olesya knocked the cigarette out of Natasha's hand. "How can you be so . . ."

"So *what*?" Natasha crossed her arms.

"I don't know . . . indifferent. Cold. Like you—"

"Cold? *I'm* cold? *You're* the cold one, devotchka. Not me. You got a gorgeous guy falling all over you, and you can't even let him fuck you."

Olesya flinched. "I thought he wasn't your type."

"Well, maybe I've changed my mind."

"Why?"

Natasha shrugged. "I don't know. Because I'm bored."

Olesya's mouth opened. "What're you going to do?"

"Seduce him for you." Natasha smiled. "Like you asked me to."

"I didn't—" The breath caught in Olesya's throat. "He's not a . . . you can't just—"

The train started moving.

"Come on!"

Natasha didn't move. "Why do you care? Are you in love with him?"

Olesya turned and ran. The snow squeaked under her boots. She reached her car, keeping pace. A short, portly attendant leaned out of the rear door, grabbed her hand, and pulled her in.

"Thank you," she said breathlessly.

"Oh, no no no. No need to thank me, dorogusha. It's all my fault." The attendant grinned, revealing a pair of golden teeth. "Got carried away kindling the boiler." He pulled the emergency brake, and the train jolted, hissing in protest. "You girls decided to stay behind, eh? I don't blame you. Better on the firm ground than on this boneshaker. Got to fetch your friend." He hopped out onto the platform with surprising agility.

Natasha strolled to him, unhurried, as though she never doubted someone would fetch her.

Dima jumped out of the front door. "What's going on?"

Olesya ducked back inside.

Where to hide? The thought of facing Natasha in their compartment made Olesya nauseated. She didn't feel like dropping in on any of the other girls either. They'd start asking questions. Where then? The dining car? It was closed until lunchtime.

Olesya's eyes fell on the gangway door. She'd freeze in there, standing between two moving cars, but it wouldn't be for long. She'd wait for them to leave. Then she could hang out in the vestibule, wait for lunch, and hang around in different cars until it was night.

She opened the door and slunk inside, her heart racing. The gangway was cold and cramped, and it stunk of piss. Olesya pressed her ear to the doorjamb, listening.

Feet stamped off the snow. A door opened, slammed shut.

"You've earned a kiss," Natasha's voice said.

Dima snickered. "No, thanks. I'm fine."

Don't look, Olesya thought. *Don't look!*

She turned and looked through the dark glass of the door's window.

Natasha wrapped her arms around Dima's neck. The train jerked forward, and Olesya's head slammed into the glass. She froze, scared stiff, but they didn't seem to notice.

"—heard you can't kiss for shit," Natasha was saying.

"Oh, yeah?" Dima looked amused. "Says who?"

"Says Olesya."

"She said that?" He peeled her arms off his neck.

Natasha touched his cheek. "You're so naïve. You've known her for, what, three months? I've known her half my life. We went to ballet school together. Who do you think advises her on all her *intimate* problems?"

"Intimate problems?" Dima said.

"Yeah. She asked me to help."

"Help. Really. Help with what?"

Natasha tilted her head. "She said you don't quite know how to . . . you know . . ."

Dima stepped away. "What do you want?"

Natasha laughed. "What's there to want from you? You can't fuck, you can't even—"

He grabbed her. Olesya could only see his back.

He's kissing her, she thought. *Oh God, he's kissing her.*

She stopped breathing. White, loud static filled her head. She watched Dima's back, watched him push Natasha into a corner, then she closed her eyes.

When she opened them, the vestibule was empty, and the attendant was looking at her through the glass, shaking his head.

TULA–ORYOL

11:42

Olesya flipped the lock. The handle rattled.

"Open the door," the attendant said.

She shook her head.

"I can't have you in there. It's against the rules."

"I want to be alone," Olesya said.

"What?" He cupped his ear to the window.

"Leave me alone!"

He looked at her, scratched his head. "Listen here, dorogusha. It's a serious offense, stopping the train. You know that. I'm taking the blame myself, for what it's worth, so your friend—what's her name, Natasha. So your Natasha won't get fined. And now this. I tell you, you stay in there and someone finds you half-dead from the cold? I lose my job."

Beneath Olesya, the ground flashed between the shifting plates and the swaying, creaking bellows. The wind pushed its fingers under her coat. She shivered.

"You'll freeze to death in there! Is that what you want?"

"I want to be alone!" she shouted.

"Fine. I give you five minutes. Five minutes, and I'm forcing the door open. Got that?" The car bumped over a gap in the tracks. The attendant crossed himself. "Damn boneshaker."

He ducked out of sight, then came back with a bucket of coal and knelt in front of the boiler. Olesya watched him open the small, blackened door and feed the coal into the fire. The orange glow danced on his face, making it look friendly. Fatherly almost.

Olesya sighed, unlocked the door, and stepped out.

The attendant grinned. "That was a fast five minutes."

"It's cold in there." She hugged herself.

"Told you." He got up with a groan and stretched out his hand. She gave hers. He shook it, his grip surprisingly soft and warm. "Temnenko, Yuri Fiodorovich. You can call me Yuri."

"Olesya."

"Pleased to meet you, Olesya. May I give you some advice?"

"Advice?"

"Don't hide from people. That's not how you fix a heartbreak."

"What are you talking about?"

Yuri studied her. "I saw you looking. Spying on those two. Who was it, your boyfriend?"

Olesya tried to get past him. "Excuse me."

Yuri blocked her way. "Hang on there, dorogusha—you don't mind if I call you 'dorogusha'? It's what I call my daughter, Lidochka. You remind me of her. Stubborn, that one, just like you. She's twelve, coming on thirteen, wants to be a ballerina." He smiled. "You're a ballerina, aren't you? From Bolshoi?"

"Yes," Olesya said. "If you'll excuse me—"

"Anyway. As I was saying, you need to talk it out. No good burying it inside you."

"I appreciate the advice, but I really need to go to my compartment."

"Sure, sure." He stepped aside and opened the door to the aisle. "Off you go. Keep lugging that dead weight inside you. I bet you're used to it by now. Bet you don't even notice."

Olesya stopped. "What dead weight?"

Yuri smiled. "Let me make you some tea, and we'll have us a little talk. A hot cup of tea is what you need right now. What do you say?"

"A hot cup of tea," Olesya repeated. It sounded perfect. She could hide in his room. Let him talk. She'd just sit there and nod. "Okay . . . I guess."

"There you go. That's what I'm talking about. This way."

He led her into his compartment. It was small and narrow, with only one bunk on the side. "I won't be a minute."

Olesya unbuttoned her coat and sat by the table.

Yuri promptly returned with two glasses of steaming tea, handed one to Olesya, and perched on a stool. "So, tell me. What's his name?"

"Whose name?"

"Your boyfriend."

"Why do you think he's my boyfriend?"

"Who is he then?"

Olesya blushed. "My dancing partner. Dima Rumyantsev."

"Dima, eh? Nice name." Yuri slurped his tea. "I knew it when I checked your tickets. Knew it from the way you looked at him."

"Knew what?"

She dared a sip. The hot tea burned her tongue, and she set the glass down.

"You're in love with him, that's what. And he's not in love with you. Which is a pity. The boy is blind. You've got a good heart, and he's not seeing it. If he was my son, I'd knock some sense into him." He slapped the table. The tea sloshed over the rim of her mug.

Olesya recoiled. "How can you know all this?"

"What's there to know?" Yuri shrugged. "It's all right there on your face, written for all to see. Most people don't care to look, that's all."

"And you do?"

"Sure I do. You're my passenger. I need to take care of you. Saw it the moment you came up to my car. Saw it buried inside you. Deep down there." He nodded at her stomach.

Olesya stiffened. "Buried . . . what?"

"Your dead weight."

"I . . . I don't understand. What dead weight?"

"You tell me." He slurped his tea, watching her.

She took a large gulp and choked on the burning liquid. "Thank you for the tea. I'd better go."

Yuri squinted at her. "Running again. Is that your solution?"

"If you'll excuse me—"

"It'll eat you—you mark my words—it'll eat and eat and eat until there's nothing left."

Olesya stood to go. "You're talking nonsense."

"You know I'm right."

"No, I don't."

"How did you get that bruise?" He nodded at her forehead. "A big one too. Looks like you worked hard at it. Want to see mine?" He pulled back his hair, revealing an ugly scar that crawled up into his hairline like a fat slug.

Olesya sat back down. "How . . . ?"

"An ax." He rubbed it. "Lost my wife, Raisa. She left us alone, me and Lidochka. Lidochka was just a baby, didn't understand where her mama went, cried and cried. And what did I do? I took to the bottle, blacked out, and—" He shook his head. "Old durak. Cost me a month in the hospital. Haven't touched vodka since." He crossed himself again.

"I'm sorry about your wife," Olesya said.

He looked out the window. "No need to be sorry. She visits me sometimes. We talk. She's proud of me, proud of me for taking care of people." He looked at Olesya. "She'll be proud I helped you. You're something, I tell you. I see all kinds of folks on the train. You're the first one with a hole in your belly."

Everything inside Olesya shrank. "What?" Was this guy crazy?

"Right there. See? Someone hurt you. Tore a hole in you and left you for dead. You got it covered up real good, but it didn't stop hurting, did it?"

Olesya looked down. There was no hole. She covered her stomach with her hands. "You're . . . you're not well."

"And who is nowadays?" He smiled. "You know I'm telling the truth. You know you've got it."

Olesya stared at him, speechless.

"Devil take me." Yuri rubbed his scar. "Forgive me. I didn't mean to dump it on you like this."

Olesya's skin prickled with goosebumps. She watched the steam rise from her tea, watched it curl and dissolve in the air. *Who was this man?* she thought. *How did he know all this?*

"What did you see?" Yuri asked.

"Huh?"

"You saw something, didn't you? On the train. Something that bothered you."

"How do you know?"

"What was it?"

TUBE, Olesya thought.

The compartment started spinning. She grabbed the edge of the table, closed her eyes. "I'm not feeling well. I need to go."

"Sure, sure. Let me walk you to your compartment."

"No!" It came out louder than she'd intended. "No, thank you. I want to be alone."

"It's a hard thing, to be alone on a train."

"I'll figure something out." She got up.

"That bad, eh?" Yuri clicked his tongue. "All right. You can sit here for as long as you need to. I'll go sit in the aisle."

Olesya shook her head. "You've got work to do. I'll be fine."

Yuri studied her. "Tell you what. The last car is empty. I can let you in, but don't tell a soul, you hear? Not a soul."

"But—"

"This way."

Olesya contemplated. Where else could she stay?

She walked after Yuri through the quiet, rocking cars.

This is good, she thought. *An empty car. I'll be alone. I'll bury my pain, and at lunch I'll face Natasha and Dima like nothing happened.*

They walked through the whole train until the very end.

The vestibule of the last car was cold and dark.

"Here we are." Yuri pulled out his keys, selected the biggest one, fit it into the door lock, and turned. Cold air rolled out.

Olesya thought she heard a compartment open. She peered inside.

All the doors were closed.

12:02

Yuri unlocked the compartment nearest the restroom.

"Here you go. As private as it gets."

Olesya didn't move but stood listening, certain someone was there. Someone was hiding in one of the compartments. Most likely it was a bum or a runaway kid, getting a free ride. All they needed was a triangular key. Any train door could be opened with it. She'd seen Papa do it countless times. It made train security a joke, yet all attendants were attached to their keys like they were part of them.

"Well, I'll be going then. You need anything, you come find me."

Olesya hesitated. Tell Yuri? And what if she was wrong? He'd think her crazy. She'd think herself crazy. It was enough seeing things; now she was hearing things?

"I'll be going then."

She nodded.

The door closed behind him.

Olesya inched toward the next compartment, tried the door. Locked. She put her ear to it. Silence. The clatter of wheels. The whine of the wind. She tried the next door, and the next, and the next. By the time she reached the end of the car, she assured herself she had imagined it all. There was no one there.

She started back, shaking her head.

A faint scratching sound came behind her.

Olesya spun around.

No one there. Every door closed.

She held her breath, listening, her heart frantic.

Nothing.

She was about to turn back when the scratching started anew.

She jumped. The scratching stopped then immediately continued. It was coming from the attendant's compartment. Olesya stilled her impulse to run. She had to know who was there. *Had* to. She took a step forward, another—

The door slid open.

A little girl stepped out, no older than five. She wore a summer dress and her feet were bare. In one hand she held something tight. With the other she rolled the door closed, taking care to be quiet. After it shut all the way, she pressed her ear to it, nodded to herself, and walked toward Olesya.

Olesya thought it was the girl in the heavy coat until she noticed her dress. It was Olesya's summer dress. Baba Zina had sewn it for her from one of Papa's old shirts. And the girl's hair . . . it was tied in two pigtails. Mama used to tie Olesya's hair into pigtails every morning. And the big gray eyes . . .

Little Olesya pressed something into Olesya's hand. "Here, I stole it from him. For you."

Olesya's fingers closed around the familiar shape—her toy train engine. She squeezed it, until its wheels dug into her palm, then lifted it to her face. It was exactly as she remembered it, as though she'd never lost it. The headlamp. The grille at the front. The tiny windows. The faded letters stamped on the side.

TUBE
Trans-Urban Blitz Express

"It can't be. It—"

"It's polite to say 'Thank you.' "

"Thank you," Olesya said automatically.

"You're welcome," Little Olesya said.

They stood for some time in silence.

"When are you going to let me out?"

Olesya blinked. "What?"

"You're so dumb. Did you forget? You locked me up here. With him." She glanced back over her shoulder. "See this?" She pointed to Olesya's hand.

Olesya gazed at her, uncomprehending. "Locked you up?"

"You *are* dumb. You locked me up with TUBE, see? It's a key. And you went the wrong way. You need to start from the first compartment and go in order. Got it? And when you get to the last one—"

"I'm going crazy," Olesya said.

"You're not crazy. You're dumb, and you're mean too." Little Olesya pushed out her lower lip, as if about to cry. "You're keeping me down here—"

"I'm not keeping you. I'm not— You're not even here."

Olesya reached for the girl. She jumped back, and Olesya's hand closed on air.

"I'm not letting you go this time," Little Olesya said. "And don't you try throwing it away. I know you. That's the first thing you'll do, you coward."

"Stop calling me names," Olesya snapped.

"Coward! Coward-coward-coward!"

Olesya launched at the girl, but she sidestepped her and slunk right under her arms. Olesya spun around. The girl stood a safe distance away, her knees half-bent for fast retreat.

"I'm not the one who did it. You did it. You *called* it," Little Olesya said triumphantly. "I thought you'd never do. I've been waiting and waiting. You know how many years?"

"Shut up."

"Sixteen."

"Shut up!"

"*You* shut up! I don't want to wait anymore! I don't want him—"

"Olesya?" called a man's voice, garbled with sleep.

The girl's face crumpled. She shrunk, dropped her face into her hands. "Now I've done it. Now I woke him up."

"Is that . . ." Olesya said. "Who is that?"

"Where are you?" called the man. "You silly thing. Get back in here."

The girl looked up. There were tears in her eyes. She wiped her face, ran to the end of the car—"I'm coming! I'm coming!"—stepped inside the attendant's compartment, and rolled the door shut.

Olesya watched the door for a long time, unconscious of TUBE in her hand, thinking about the last thing she saw before the girl disappeared—dark lines on her legs. And then she understood what they were.

"Tracks."

The girl drew train tracks on her legs. With a red marker.

Olesya had the unpleasant feeling of nausea rising in her stomach.

13:13

You silly thing rang in Olesya's head. Papa called her that, when they were playing TUBE. Could it really be him in there?

He sometimes took Olesya with him on trips when she was little. They had a grand time. They played games and had cookies with tea and watched the scenery roll by. Papa would sit her on his lap, point out the houses and the trees, give her candy and kiss her, calling her "my little ballerina."

Was he really here, on the train? Right now?

But he was dead. Long dead.

Olesya tiptoed to the attendant's compartment to listen. Silence.

She tried the door. It was locked.

Olesya shook her head. There was no Papa. No Little Olesya.

No TUBE.

She looked at TUBE in her hand. The solution was simple.

First she tried a few windows, but they were sealed for winter. Of course. She walked to the vestibule and tried the exit doors. Locked. Where else? The gangway. She stepped on the shifting, grinding plates, the wheels' rattle deafening, the cold freezing. She crouched on all fours and shoved TUBE through the gap between the plates and the bellows. Then she let go.

Done.

She got up, brushed her knees, and went back to the car.

On the floor of the aisle sat TUBE.

The moment she saw it, its headlamp lit up and it whistled and rolled at her.

Olesya broke into a sweat.

It bumped her feet until she picked it up and switched it off. Her hands were shaking.

She went back to the gangway, put her face to the gap, and let go, watching TUBE fall onto the frozen railway and disappear.

She returned to the car.

TUBE sat on the floor.

Olesya stifled a scream.

She grabbed it and flushed it down the toilet.

Same result.

She closed it in storage bins, rolled it in blankets, pushed it inside the radiator grille. No use. Desperate, she smashed it in the compartment door, and when that didn't work, she chased it with an ax she found in the vestibule closet. But TUBE was always one step ahead of her.

The train pulled into a station and slowed to a stop. The loudspeaker announced their arrival at Oryol station. There were shouts on the platform, the clatter of luggage carts, the attendants' calls.

Olesya sat on the aisle floor, drenched in sweat. TUBE sat in her lap.

"You think you won?" she said. "You didn't. I'll get rid of you. You'll see."

She scooped it up, grabbed her things, and went to the next car. No one was getting on or off here. Olesya walked through a few more cars and suddenly stopped. An imposing woman swaddled in a fur coat huffed along the aisle, dragging a boy of about seven behind her. Olesya set TUBE on the floor and stepped aside, letting them pass.

She saw the boy spot the shiny red engine. He let go of his mother's hand and snatched it.

"Look, Mama. Look what I found!" He held it up.

She barked without looking, "Get moving, Nikita, or I'll whip your ass. Hear me?"

Nikita's eyes widened. He put TUBE in his pocket and hurried after her.

Olesya walked toward her car, smiling. She did it. TUBE was gone.

On her way back, she managed to avoid meeting any of the dancers, but the moment she closed her compartment door, someone knocked.

"Yes?"

Yuri stood at the door, his golden teeth shining. "Back already, eh? Feeling better?"

Olesya laughed. "No. Yes. I don't know. I guess."

"Well, seems you've forgotten something." He smiled and stretched out his hand.

On his palm sat TUBE.

ORYOL-PONYRI
14:23

Lunchtime was coming to a close. The dining car was empty save for a few passengers finishing their food. Olesya, Natasha, and Alla Borisovna sat in silence at a table in the back.

The silence stretched to a breaking point.

Natasha sipped her tea.

Alla Borisovna sipped her coffee.

Olesya kept her eyes on her plate of untouched food: steamed fish with colorless, soggy cabbage. She didn't have to lose any more weight—there was hardly any fat left on her frame—but eating anything fatty, starchy, or sweet in the presence of Alla Borisovna was a crime. This rigid abstinence was supposed to demonstrate their dedication to ballet. Alla Borisovna weighed them often, sometimes every week, and those who went over her prescribed weight were disposed of without a blink. Some girls subsisted on crackers with sliced cucumbers. Others would gorge themselves and vomit afterward. Olesya practiced moderation. Besides, she worked so hard that she burned it all off.

She glanced at the jar of raspberry jam the waitress had forgotten to remove. Her favorite jam. Her stomach grumbled. She wondered what would happen if she ate a spoonful of it—or, better yet, the entire jar.

"You missed the meeting," said Alla Borisovna. Her ratlike eyes bored into Olesya's face.

"I didn't know there *was* a meeting."

"We couldn't find you," Natasha said.

"I—"

"I don't need your explanations." Alla Borisovna waved a dismissive hand. "My decision is final. You're moving to the second cast. Natasha will take your place in the first."

Natasha smiled.

Olesya felt numb. She had expected a scolding, at worst a threat. But not this.

"You can't . . . you can't demote me for missing a meeting. I didn't know about it. I didn't—"

"Missing the meeting has nothing to do with it, and you know it, so don't act so surprised."

"But—"

"I gave you the part of the Swan Princess under one condition. You were to deliver emotion. I personally vouched for you to Gennady Romanovich. *Personally.* And what did you do? You managed to fail at every rehearsal. Not only that, you failed to do what I asked you to do." She paused for her words to sink in. "You know Gennady Romanovich. There is no middle ground with him, only black or white. So here we are." She steepled her fingers, leaned forward. "Either you dance in the second cast, or you're out."

Olesya glanced at Natasha. Natasha averted her eyes.

"I can't accept this, Alla Borisovna," Olesya said. "I spent years preparing for *Swan Lake.* Years. I was promised a principal position, I was— Please. Let me talk to Gennady Romanovich. Maybe he'll—"

"Quiet!" Alla Borisovna looked livid. "Where is your common sense? Keep your mouth shut, girl, before you do more damage. We've talked about this at length. I don't need another wind-up doll who can leap and jump and turn. There're plenty of those, and none of them work at Bolshoi. I need an artist, someone who can transform into a living, breathing swan. Living, not dead." She grabbed Olesya's wrist and shook it. "Look at you. I'm telling you your career is in danger, and there you sit, frozen stiff. Can't you feel *anything*? Oh, this is pointless." She dropped Olesya's arm on the table. It made a dull *clunk*.

Olesya stopped breathing.

In the silence, the clatter of wheels came in sharp and loud. The car swayed as it turned the bend, and Olesya swayed with it, watching the tea jitter in Natasha's cup.

Natasha. She'd always outshined Olesya in every way. But when Dima rejected Natasha, something in Olesya had shifted. She started to believe she had a chance at a life beyond hard work. She had a boyfriend, she had the leading part in *Swan Lake*. Things were looking up for once—until Natasha stole them both, with her beauty, her guts, her . . . sex. It all came down to sex, didn't it?

The thought made Olesya's face burn.

What Alla Borisovna asked her to do, like it was nothing—a chore, an errand. Gennady Romanovich was an old man, and when she imagined . . . the idea alone made her gag. Olesya looked at Natasha. Did she . . . ? Of course she did. It was nothing to her, like changing socks.

"What is it you have that I don't?" Olesya asked her.

Natasha glanced at Alla Borisovna.

"Go ahead," Alla Borisovna said. "Explain it to her. Seems she's clueless."

"What Alla Borisovna means is, you need to open up emotionally," Natasha said. "To experiment. You know. Push yourself beyond your comfort zone?"

"But I'm already pushing myself—"

"No, not your technique. Your technique is flawless. You need to practice feeling. You know. Emotion." She smiled.

Olesya wanted to punch her pretty face, make it bleed.

"Emotion. Okay. All right. Are there some ballet recordings you suggest I watch?" she said icily. "Documentaries? Maybe hire an acting coach?"

Alla Borisovna pursed her lips. "Let me ask you something, Olesya. Are you a virgin?"

"Excuse me?"

"Yes or no?"

Olesya gaped. "I— This is—this is private. I don't understand what is has to do—"

"I was afraid of that." Alla Borisovna sighed. "Listen, my dear, if you don't know what it's like to experience passion, you can't fake it onstage. I think it'd be a good idea to remove you from *Swan Lake* altogether until you *remedy* the situation. Natasha, think you could handle the load?"

Natasha beamed. "Absolutely."

"Good. You'll partner with Dima. I'll coach him, don't worry."

Olesya put her hand in her pocket and gripped TUBE. Old habit. As a child she would carry it with her for reassurance, gripping its sharp edges when she needed calm. "Alla Borisovna. Please. May I say something? I understand— I mean, I apologize for disappointing you. I—I see that my failure is putting our whole tour in jeopardy. Can I ask—can you please give me one more chance? Just one. Let me dance at the opening night. I'll prove it to you. I'll prove I can deliver *both* technique and emotion. I swear."

Alla Borisovna studied her with interest. "Will you?"

"Yes."

"How?"

Olesya took a deep breath. "I'll . . . I'll sleep with Dima. It'll help us with chemistry."

"You mean to say, you'll lose your virginity to him?"

Blood rushed to Olesya's face. "Yes," she whispered.

"Louder."

"Yes."

Alla Borisovna raised her eyebrows. "Well, that's the most abominable thing I ever heard you utter, my dear. You're planning to force one of my dancers to sex. Why, that's sabotage." She stood. "That seals it. I'm putting you in corps de ballet. One of the girls will take your place."

Everything inside Olesya dropped. "What? No—no. Please. Please, Alla Borisovna. Ballet is my life. You can't—"

"Ballet is your *job*. And when one can't do their job, they find another."

"But it's only—"

"Do us all a favor, girl. Quit. Find yourself a man. Have sex. Enjoy life."

"Enjoy life." Something snapped in Olesya. She felt a curious lightness. She opened the jar of raspberry jam, stuck in her finger, scooped out a dollop, and popped it in her mouth. "Oh God, this tastes good. So sweet. Want to try?" She scooped out another dollop and offered it.

Alla Borisovna stared in horror.

"Maybe you need to eat more sweets, Alla Borisovna," Olesya said, licking her finger. "You might start enjoying life, you know?"

"Stop it," Alla Borisovna hissed. "You're embarrassing yourself."

"Why? Isn't this what you suggested? That I enjoy life? What about you, Natasha? Am I doing this right? Practicing emotion?"

"You're crazy," Natasha mouthed.

"Is this how you get men to fuck you? Make yourself taste swee-e-et?" Olesya smeared the jam on her blouse and started unbuttoning it.

Alla Borisovna forced the jar out of her hand and slammed it on the table. "Enough. You're getting off at the next station. You're off the tour." She turned and left.

The waitress stared after her for a moment, then got back to wiping the tables.

Olesya picked up the jar and stuck her finger inside, but the desire was gone.

"Idiot," Natasha said. "Where have you been? I was going to warn you. She told me about your demotion before the meeting. I had a plan for how to pacify the Old Bitch so you could keep your part. But no, you had to fuck it up. Good job." She walked out.

The train started slowing. The snowy fields gave way to gray apartment blocks and barren trees. Olesya watched them roll by, feeling nothing.

"Miss?" the waitress called. "The dining car is closed. You need to leave."

Olesya looked at her. "Do you have any vodka?"

PONYRI–KURSK
15:19

In the last car, in the compartment closest to the restroom, on the table were arranged a faceted glass, a bottle of vodka, and an ax. Olesya's plan was to get drunk to forget it all and then destroy TUBE. She sat at the table, filled the glass with vodka, and downed it. Her eyes watered. She poured another glass, downed it, poured more. Her hand shook, and half the vodka spilled.

Someone rapped on the door.

Olesya started. The bottle clinked to the floor. "Who is it?"

"Dima."

"Dima?"

"Yes."

"What do you want?"

"Can I come in?" He opened the door. His eyes widened. "Oh dear God, Olesya. What are you doing?"

"What does it look like? Hand me the bottle, please."

"You drank half of it? What are you, crazy? You'll get poisoning." He picked up the bottle and put it outside the door.

"What do you care?"

His face clouded. "Don't."

"Listen. I've got to tell you something—"

"Olesya—"

"Shut up!"

He recoiled as if slapped.

She smiled. "Here's the deal, my dear Dima. If you came here to lecture me, then I don't want you here. Got it? Get the hell out. Now." She burped. Her stomach felt queasy. "How did you find me anyway?"

"The attendant—"

"Who, Yuri? He told you? Damn him."

"No no no no. It wasn't like that. I just asked—"

"Look, I'm not in the mood for talking. Can you get me the bottle?"

Dima closed the door and sat next to her.

"I wanted to say . . . I'm sorry about what happened."

"Really? You're sorry."

"I am."

"You're *sorry*. Is that why you came? To tell me you're sorry?"

"Olesya, please."

"What? What do you want? You want to pity me?"

"No, it's not like that."

"Why don't you save your 'sorry' for someone else?"

"Olesya, listen."

"No, *you* listen!" She poked his chest with a finger. "It's done and done, okay? It's over. And I'm fine. I'll be fine. Isn't this what you always tell me?"

He took her hand. "Please. It's important."

She pulled away. "No, this is what's important." She took TUBE from her pocket and set it on the table.

"What's that?"

"TUBE."

"TUBE? Your toy train engine?"

"Yep."

"But I thought . . ."

"You thought I imagined it."

He picked it up and twirled it in his hand. "Huh. Strange. Did you bring it with you?"

"I didn't." Olesya's tongue felt thick. It was hard to talk clearly. "I didn't bring it with me. I lost it sometime after Baba Zina's funeral. Then this morning . . . well, this morning— I don't know how to say it. You'll think I'm crazy."

"No, I won't."

"Promise?"

"Promise."

Olesya sighed. "Okay. So this morning I met . . . I met a little girl. She's . . . she was me. You know? I mean, like when I was five. The . . . I don't know how to call her. Little Olesya? And she was real. She stood right next to me. Then she gave me this." Olesya motioned to TUBE.

"Little Olesya? Are you sure?"

"Yes, I'm sure. See, I knew you wouldn't believe me."

"No, no, I do. Honestly. I do."

Olesya searched his eyes. There was no laughter in them, only worry.

"Well, she said she stole it from 'him.' I think she meant Papa. I heard his voice. It wasn't very clear, but I'd recognize it anywhere. And . . . anyway, he couldn't be there. TUBE couldn't be there. So I tried getting rid of it, but it always comes back. I swear to you, I threw it off the train. Several times. And every time it comes back, every time. Like it's mocking me."

Dima smiled.

"What?"

"Nothing."

"No, what?"

"You're drunk. That's what."

"Fuck you."

"Olesya, look." He squeezed his eyes shut, pinched the bridge of his nose. "I screwed up. I should've stayed with you when you wanted to . . . you know. I should've tried, one more time. But you scared me. I didn't know what to do."

"You knew what to do with Natasha."

Dima paled.

"I saw you kissing. I was in the gangway. Damn. You never kiss me like that. I understand though. I mean . . . who wants to kiss a doll, right?"

"I didn't," he said. "I didn't kiss her."

"Sure, you didn't. That's what you came here to apologize for, didn't you? For not kissing Natasha. Well, I accept your apology. Now, can you please go? I'm rather busy." She picked up the ax.

"Um." Dima reached for it. "Let's not—"

Olesya brought the ax down on TUBE and missed. TUBE fell to the floor. "Did you see it move? It moved. Oh my God, it moved! Did you see it? Grab it. Grab it, before it escapes!" She sprang after it.

"Olesya!" He followed her into the aisle, forced the ax from her hand, and clutched her against him.

"Let go of me. Let go!"

She thrashed. He tightened his grip. The train bumped on a gap in the tracks and her stomach lurched. She bent over and vomited. Dima held her hair back until it was over. She sunk to her knees, shaking, sobbing.

"I missed it. Again. I missed it. I can't destroy it, no matter what. Every time I try, it runs away, and then it comes back, and we start all over again. Why? Why is this happening to me? What did I do wrong?"

"You did nothing wrong." Dima's face was stony.

"You don't believe me," she said.

He shrugged.

"Can you at least try?"

"Yeah, I can try. But it does sound strange. All of it."

"Didn't you ever have something like this happen to you?"

"Like what?"

"Like, I don't know." She wiped her mouth with the back of her hand. The taste on her tongue was foul. "Like something you're sure of, but everyone else thinks you're crazy?"

He shrugged. "Maybe."

"I swear to you. I swear I didn't imagine it. I saw her with my own eyes. But then . . . then I started doubting because it's impossible. Of course it's impossible. It can't be, right? But I did see her. So does that mean it really happened? Or did I imagine her after all?"

Dima was silent.

"Haven't you ever experienced something like this? At least once?"

She waited.

"You know what? Go. Just go."

"Yeah," Dima said.

"Yeah, what?"

He leaned his back on the wall, his eyes vacant. "Yeah, I did."

She waited.

"My mom's flats," he said.

"Your mom's flats?"

"They came to me three days after she hung herself."

"Oh. Oh, I'm sorry. I didn't know."

"It's okay, It was a long time ago."

Olesya was afraid to breathe. "So . . . what happened?"

"I was in bed, nodding off, then suddenly I hear her moving around the kitchen. Not cooking or anything, just moving around. Like she's looking for something. I didn't dare breathe, listening. Half hoping it was true. I mean, I knew she couldn't be there. She was dead. But I heard her. It was real. Like I'm talking to you now." He fell silent.

She touched his arm. "And then?"

"And then I called her. 'Mom?' I couldn't help myself. She stopped. Then I heard her walking to my room. I closed my eyes from fright. Heard the door open. She walked right up to my bed and stopped. I sat there in silence, afraid to open my eyes, waiting for her to say something, to touch me . . . Those seconds were probably the worst seconds of my life. I thought I'd die. Thought my heart would burst from beating.

"I don't know how long I waited. Seemed like a whole night. Then I thought, What if Dad woke up and barged in? He'd spoil everything, scare her off. So I looked, but she wasn't there. I looked all around . . . then I saw her flats on the floor. They just stood there, right by my bed. They couldn't get there by themselves, right? So I thought, Well, maybe I put them there myself. Maybe . . . I don't know, I sleepwalked or something. Went through her wardrobe. Whatever. Then it dawned on me." He looked at Olesya. "We buried her in them. They were her favorite flats. Red patent leather. She got them on the black market, imported. French. Only wore them for special occasions." He paused, looked down at his hands. "I was a big boy, Olesya, twelve going on thirteen, and I wet myself." He was silent. "I can't believe I'm telling you this. I never told anyone."

She squeezed his hand. "Thank you for telling me."

He nodded.

"So what happened next?"

It took him a while. "They kept coming every night. For weeks. Until I finally got fed up and tried getting rid of them."

"How?"

"Tried throwing them away."

He fell silent.

"But they came back," Olesya said.

"Yeah, they came back."

"Like TUBE."

"Yeah." He looked at her. "I'm sorry about the way I reacted. When you told me. I tried to forget. It took me years to forget. I didn't want to remember."

Olesya's heart beat faster. "No, it's okay. I understand."

They sat in silence, listening to the wheels knock their rhythm, swaying with the car. A cold draft brushed Olesya's legs, and she shivered. Dima put an arm around her shoulder. She moved closer.

"Do they still come?" she asked.

"No."

She sat up straight. "How did you get rid of them?"

"You won't believe me."

"How?"

"Well, I went back to the day she died—"

"What do you mean, 'went back'?"

"See, I told you." He turned away.

"Please. Please." She pulled on his sleeve. "I didn't mean it like that."

"Well. Okay." He picked up her hand and held it, caressing her fingers. "You're cold."

"I don't mind."

"Let me warm you."

"No, please. I really don't care. Tell me."

He looked into her eyes, then at her forehead, and frowned. "Where did you get this bruise?"

"Never mind the bruise," she said impatiently. "Just tell me."

"Well, I sort of recreated the day she died. Like, I went back there and talked to her." He paused. "I was the one who found her."

"You did? That's horrible." Cold brushed its fingers down her back.

"Yeah. I remember it like it happened yesterday. I opened the door, and the whole apartment smelled of meat cutlets—she made the best meat cutlets. I was so hungry. I dropped my school bag and called to her, but she didn't answer. That was strange. She always waited for me to come home, to stuff me with food before ballet school. Something was wrong.

"Then I had this awful thought. Dad had finally killed her. He'd always promised her when he'd got drunk. He'd beat her and yell, 'I'll kill you, you bitch. I'll kill you.' So I thought, That's it. He did it. I was so scared, I was shaking. What if he wanted to kill me too? What if he was there, waiting for me? So I took out my jackknife, went to the kitchen, and that's when I saw them. Her flats. They just hung there, above the floor—"

He closed his eyes.

Olesya waited, her hand warm in his, her breath still.

"So I went back to that day. I tried recreating it."

"What for?"

"I don't know. To remember."

"Remember what?"

"Something I could've done. I thought it was my fault, you see? Thought I did something wrong. Maybe I could've saved her somehow. It was a kid in me. I had to know. *Had* to. So I took a day off work, waited for Dad to leave, dressed in this old navy suit I had, to look like I was wearing my school uniform. I even dug up my old schoolbag from storage, couldn't believe it was still there. Then I went to my school. God, I hadn't been there for years. It looked so small, so shabby. I walked around the building to pass the time, ate lunch at the cafeteria, and went home. The weather was about the same, cloudy—the snow had just started melting. I opened the door and repeated every step: dropped my schoolbag, took out my jackknife . . ." He fell silent.

Olesya put her head on his shoulder.

He stroked her hair. "In the end, I don't think any of it mattered. All this recreating. I was simply ready to face her. I went to the kitchen, and there they were."

"Her flats."

"Yeah. I could've stopped right there, but I made myself look up, at her face. It was awful. Gray. The tip of her tongue was stuck out like she was licking her lips. I started yelling at her. I was so mad at her for leaving me alone with an alcoholic father. She got the easy way out. I called her a coward, a selfish bitch. And then something happened. Something left me. I sat there and cried, I don't know for how long. When I looked up, she was gone. That night the flats stopped coming. I slept like a baby for the first time in years. It was wonderful. I forgot what it was like, you know?"

"Yeah."

He took her face and kissed her. Kissed the bruise on her forehead, kissed her lips. It was so simple, so sweet, Olesya felt like crying. She pulled away.

"What?"

"Nothing."

"No, what?"

"I . . ." She hesitated. "I wish it was so easy for me."

"Easy?"

"At least you remember. I don't. That's the worst part, see? I remember nothing. There is something there, I can feel it, but—" She dropped her head.

He lifted her face by the chin. "Is that what you were trying to do? To remember?"

She shrugged. "I don't know. I think I tried to forget."

"But if you don't remember . . ."

She thought about it. "Yuri, the car attendant. I had tea with him. He said something strange. Like he could see . . . like he knew someone hurt me. How is that possible? I mean, he doesn't even know me. And then TUBE and Little Olesya and Papa—" She hugged her knees, trembling. "I guess it's like with your mother, except . . . I don't understand. Why did she give it to me? And why was she afraid of Papa? She looked like she was afraid. I was never afraid of him. Is it because he's dead? I'm so confused, Dima. What does this all mean?"

"What do you think it means?"

"Well, she said she stole TUBE from 'him.' From Papa, right? He was in the attendant's compartment, he called her, he said, 'Where are you? You silly thing. Get back here.' She was terrified of him, I could see that. And then, just as she was stepping back in, I saw . . . There were tracks on her legs, Dima. She drew them with a red marker. Train tracks. Isn't that bizarre? Why would she do that? I mean, why would *I* do it? I don't remember doing it."

"Maybe it was important."

"But I don't remember doing it! I played TUBE with Papa all the time, but I don't remember drawing on my legs. It's just so crazy. I think I'm going crazy. Am I going crazy?"

"You're not. You're not crazy."

He held her. And his closeness, his simple gesture of love, undid her.

She cried long and hard, and for some time she forgot herself, letting go, her face wet, her tears soaking into his shirt. His warmth enveloped her. She leaned into it, trusting. He squeezed her shoulders, rocking her, kissing the top of her head. Her fingers found his shirt buttons, undid them. She slipped her hands around his torso, stroked, pushed them down his pants. He tensed.

She looked up at him, flushed. "You don't want me."

"Of course I want you. I always want you."

She pulled her hands out. "You just say that."

"No, really."

"Then let's do it."

He glanced around the car aisle. "What, right now?"

"Yes."

He balked. "Not *here*."

"Why not? There's no one here. We can go into the compartment."

"I . . . I don't know."

"Okay." She scooted away from him, stood.

"No, wait."

"I get it. I understand."

"What do you get?"

"I'm just broken."

"Don't say that."

"Well, I am." She felt tears well up, swallowed them. "I can't relax. I can't come. Who'd want to sleep with a girl like that? Like me. That's why you want Natasha. She can come ten times in a row. She told me."

Dima shook his head. "Look, it has nothing to do with—"

"Yes, it does."

"I don't care if you come."

"Bullshit."

"Stop it. You've no idea—" He broke off.

"Go on."

"It's not important."

"No, go ahead. Finish. I've no idea about what?"

"Look . . ." He reached for her.

She backed off.

"Olesya, please."

She jumped back. "Don't touch me!"

He stopped. His cheeks colored. "Okay. Okay, I won't touch you. Is that what you want?"

"Yes. No. I don't know. I don't know!"

She felt like crying again, confused where it was coming from, unable to hold the tears from spilling. Her face hot. Her thoughts in disarray. He stood watching her, and it unnerved her. She wanted to hide from his gaze. Wanted to run away.

"What do you want me to do?" he said.

She couldn't think of an answer.

"Okay. Okay." He turned to leave, looked back at her.

But she didn't call to him like last time, didn't plead. She was wooden.

He picked up the bottle of vodka and the ax and left.

Olesya walked into her compartment, closed the door, then stuffed a towel in her mouth and bit on it, to stop herself from screaming.

CONNECTING
THE CARS

KURSK-BELGOROD
16:05

The bruise on Olesya's forehead helped her calm herself. She pressed on it. The pain was clear and sharp. It brought her back to her practical needs—it always did, like the pain in her feet from too much dancing. She was addicted to it. Not many understood. It helped her function. Helped her clear the mess of anxiety, fear, confusion. Focused her. Gave her a reason to move forward.

And so she got up, went to the restroom, rinsed out her mouth, wet the towel, and scrubbed the vomit off the floor, then sat down to think.

She had two choices: forget everything and go back to Moscow, or try to remember and continue to Simferopol. The first choice was bad. TUBE wouldn't let her forget. It would haunt her, just like those flats haunted Dima. She was sure of it. That left Simferopol, and then Alupka. Besides, if she did go all the way, she might as well stay longer, sneak into the theater, watch Natasha and Dima dance *Swan Lake*—

No, it'd only further her misery.

"Okay," she said. "Okay."

She would do it.

She'd get to Simferopol, take a trolleybus to Alupka and stay at Baba Zina's house. She hadn't been there since the funeral. It was on their trip back that she'd lost TUBE. Maybe she could retrace her steps like Dima. Maybe she'd remember something—anything. It was worth a shot. The house would be locked up for winter—Uncle Shurik was surely gone on one of his expeditions—but she knew where to find the key. She'd stay there for a few days, sleep in her old room, take walks along the sea—

It sounded good. In fact, it was just what she needed.

She glanced at her watch. 16:35.

Two hours till Belgorod. A big station, crowded, with lots of restaurants, food kiosks. Good. Since she couldn't eat in the dining car, she'd sneak off the train, eat, then call Mama.

Mama for sure would remember something. If someone really did hurt her, Mama would've noticed, wouldn't she? Of course she would have.

Olesya sighed, satisfied.

Now there was one more thing left to do. After all, what was the worst that could happen? So she'd stumble on some free-ride squatter. So what? At least she'd know there was no Papa in there.

There couldn't be. He was dead.

"All right," Olesya said, to encourage herself. TUBE lay heavy in her hand. "Start from the first compartment and go in order."

That's what Little Olesya had told her. TUBE was the key.

She touched the headlamp, the engine grille, flipped TUBE around. How was this going to work? It had nothing on it that could fit into locks—nothing resembling a triangular key. How could it open doors?

"Come on," she said aloud, "give it a try. Maybe it'll reveal something." It sounded so ridiculous, she scoffed, looked out the window at the gray, boiling sky and the frozen fields, and shivered. She could see her breath.

"Might as well move around to warm up."

She buttoned up her coat and walked the length of the car to the first passenger compartment, No. 1. Tried the door. It was locked. She squatted down, studied the keyhole, then tried inserting TUBE. Of course, it didn't fit.

"This is just stupid."

She got up and stepped over to try the attendant's compartment. Locked. Frustrated, she walked back and tried every door on her way, just to know she did it.

"I'm wasting my time." She plopped down on the bunk, set TUBE on the table. "You can't open doors, can you?" she said to it. "Didn't think so. Then why—"

She was interrupted by the sound of a door opening.

Olesya sat up straight. Through the compartment wall, she heard water hit the toilet.

16:59

The sound was thick and bright. A man was urinating in the restroom, separated from Olesya by a thin wall.

Her palms broke into a sweat. She froze, listening. "Papa?"

The toilet flushed, the door swished open, the footsteps—

Her legs wouldn't move, so she had to force herself up, force her hand to open the door. She peeked out, only to catch sight of the attendant's door closing.

She ran to it.

"Who's there?"

No answer.

"Open up! I know you're in there!"

She pressed her ear to the door—nothing.

"You can't stay here," she said, keeping her voice steady What if it *was* Papa? No, it couldn't be. It was a bum. "You hear me? You have to leave, or I'll call militia."

Not a sound.

The wheels rattled off the kilometers, and her heart pounded hard in her head.

"Look, you really need to leave." Olesya waited. "I won't rat you out, I promise. Just go, okay?" She looked at her watch. "We'll be in Belgorod in about an hour. I'll stay in my compartment so I won't see you. I'm in number nine, at the front of the car, okay?"

Silence. Then something dropped to the floor. A body. A child whimpered.

"Hey!" Olesya pounded on the door. "Open up! What're you doing in there?" Her heart hammered. "I'm calling militia!"

She stomped down the aisle, slammed the vestibule door, then crept back to spy.

No movement.

She was shaking, certain now. It wasn't Papa. How could she even *think* that? She didn't believe in ghosts or in reincarnation or in any of this idiotic superstitious stuff. It was that man with the girl in the heavy coat. Yes, that's right. He was hurting her—hurting his own daughter.

All fear of stumbling into Alla Borisovna or any of the dancers evaporated from Olesya's mind. She turned and ran, through one car, another, pushing past startled passengers, ignoring attendants' calls.

She burst into her car and banged on Yuri's door until he opened it.

"Yuri! Yuri, quick!"

He looked at her, his shirt sprinkled with crumbs, a cookie in his hand. "Why, that's a surprise. Back already? Couldn't stand the cold anymore, could you?"

"That man"—Olesya swallowed hard—"that man. The girl. He's hurting her."

"What man?" Yuri brushed crumbs off his shirt.

"In the empty car. I need your keys."

"My keys?"

"Yes. *Now.*"

"What's this about? Did that boyfriend of yours—"

"No!" Olesya groaned. "It's not him, not Dima. There's a man in my car, in the empty car. He's got a girl with him. His daughter. He used the restroom, and then—he's in the attendant's compartment. They got on in Tula. She slipped, and he yelled at her. I saw them, Yuri. He's hurting her."

Yuri's face darkened. "You sure about that?"

"I'm sure."

"Well. That son of a bitch." He put on his attendant's cap. "Lead the way."

Olesya rushed out, pushing past startled passengers, Yuri puffing and sweating behind her.

She got there first and waited for him.

He pounded on the door with a fist. "Open up! Head attendant here."

Silence.

He slipped the key in the lock, turned it, and rolled the door open.

Olesya's knees buckled.

Yuri stepped inside. He traced his finger on the table, then lifted it to his nose. It was dusty.

"I heard them, I swear to you," she said. "They probably left—"

"You said you saw them?"

"At the station. Yes." Her face grew hot. "You don't believe me."

"Did I say that?"

"No. But I heard him"—Olesya's voice caught—"I heard him . . . urinate. He flushed the toilet. Right next to my compartment. The walls are so thin . . ."

"Let's take a look."

They went to the restroom.

Yuri stepped in. "The bowl is dry. Want to see for yourself?"

Olesya grabbed her head.

Yuri scratched under his cap, pushed it back down. "Tell you what. I think I know who it was."

"Who?"

"A ghost, I think." He crossed himself. "I should've known. It's the haunted car, that's what it is."

"What?"

"A haunted car."

"There is no such thing."

Yuri smirked. "It sure is. I worked the rails for twenty-three years, and, mind you, never seen it myself, only heard of it. No wonder it's empty. No one stays here long. People sense it, you see? They say a man offed himself in here. I'll bet you anything it was him."

Olesya gaped at him. "A ghost? Are you serious?"

"Sure I am. And don't look at me like that. You never heard of a haunted car? A haunted house?"

"Of course I did. But—"

"Have you ever seen one yourself?"

"No."

"Then why do you think you know better than me?"

Olesya thought of Little Olesya and fell quiet.

Yuri stepped out of the restroom, looked down the length of the car. "They keep hitching it from train to train. Can't send it to the wrecking yard. What would they tell the boss? Can't park it in the depot either. The ghost didn't like it. Came out at night and howled, scared the crap out of the boys. So they keep him moving. Seems he likes the ride, stays quiet that way. Poor soul." Yuri shook his head. "I'll ask Raisa about him. She'll know."

Olesya shifted uncomfortably. "I heard them, Yuri. There were people in here. *Real* people."

He touched her arm. "Let's go, dorogusha. It's not good for you to stay here."

"I need to know who it was."

"There you go again, stubborn like my Lidochka. She has to see everything herself too. There's no one here." He

71

walked from compartment to compartment, opening the doors, closing them. Olesya followed him as though in a trance.

After he locked the last door, he pocketed the keys. "Seen enough? Go get your things."

"I'm not going."

"You're not going."

She sat on the floor.

"So that's how it's going to be." He squinted at her.

"I can't. I have to know."

Yuri rubbed his scar, his expression vacant. "You'll regret this."

"Why?"

"You're not ready, that's why."

"Ready for what?"

But he was already stepping out.

"Yuri!" Olesya jumped to her feet. "Ready for what?"

He stopped, looked back. "Your hole got bigger."

Olesya looked down at herself.

When she looked up, he was gone.

"Oh, that's just great. That's just fucking terrific. Tell me the car is haunted, then leave me alone in here."

She went back to her compartment, picked up TUBE. It was no ghost. It was solid, real. She traced the letters on its side, spelling them out as Papa had taught her.

"TUBE. Trans-Urban Blitz Express."

What was it that he said after? *Do you want to play TUBE?* How she loved it. The rare days that he was off work, when he had time for her, when he wasn't busy. She didn't care what they did, eager to please him. He loved trains, and he loved playing TUBE.

"Yes, Papa," she said. "I want to play TUBE. I miss you so much—"

The train lurched around the bend, and she swayed, sitting back hard on the bunk.

TUBE slipped from her hand and into her lap. Its headlamp lit up. It whistled. The wheels started spinning. She felt it nosing, crawling under her sweater. She gasped, beat at it. It was now under her shirt, pushing at her belly button—

A curious sensation opened up in her stomach, as if it were hollow somehow, and TUBE rolled inside it. The bulge in her sweater disappeared. Olesya panted, wheezing. With shaking hands, she lifted her sweater.

Oh God.

Her belly button was gone. In its place was a black hole the size of a rodent's burrow. Inside it sat TUBE. She screamed, but as she grabbed for it, it wiggled in deeper. Pain shot through her. She shoved her fingers in the hole, clasped TUBE, and yanked it out.

Shaking, she tossed it to the floor. It blinked its headlamp, whistled three times, and shot into the aisle as if it had been waiting for her to do exactly that.

Olesya scrambled after it. "Wait. Wait!"

TUBE stopped in front of compartment No. 1.

Olesya leaned on the wall, nauseated. This couldn't be happening. There was no hole in her stomach. There couldn't be. She steeled herself, gritted her teeth, and lifted her sweater.

A moan escaped her. "No. No!"

TUBE bumped at the door, impatient.

"What? What do you want?"

Then she knew.

Key.

Sweat rolling down her back, her breath shallow, she bit on her coat sleeve to keep from screaming, picked up TUBE, and slid it into her hole. It wiggled in there, and she understood. Clasping its tail end, she turned.

At the faint sound of a lock clicking, the door rolled open. Inside was dark, then a voice.

"Where did you hide it, Olesya? *Where?* And don't give me this look. I'll find it, you know it, so your silence is pointless, yes?"

Olesya reeled. "Mama?"

MOSCOW, BELY APARTMENT
25 January 1979
17:13

Olesya crossed the threshold and stepped into her room in their two-room apartment. Her bed was neatly made, her desk clean, her dance bag packed and sitting on the chair by the door.

The clock read 17:15. Ballet class started in forty-five minutes. She needed to hurry.

Mama stood by the window, her arms crossed. "Silence is a form of lying, you know that, yes?"

Olesya said nothing.

"All right. We have the whole night ahead of us."

"But I have class!"

Mama turned to face her. "You're not leaving until you tell me where it is, Olesya."

"But—"

"I want you to listen to me carefully. Tomorrow we'll start new, fresh . . . together, you and I both." She stepped toward Olesya, and the floor creaked. Olesya took a step back. "The past belongs in the past, you understand that, yes?"

Olesya said nothing. Her eyes were glued to the clock. 17:16.

Mama picked up her dance bag and unzipped it.

"No!" Olesya's throat constricted. "Please. It's not in there."

"Then *where*? Where did you hide it?"

"Please, Mama. If I'm late again, Ekaterina Petrovna will kill me."

Mama upended the bag over the bed.

Olesya moaned. Her meticulously prepared and neatly folded dance attire now lay in a heap: leotard, dance skirt, pointe shoes, tights.

Mama rummaged through the bag, checked the bag pockets, turned it inside out. "Well?"

Tears prickled Olesya's eyes. "Why?"

"Why *what*?"

"Why do we have to throw away Papa's things? Why can't we keep at least *something*? Something small?"

"Like your toy train engine?"

Olesya stiffened.

Mama walked up to her and stroked her head. "It's hard for you, I know. It's hard for me too. But you need to let go, Olesya. We both need to. We need to move on."

"But can't we keep something for memory? Just for memory."

"Memories belong in the past." Mama took Olesya's face in her hands, lifted it up. "I want you to focus on your future. Think about your life, what you want to accomplish. Your goals."

"I don't have any goals."

"Yes, you do. You want to be a ballerina, don't you? You want to dance on the Bolshoi stage. Isn't that a goal?"

Olesya bit her lip.

"So you see. Your life is in your own hands, Olesya. I can't live it for you. Nobody can. You need to stop sulking—"

"I'm not sulking."

"Don't interrupt me."

"I'm not sulking!" She pushed her mother's hands away. "I'm remembering."

"Remembering."

"Yes."

"I see." Mama's voice was cold. "And does *remembering* require you to hide from people and stop talking?"

Olesya scoffed.

"Answer me."

"I don't care."

"Answer—"

"I don't care, okay? Leave me alone! Why won't you leave me alone?"

Mama's face hardened. "You've hardly spoken a word to me since we buried your father. You don't go out with Natasha anymore. You don't go anywhere except school or ballet. Yesterday your teacher Anna Mikhailovna called. You know why? She said you stopped participating in class. You don't answer her when she calls on you. How long is this going to continue?"

Olesya glanced at the clock. 17:22. Her belly squeezed. She'd have to sprint to make it.

"Did you hear me?"

"I need to go." She made for the bed.

Mama blocked her. "All right," she said softly. "I'll make it easy for you. No more ballet classes, starting today."

Olesya's breath caught. "What?"

"Ballet was your father's idea. I never approved of it. It'll save us a great deal of money too. So you can take your time. One way or another—"

"I hate you."

"What did you say?"

"I said, it's mine," Olesya blurted. "TUBE is *mine*. It's my birthday present. It belongs to me."

"Did you pay for it?"

"No."

"Then it doesn't belong to you. Your father paid for it. Actually, he got it as a bribe from a smuggler—a criminal."

"That's not true."

Mama ignored her. "It's not a good idea to keep American contraband at home. It's risky. I could go to prison for it. You know what they'll do to you? If I go to prison? They'll put you in an orphanage, where you'd be lucky enough if there's food, never mind ballet."

The minute hand moved. 17:30.

"Well?"

Olesya hung her head. In thirty minutes, Ekaterina Petrovna would lock the studio doors, and Olesya would have to stand by the glass, humiliated, avoiding the girls' pitiful looks, until class was over. And then she'd have to stand in front of them and explain why she missed it. She couldn't blame Mama, so she'd have to come up with a lie.

All was lost.

Olesya walked to the wardrobe, pulled out the bottom drawer, swiped her underwear out of the way, and lifted a box stamped with English letters.

TUBE
Trans-Urban Blitz Express
HO SCALE ELECTRIC TRAIN SET
COMPLETE AND READY TO RUN

Quickly, before Mama noticed, she slipped her hand under the lid, pulled out the engine, and slid it under her sweater.

Mama took the box from her. "Get dressed."

Olesya was ready in two minutes flat, TUBE safely deposited in her coat pocket.

While Mama waited for the elevator, Olesya raced down the stairs and burst out the doorway, gulping cold air. Mama emerged moments later, and they walked to the dumpster area across the yard.

It was a crisp winter evening. The sky was dark, and the snow was bright in the glow of the streetlamps. Olesya watched shouting children sliding down the snowbanks, young mothers walking their prams, old babushkas gossiping on the benches, and she wondered how life could continue. How could these people live when Papa was dead?

The snow crunched under her boots. She stopped by the dumpster and covered her nose—even in this cold the garbage stank.

Mama handed her the box. "Quickly."

"Me? Why me?"

"Because." Mama waited. "I thought you were late?"

Olesya looked around for help. None was coming. She flung back the dumpster lid, lifted the box.

"Wait. Open it."

Dread gripped Olesya's heart. Any moment now Mama would see that TUBE was missing. Then she'd pat her pockets and find it. Why, oh, why didn't she leave it at home or stash it somewhere? Oh, she was so stupid, so—

A door creaked open, banged shut. A dog yipped excitedly. A man's voice hushed it. Footsteps approached them.

This was her chance.

"Someone's coming!" she said.

Mama turned to look, and Olesya took TUBE from her pocket and shoved it down her pants.

"Just a man walking a dog." Mama opened the box. There they sat, the shiny cars, the bundles of tracks, the speed dial— "Where's the engine?"

Olesya shrugged.

"Come here."

She came up slowly.

"What's with the funny walk?"

The lie came easy. "Ekaterina Petrovna made me do extra *pliés*. My legs hurt."

"You walked just fine a minute ago."

"I was warm, and now I'm cold."

It was easy to fool Mama. She didn't understand ballet. She frowned but made no comment and reached inside Olesya's coat pockets.

"Maybe it's still in the drawer?" Olesya said. "Fell out?"

"All right." Mama exhaled a cloud of breath. "I'll go look." She threw the box in the dumpster. It hit the garbage with a wet smack.

Olesya flinched at the noise.

"You better hurry," Mama said.

"Okay."

Olesya walked around the dumpster area, looked back. Mama was gone. Olesya crossed the street, hid in the shadow of an apartment building, and pulled TUBE from her pants.

"Don't worry," she said. "I won't let her find you. I'll hide you well."

She put it in her coat pocket, adjusted her dance bag, and walked out into the aisle of the haunted car.

15KM TO BELGOROD
5 February 1989
18:11

She was back on the train. She was back. She was *back*.

From where?

Olesya looked into compartment No. 1. It was empty.

"Did I . . . did I just . . . ?"

She blinked, looked down at her hands, at her sweater, felt her coat pockets, pulled out TUBE. "Where did you take me?" she said. "What was it that I saw just now?"

But she already knew.

A memory. She'd seen a memory she'd long forgotten.

She flipped TUBE around, rolled its wheels, set it upright on her palm. It seemed improbable it had been inside her, in the hole where her belly button should've been—where she was hollow. It was the stuff that nightmares were born from. It was something that happened to other people, not to her. Not to Olesya Belaya, an ordinary Soviet citizen and a Bolshoi Ballet soloist. A normal woman, by all counts, who didn't believe in ghosts or visions of any kind, who didn't fall for any superstitions, delusions, or untruths. And yet, she held in her hand a toy that had no business being here. She talked to her own five-year-old self. She believed Dima's story about his mother's flats, and now she'd opened a compartment that held her forgotten memory—not with a key but with TUBE, and not by inserting it into a lock but by inserting it into herself, into a hole in her. A hole Yuri saw . . . a hole he said grew bigger.

Olesya gazed down at her sweater until every yarn pattern was etched in her mind, until her eyes watered and her head started swimming. She gripped the hem, lifted it up.

Nothing.

Her belly was fine. No holes, no marks of any kind.

She exhaled.

"Mama."

The memory was so fresh, she felt she was still in it, sprinting to her ballet class, horribly late. Was that what Little Olesya wanted from her? To remember? Remember what exactly?

Olesya looked down the length of the aisle and counted the doors. Nine compartments total. Eight more memories to visit? The thought gave her chills. What if there was something she didn't want to see, didn't want to remember? She glanced at the attendant's compartment. Could TUBE open it too? But Little Olesya said—

She didn't want to think about that. She wanted out of here, out of this car.

And where would she go?

Dima? No. He clearly didn't want her. Natasha then. Olesya shook her head. No, it'd turn into a fight, and she didn't feel like fighting. Didn't feel like talking to anyone, except maybe Yuri. Maybe he'd find her a vacant bunk in some car. She wouldn't mind neighbors, someone who didn't know her. Yes, that would work. She'd ask him about the hole, about ghosts.

But first she'd call Mama.

Olesya went to her compartment, gathered her things, looked at her watch. 18:20. Fifteen more minutes or so till Belgorod. If they were on time. She sat down to wait, looked out the window at the snowfields rolling in the dark, at the yellow lights of the distant buildings.

Why did Mama throw away Papa's things? Did she hate him that much? She must have. They always fought, *always*, Mama and Papa. For as long as Olesya could remember. Their fights were loud, long and ugly. And it was always about Olesya. Why, she didn't understand. It seemed they used her as an excuse to start blaming each other, and then it went downhill. Olesya would flee to her room, put a pillow over her head. Not that it helped. She still heard every word through the thin walls of their apartment. Every slur. Every insult. Every shriek and slap.

It was her fault. She had to do better. In school. In ballet. And she had to stay quiet. Invisible. So as not to provoke them.

Her family wasn't different from the others she knew. Natasha's parents fought too. Everyone's parents did. It was a way of life. And yet she felt dirty somehow. Guilty. As though there were a family secret that caused all this fighting, and she the center of it.

Why couldn't she remember?

Her head hurt from thinking, and she squeezed her eyes shut, swaying with the car. An image struck her. She sat up straight, startled. Little Olesya. The tracks on her legs. That feeling of nausea that hit her. Why did she feel nauseated? It made no sense. And yet it did, somehow, for a brief moment. But then it slipped her mind. It was gone. *Poof!*

It was over before it started. What was it though? *What?*

"I don't know," Olesya said.

Yet she knew. There was something, all right. Her body felt it.

Olesya got up and stepped into the aisle . . . and froze.

The door to the attendant's compartment was open.

She didn't dare breathe.

"Attention, passengers," the intercom squawked. "We're now arriving at Belgorod station. Mind the doors. Don't forget to check for your belongings."

In the window the platform rolled into view, dwarfed by the imposing station building. Olesya's legs acted before her mind. The train was still moving when she jumped out and bolted for the entrance, feeling eyes on her back, afraid to turn and look.

Afraid to see who it was.

Afraid to know.

BELGOROD STATION BUILDING

18:59

"Who is it? Misha? Misha, is that you?" a woman shouted in the telephone booth.

Olesya fidgeted, scanning the crowd for familiar faces. She'd waited in the queue for half an hour now, and her turn was next. So far luck was with her. No dancers, no Alla Borisovna, no one she'd have to explain herself to—what she was doing here, why she wasn't on the train back to Moscow—

The wall clock struck 19:00. Twenty-six minutes till departure.

"Come on," Olesya muttered to the back of the woman's head. "Hurry up."

As if the woman had heard her, she slammed the receiver down, banged the door open, and shoved Olesya aside, cursing under her breath. Olesya didn't mind. The phone was hers to use, the receiver still warm from the woman's grip.

Olesya dropped a two-kopeck coin into the slot and dialed her home number.

The phone rang a few times before Mama picked up.

"Hello?"

"Mama? It's me. I'm in Belgorod."

"Olesya?"

"Mama, I need—"

"I'm grading papers. Call me tomorrow, when you get to Simferopol, yes?"

"Wait! Wait. I need to ask you something. I remembered something . . . when I was five, I think—I think something happened. I mean . . ." How could she put it?

"What is it?"

Olesya closed her eyes. "When Papa took me on the train for the first time, on the ride . . . How old was I, do you remember? Five? Six? Older?"

"What's this about?"

"Mama, please. How old was I?"

"Why, don't you remember?"

"No." It hurt to say it.

"You were five."

Olesya nodded. Five. "And . . . did I like it? I mean, when I came back, were there any signs—"

"Olesya, I don't have time for this right now. We'll talk tomorrow."

"Wait!" Olesya's hands shook. "Mama, please. I remembered something. I . . . we played TUBE, Papa and I, and I drew on my legs. Train tracks. It sounds strange, I know. I think I drew them with a marker. So when I came back, did you see anything?"

"Like what?"

"Like—I don't know—train tracks on my legs? When I came back . . . were they there?"

Silence.

"Mama?"

Breathing.

"Mama, you okay?"

"I need to go." Mama's voice was quiet.

Olesya's gut pricked. "So they were there. The lines. Weren't they?"

"Call me tomorrow."

"No, please. Listen to me. I think something happened on that train. I think . . . maybe the game went wrong, I don't know. Maybe I did something wrong. But somehow those tracks are connected . . ." How could she put it exactly? What was it that Yuri said? He said someone tore a hole in her and left her for dead.

"Someone tore a hole in me," she said, horrified at how insane this sounded.

"No one tore a hole in you." Mama's voice trembled. "Where did you get this crazy idea—"

"I think it was me," Olesya said, suddenly certain. "Yes, it was me. I don't know how I did or why, but I did it to myself. With TUBE, maybe? I think so. I'm not sure. I think I did it and was terrified Papa would discover it. Yeah, that sounds about right. That's why I was so afraid of him. Afraid he'd scold me. Punish me. Do you know anything about this, Mama?"

Silence again. Then: "This is not a phone conversation."

"So I did do it. Tell me."

"Olesya, I—"

"Tell me!" Olesya wiped the sweat from her face, unbuttoned her coat.

"Have a good time in Simferopol. Goodbye."

"You lying, selfish bitch!"

Fast breathing. "What did you call me?"

Olesya was stunned. It was Papa's words she'd repeated. He called Mama that and worse when they fought. But Olesya—never in her life did she swear at her mother. Not once. But now something broke in her.

"You heard me. Good. Then I hope you'll hear this too. Someone hurt me on that train. Do you understand?"

No answer.

"Are you there?"

"Then why didn't you say something?" Mama snapped.

"What? When?"

"When you came back."

Olesya gasped, incredulous. "What? I was five! For God's sake, Mama. What could I possibly say?"

"So you remembered it now, out of the blue? That's not how memory works."

"Oh. How *does* it work?"

"You don't forget things like that."

"Things like what?"

"Awful things like that. You remember them for the rest of your life."

Olesya gripped the receiver in mute shock.

"Olesya?"

Words fled her.

"Olesya, you there?"

"You made me like this."

"What? I don't understand—"

"You and Papa both. I never cried, never complained, did I? I never told you I was hurting. Wasn't that convenient, Mama? The perfect child. Perfect little doll. All you had to do was dress me up and show me off."

"How can you say something like this to me? I'm your mother. Your mother! I gave birth to you."

"That's not an excuse, Mama. Not an excuse to torture me."

"*Torture* you?"

"You made me throw away TUBE, the whole train set. You didn't think I'd remember?"

"It was for the best—"

"It was *torture*. Why did you do this to me? Why?"

"I'm tired of this conversation."

"Of course you are. It's your usual cop-out. Next you'll tell me you don't want to talk about this, that you're busy. Am I right?"

Silence.

"I can't believe it. Really, I can't. How did I not see it until now? I mean, at least Papa showed me some affection. You showed me none. Why did you even have me?"

"You want to know why?" Mama's voice changed.

"Yes."

"I'll tell you why. Your father—"

A man knocked on the glass. When Olesya looked at him, he tapped his watch. She put the receiver to her other ear. "What was that? I missed it."

"I've nothing else to tell you."

"No, I missed it! I didn't hear you."

The man rattled the door. Olesya held it shut, her temples pounding.

"What did you say?"

"—ask your uncle Shurik."

"Mama, wait!"

The line beeped. Dead.

Olesya picked up her bags.

The man yanked the door open. "You're not alone here—" he began.

"Fuck you!" She shoved past him.

"Attention," boomed the intercom. "The Moscow–Simferopol train is leaving from siding number one—"

Olesya sprinted, slinging her backpack and dance bag over her shoulder, pushing people apart. When she burst onto the platform, the train was already moving. She snatched a handhold on the nearest car, then heaved herself up.

"Another one." The attendant woman shook her bleached head. "Every stop it's the same. When will you learn to get back on time?"

"Sorry." Olesya leaned on the wall, catching her breath.

"Your ticket."

"It's in my compartment."

"Then go there." She waved impatiently, and Olesya walked down the train, to the haunted car, her steps automatic, a single question on her mind.

What did Uncle Shurik know?

KHARKOV STATION PLATFORM

19:52

The terror of facing Papa—if it was indeed him—stopped Olesya a car short. Thankfully, the next station was only twenty minutes away. She whiled away the time in the vestibule, in the company of the smoking soldiers, ignoring their jabs and attempts to hit on her, staring straight ahead, relieved she was on the train and not in some deserted alley.

The moment the train stopped, she hopped off and smiled.

Snow. Fresh snow.

The platform was swept with it, bright in the light from the posts. She set her bags down, scooped a handful, made a snowball, and threw it at a post and missed. Made another one and missed again. Made a third one, turned, and hurled it at the haunted car.

The snowball burst in a spray of white.

"Score!"

Olesya looked up at the dark windows and shuddered. Did she see someone move? No, it was just a shadow. Still, it shook her. The dread came back, and with it the fear, the guilt, the shame. The sting of pain. She wanted to hurl herself at the car, smash to bits. The pain was too much, *too much*.

Mama lied to her.

Mama betrayed her.

It didn't even matter what happened anymore. Train tracks on her legs, a hole in her stomach—whatever it was, whatever game had gone wrong—Mama knew about it, and she'd covered it up. Olesya felt sick. She picked up her bags and sat down on a bench, shivering.

Uncle Shurik.

What did he have to do with anything? He was the only adult in the family who spoke to Olesya like an equal. Never treated her like a child, never disciplined her or ignored her. She loved him, loved spending time with him when they visited Baba Zina.

She'd always hated it when Baba Zina ridiculed him, praising Papa, his older brother, her beloved Grisha. In her eyes, Uncle Shurik was a failure, and Papa a resounding success. He'd had a stable job as a car attendant. He had been married, and not just to some empty-head, but to a schoolteacher. A respected position. They'd had a daughter, the latest model Zhiguli, a two-room Moscow apartment. And what did Uncle Shurik have? Nothing. No job, no wife, only his rocks and caves. And his vodka.

"An embarrassment," she'd say the moment they arrived, loud enough for Uncle Shurik to hear. "Still lives off his mother. Sucks all the blood out of me. Just yesterday . . ." Then she'd launch into some story that always had the same ending. Uncle Shurik borrowed money from her, disappeared for a few days, then came home drunk. "Do something, Grisha," she'd implore Papa. "Talk to him. He always listens to you."

Olesya sat up straighter on the bench.

Did they visit Uncle Shurik that summer? When she was five? When Papa took her on the train? A vague recognition stirred in her. It felt true. She could almost smell it. The dusty platform, the tar, the stuffy car—

"Olesya!"

She turned. The memory fled her.

Dima walked toward her, in his hands a bulging grocery bag. "Are you all right?"

She wanted to return to her memory. "Why wouldn't I be?"

He sat next to her. "I don't know. Just wondering."

Olesya said nothing.

"I was worried about you."

She nodded.

"Alla Borisovna—"

"I don't want to talk about this."

"Okay."

She longed for him to reach out, to embrace her. He sat erect, stiff, his breath white.

"Well," he began, "I need to tell you something."

"Tell me what?"

"I talked to her."

"Who?"

"Alla Borisovna."

"You talked to the Old Bitch? About what?"

"About us."

Olesya stared. *"Us?"*

"Yeah. She doesn't want to reinstate you, at least not yet, but when we're back in Moscow—"

The memory of Alla Borisovna's request rushed at Olesya. Gennady Romanovich—the looks he gave her, the way he squeezed her naked shoulder when he dropped by at the studio . . .

"No."

"No what?"

She stood. "I'm not . . . I don't think . . . Dima." She looked at him. "I think I'm going to quit."

"Quit?" His mouth opened. "You're serious?"

"Yes. I'm going to quit ballet." The moment she said it, it felt right. She scooped up some snow, pressed it into a ball, and threw it at the car. It smashed satisfactorily. She bent to make another snowball.

Dima grabbed her by the arm. "You can't do that."

"Let go."

"Olesya."

"I can and I will." She wrested her arm from his grip, her face flushed.

"You're crazy."

"Of course I am. To you anyway. Not to me."

"But why?"

She looked at his grocery bag. "You were on your way somewhere, weren't you?"

He looked down at it. "Yeah. I was. Look—"

"Where were you going?"

"It doesn't matter."

"No, where?"

"Listen, it's not important. Really."

His eyes shifted and he got up. Olesya followed his gaze.

At the far end of the platform, in the glow of the lampposts, two figures walked toward them, both easily recognizable by their gait and poise. They were laughing at something, some private joke, their arms linked as if they were mother and daughter. A thought pierced Olesya. Natasha looked up and their eyes met for a moment, then she looked past her and waved. Dima waved back.

"That's a lot to eat by yourself," Olesya said.

"It's not for me."

"I know." She smiled bitterly. "Delicacies for Natasha."

Dima started to respond, but Olesya spoke over him.

"Just one question, can I? How is she, you know . . . is she really that great? Can she really come ten times in a row?"

"What the hell—" Dima's eyes narrowed. "Whatever gave you that idea?"

She peered into the bag. "Beef cutlets, piroshki, kefir. Oh, raspberry jam. A whole jar, wow. What's that for? To smear on her butt and lick it?"

"It's for you," Dima said, his voice flat. "Dinner. Since you can't eat in the dining car."

"Oh." Blood rushed to Olesya's face. "I didn't—"

"Yuri wanted to bring you leftovers, but I stopped him. Thought I'd get you something better than train fare. Should've known it'd be a waste of my time."

He thrust the bag in her hands and stepped away before Olesya could take hold of it. It dropped and opened, scattering its contents. The jar cracked and leaked red syrup, spilling dark and thick on the snow.

"Oh no! Was that raspberry jam? For practicing emotion?"

Olesya turned to look.

Natasha smiled at her.

"Bitch."

"Excuse me?" Alla Borisovna said.

Olesya swayed, heady with emotion. It hit her hard. Rage, envy, spite. She felt she could kill them both—right now, right this very moment—reach out and break their scrawny necks. The thought chilled her.

"I see you decided to stay." Alla Borisovna crossed her arms. "There will be consequences."

"No, there won't."

"I beg your pardon?"

"I quit."

Natasha stared at her. "Quit?"

"Olesya, don't." Dima touched her arm.

She shook him off. "This is my official resignation." She turned to go, then stopped and turned back. "Oh, one more thing. Alla Borisovna, may I ask for a favor?"

Alla Borisovna raised her eyebrows. "And that would be?"

"It's nothing big, really. Won't take you a moment. Can you please relay a message for me to Gennady Romanovich?"

Alla Borisovna studied her for a moment. "Go ahead."

"Next time you see him, can you please tell him to go fuck himself?"

The stung look on Alla Borisovna's face was worth it.

Olesya turned and walked away, smiling, as she slipped her hand in her pocket and felt for TUBE.

MOSCOW, VAGANKOVO CEMETERY

9 January 1978

13:21

Compartment No. 2. Olesya steeled herself. It was going to be painful.

She was no stranger to pain. Pain didn't scare her. What scared her was what lay beyond this door. Did she want to remember?

Yes, she did. And she needed to do it now. While the car was empty.

Was it?

When Olesya stepped in, after leaving Dima, she forgot her fear. Forgot she'd felt eyes on her back the last time she left. But there was no one here. No Little Olesya, no Papa. Her curiosity was impossible to ignore, and she decided to go for it. She knew a shortcut now, knew how it worked.

"I want to play TUBE," she said.

TUBE turned on.

She closed her eyes, pushed it under her sweater. The hollowness opened. She felt TUBE crawl in, gritted her teeth. The pain shot through her, made her cry out. She clasped TUBE's tail end and turned it, watched the door open—

"Vagankovo cemetery."

The city for the dead.

The iron fences and the gravestones and the denuded trees formed a maze that one could get lost in. The alleyways were numbered, and many plots had statues of the dead—a symbol of wealth. It was a prestigious cemetery, the oldest in Moscow. Lots of famous people were buried here: actors, singers, poets.

It was always Papa's ambition to belong to the Moscow elite. The car attendant job was his duty to the Motherland, he explained. At heart, he was an actor and a ballet lover. From what Olesya had overheard in their fights with Mama, he'd paid a hefty bribe for their burial plot. What for? She couldn't understand. It was just a square of earth, wedged between a crypt and a granite obelisk of some war hero.

The freshly dug grave yawned black in the ground. On the trestles sat a closed coffin. Mourners huddled around it, talked quietly. Uncle Shurik stepped up to it. Everyone hushed.

"My dear brother . . ." he began.

Olesya clutched TUBE in her pocket, her hand numb in Mama's grip, her feet cold.

"My dear brother," he said again. "No, this is . . . please forgive me, I need a moment."

The mourners shifted. Someone coughed. Olesya flexed her toes in her boots to warm them, afraid to move too much lest Mama scold her.

Uncle Shurik put a hand on the coffin, smiled. "Hey, Grisha, listen, you silly thing—"

Olesya's heart skipped.

"—I want to tell you something. Something important. Should've told you this while you were alive but . . . somehow never did." He sniffled. "Listen. I never thanked you for saving my life. Always took it as a given, the older brother protecting the younger, that sort of thing. And now look at us. I'm standing here, and you're lying in there, and I feel like I've failed you. Like it was my turn—"

He choked back tears. The sound sent chills down Olesya's back. She jerked her hand out of Mama's hold and covered her ears, which were already covered by a woolen hat. She hated—absolutely *hated*—the sound of crying. What was he, a baby? Couldn't he hold it in?

"Stand still," Mama whispered.

Olesya stood still.

". . . I was only five," Uncle Shurik was saying, "and I'd already got into more trouble than you ever did, climbed every tree in the yard, scraped my knees bloody. You seemed so grown-up to me, thirteen, dreaming of becoming an actor. Remember our walks on the train tracks? You'd come home after school, and I'd be already sitting by the door, waiting—"

"I went on walks with Papa too," Olesya interrupted.

"Olesya." Mama looked at her, aghast.

"What? I did."

"Oh, Grisha. My dear Grisha. My only—" Baba Zina uttered a strangled, agonized wail. Her legs gave out under her and she swayed. Hands caught her.

"Mama!" Uncle Shurik rushed to her.

She waved a dismissive hand and fixed her black kerchief.

Olesya fidgeted. It was getting colder.

Uncle Shurik cleared his throat. "Where was I? Ah yes, our walks." He paused, his eyes unfocused. "We never went past the tunnel—it was too dark, too dangerous. It turned, so you couldn't see the train coming at you till the last moment, but on that day . . . it was September, first day of school, the day when you . . ."

He stood silent for so long, it seemed he wouldn't continue. Seemed he was frozen.

Olesya stared at him, and he looked at her and held her eyes. She couldn't look away. Something passed between them. Something painful. She couldn't tell what it was, couldn't explain it, but suddenly Uncle Shurik straightened, coughed into his fist, and rattled off, "We were playing cops and robbers, and I wanted to win so bad. You'd always won before, you were bigger and faster than me, so I decided to chance it. I ran into the tunnel, and the next thing I knew a train was coming right at me. I froze. It blared at me. Didn't do any good. I couldn't move. I was scared stupid.

"Then I heard you scream. 'Shurik! Shurik!' You rammed into me, and we tumbled down. The dirt stuffed my eyes, my mouth. Then this great wall of sound rushed by, rumbling and creaking and shaking the ground so hard my teeth rattled. So you see, Grisha, if not for you—" His voice caught. He looked directly at Olesya again. "It's ironic you died the way I almost died, isn't it? I think about that a lot. I think you saved me for a reason, even if you didn't know it back then. You saved me so I could take care of your little girl."

He smiled.

Olesya stopped breathing.

"I promise you, brother. I'll take good care of her. May you rest in peace."

He bent his head and quickly stepped away. The mourners parted.

"Can I talk now, Mama?" Olesya asked.

"What?"

"I want to tell a story too, like Uncle Shurik."

But Mama didn't hear her. She was whispering something to Baba Zina, who nodded quietly and dabbed at her eyes.

Olesya filled her lungs with breath. "I want to say something about Papa," she announced.

Mama turned to her. "Olesya. We talked about this, yes? This is not the place—"

"But it's about Papa!" She gripped TUBE in her pocket. "Uncle Shurik told his story, and now I want to tell mine."

Uncle Shurik squatted down in front of her, took her hand into his. She tried to jerk it out, but he held on. "Olesya, look at me."

"It's not fair."

"Look at me."

"No." Tears burned her eyes.

"Please. Just for a moment."

She started crying.

"Valya," he said to Mama, "can I talk to her alone for a moment?"

"Sure." Mama gave Olesya a blistering look.

Olesya wanted to punch her.

"Come on." Uncle Shurik led her out of the plot.

They walked along the alleyway. Olesya looked at her feet.

"Can I make you a deal?"

She shrugged.

"Is that a yes or a no?"

She shrugged again.

He stopped and lifted her face, took off his glove, wiped her tears. "How about you tell me your story later? When it's just the two of us?"

He smiled.

It made Olesya uneasy.

"Why can't I tell everyone?" She kicked at the snow.

Uncle Shurik put his face to her ear. He smelled of alcohol, and Olesya grimaced. "I don't think they'll understand . . . not the way you want them to understand.

Can you trust me on this?" He looked her in the eyes. His eyes were so similar to Papa's, big and gray and round. "I'm not your enemy, kid. I'm on your side—"

Olesya stepped back.

"Come on." He reached for her.

She turned and sprinted and hid behind a giant gravestone, catching her breath.

Nobody came for her. Not Uncle Shurik, not Mama. By the time she made it back, it was almost over. The pallbearers picked up the ropes, heaved the coffin off the trestles, carried it over to the hole and lowered it in, then pulled the ropes out. A man in a dark coat brought a stand with a bowl filled with earth.

"Three handfuls each," he said tiredly, "and don't crowd."

The mourners moved in.

Olesya shuffled behind Mama, her hand on TUBE. Mama sprinkled the earth on the coffin and pushed Olesya forward. "Be quick about it. There are people behind you."

Olesya looked in. The lacquered wood reflected the gray winter sky and the shape of her head, and she had a sudden impulse to throw TUBE instead of earth. She shrunk back, afraid.

"Those who said goodbye, move over to this side," the man said, then spat on the ground.

"Olesya," Mama urged.

Olesya looked at Uncle Shurik.

He walked up to her. "It's like this." He scooped a handful of earth and threw it on the coffin. It made a scattering noise.

Olesya's breath rasped.

"You can do it." He moved her hand to the bowl. "Come on."

Olesya didn't move.

Mama let out an exasperated sigh. "Shurik, just—"

"It's okay," he interrupted. "She's in shock. She needs time. Come on, Olesya. Think about Papa. What would he want you to do? He'd want you to fight, fight your fear. Show him. Show him *you can do it.*" His voice hardened.

Olesya swayed.

Uncle Shurik steadied her. "Repeat after me. 'I can do it.' "

"I can do it," Olesya whispered.

"Louder."

"I can do it." She grabbed a handful of earth and threw it in. "I can do it." She threw another one. "I can do it!"

"That's enough," Uncle Shurik said.

She couldn't stop. Her arm worked like a piston. She scooped and threw, scooped and threw. When Mama tried pulling her back, she windmilled her arms and hit the bowl. It flew and crashed on the coffin with a loud, metallic clang.

"You can't do anything right," Mama hissed, dragging her off by the arm.

Olesya slumped, numb, her cheeks burning.

She walked mechanically, putting one foot in front of the other, and in that moment she decided not to tell anything to anyone anymore. It was useless. Nobody wanted to hear what she had to say—not even Uncle Shurik. So she'd bury it—bury it deep, lock it up—and if they asked, she'd tell them she forgot.

It was the truth.

She was good at forgetting.

KHARKOV–ZAPOROZHYE

5 February 1989
21:28

"What game did we play, Papa? Was there something more to it? More to TUBE?"

Olesya closed her eyes, leaned her head against the window.

She remembered the feeling of excitement, and some fear that she might do something wrong, but not the game itself. How complicated could it be? Lay down the tracks, connect the cars, turn on the engine . . .

Something was missing.

But she'd forgotten what it was. The same way she forgot many other things. It was like her mind was full of dark holes—the kinds of holes TUBE crawled into, to unlock the compartments.

She walked out into the aisle, swaying with the train.

It was strange, what she'd done to her legs. Why would she draw train tracks on them? Yet she did remember how she liked to draw on the wallpaper, and on her mattress. She'd doodle. So what? How was it connected to what Yuri said? And what was it that Uncle Shurik knew?

Maybe she told him something. Maybe—

It didn't make much sense. Olesya sighed.

"Uncle Shurik. I miss you."

He loved her very much. He'd never had kids of his own, and he loved Olesya like his own daughter. That is, when he was sober and when they visited Baba Zina. The other times he disappeared. Never called her in Moscow, never answered her calls. So it'd be no good, trying to call him. She had to go there. Had to go to Baba Zina's house and hope he was there. Or leave him a note at least. Leave him a note and hope he'd call back.

Olesya's heart sank. She was scared. She was confused and scared and bewildered.

How did she hurt herself? *Did* she?

She looked the length of the aisle. Six more compartments.

"All right. Here we go. I want to play—"

The train whistled long and hard, and the car rocked.

Then a faint sound. Notes of a piano.

Olesya listened in wonder. *Dance of the Little Swans?*

Her belly burned as TUBE slid in, but she barely noticed the pain. The music was around her, in her, with her. It was the dance she performed in ballet school, at her first pointe recital—the recital that had been interrupted by Uncle Shurik and the bad news. She'd forgotten that too, and now it came back to her.

Her heart hammered.

The door to her right rolled open.

Olesya stepped inside compartment No. 3.

MOSCOW, CHOREOGRAPHIC SCHOOL

6 January 1978
18:32

A clap of the hands. The music stopped.

Ekaterina Petrovna barked, "Bellies in! Butts in! What are you, asleep? Again."

The music started.

"And one, and two, and three, and—point your feet! Olesya! Your feet!"

The music stopped again.

Olesya blinked at Ekaterina Petrovna's mean little face. She was short and thin and ancient, and she always dressed in black and smoked. Her favorite teaching method was to walk up to a girl and hold the cigarette next to her butt. The poor girl would clench her rear and stand higher, trembling with effort, her eyes rolling like that of a crazed horse. The parents didn't dare complain. A former prima of Plisetskaya caliber, Ekaterina Petrovna accepted only the best in her class and was Choreographic School's most prized Mistress. It didn't stop the girls from calling her behind her back Suka Zlyuka—Cruel Cunt.

"What's this?" Ekaterina Petrovna pointed at Olesya's shaking leg lifted in the air, the cigarette tip nearly touching it. Olesya gripped the bar, lifted her leg higher, sweat trickling down her back, her calf muscles cramped.

"I need a swan, an elegant swan, not a dumb goose."

The girls giggled.

Olesya dropped her leg with a *thump* and exhaled sharply.

"First group!" Ekaterina Petrovna clapped. "Hurry! You still have your costumes to put on. I said, *hurry!*"

Olesya ran out into the center of the floor, linking hands with Natasha, Lena, and Tanya. She caught her breath, steadied herself. The piano started.

They did *Dance of the Little Swans* without a hitch, all one minute and forty seconds of it—Olesya timed it exactly. Papa was coming to watch her today, and she was going to be perfect for him. Absolutely perfect.

"Go change. Quickly!" Ekaterina Petrovna ushered them out.

Olesya was the last to enter the dressing room. She stopped short.

Natasha stood over her dance bag, TUBE in her hand.

"What's this?" she demanded.

"Nothing," Olesya said.

"Where did you get it?"

"Give it back."

Olesya reached for it, but Natasha passed TUBE to Lena, who twirled it in her hands.

"Imported," she said. "Look. Something in English."

"I know English," Tanya piped up. She took TUBE from Lena and read aloud, " 'TUBE.' Girls," she addressed the dressing room, "our Olesya likes to play with imported toys. I bet her Papa is a big shishka."

Olesya lunged at her.

Tanya tossed TUBE to Natasha, who caught it and flipped the switch. TUBE whistled, and its wheels started spinning.

"Look! It's moving!"

She set it on the floor, and it raced by Olesya's feet. Lena kicked the door open. TUBE rolled out. Olesya ran after it. The girls laughed.

When Olesya returned, they were gone. She exhaled in relief and put TUBE in her boot, where she was sure they wouldn't look. Then she pulled off her damp practice leotard and changed into a clean white one, slipped on her tutu, her new pointe shoes, tied the ribbons, tucked them in, and ran backstage.

"Where the hell have you been?" Ekaterina Petrovna snapped. "Go warm up. You have five minutes."

"She was playing with her toy," Natasha said, and snorted into her fist.

Lena and Tanya snickered.

"Hush! No talking. Stretch." Ekaterina Petrovna walked off.

"Suka Zlyuka," Natasha hissed at her back.

"Shh!" Lena's eyes rounded. "She'll hear you."

"I don't care."

"Idiot."

"You're an idiot yourself."

Fast piano chords drifted from the stage. The older girls were finishing their number.

Olesya picked up her leg and lifted it, stretching. Natasha stared at her, whispered to Tanya. Tanya's eyes widened. She covered her mouth, giggled, then whispered to Lena.

Olesya turned away. Let them make fun of her. She didn't care. All that mattered was that she was going to be perfect—for Papa. It was his dream to see Olesya on the Bolshoi stage. She could do it. She knew she could. She was good. Ekaterina Petrovna picked on her for a reason. She only picked on those she believed had potential. The girls knew it too, and they were jealous, most of all Natasha. Olesya was plain as oatmeal next to her, and yet Olesya danced better. Natasha couldn't stand it. She had to be the best. Her parents spoiled her. She had the best clothes, the best snacks—imported candy and gum—and the best friends. And she was pretty, very pretty. So pretty it hurt Olesya to look at her.

The piano finished playing. A gaggle of sweaty, pink-faced girls rushed backstage, their tutus swishing, their eyes gliding over the younger girls with disdain.

"Ready?" Ekaterina Petrovna said.

They crossed their arms in front of them and grasped hands—Natasha first, Olesya second, then Lena and Tanya. Olesya's cold fingers burned in Natasha's hot hand.

Feet shuffled in the audience, chairs scraped the floor.

Ekaterina Petrovna walked onstage. "Tchaikovsky," she announced. "*Dance of the Little Swans* from the ballet *Swan Lake*. Choreographer Rozanova." A few claps. "Thank you. Performing: Natasha Ryzhik, Olesya Belaya, Lena—"

Natasha pushed her face in Olesya's ear. "If you screw up, I'll give your toy to my papa, and he'll put your papa in prison."

Olesya recoiled. Then a memory came to her, something Papa yelled at Mama in one of their fights. "My papa says militiamen have rotten genes. I guess that means their daughters make rotten ballerinas."

Natasha pinched her hand.

Olesya pinched her back.

The piano started.

They entered the stage in a line, moving together in unison.

Olesya's heart beat faster. She knew Papa was there, watching her. She wanted to see him, wanted to see the expression on his face, but she knew she couldn't. They had to pretend to be little swans huddling for protection, crossing the stage in a chain, moving as one. Their heads had to turn like those of birds—up, down, sideways. If she looked straight ahead, she'd break the pattern of movement, break the illusion.

Finally.

They stopped in the center to do jumps, and Olesya could keep her head straight. She glimpsed Mama in the second row and an empty seat next to her. She stumbled. Natasha crushed her fingers. Olesya righted herself.

He's not here pounded in her head. *He's not here.*

The exit door opened. Olesya's heart leapt. A man stepped in, closed the door. Next time she looked up, the man was walking with Mama toward the exit. Her legs nearly gave out. Her body kept dancing automatically, her mind blank.

The music stopped. The dance was over. Olesya kneeled in a curtsy, breathing hard.

As the girls got up, she jumped offstage.

"Olesya!" Ekaterina Petrovna hissed from the first row.

She ignored her and sprinted out the door and into the hall, where Mama stood crying in Uncle Shurik's arms.

"Uncle Shurik?" She walked up to them. "Where's Papa?"

"Olesya." He smiled. "That was some good dancing."

"Where is Papa?" she repeated.

Uncle Shurik looked at Mama.

"What's wrong?" Olesya's voice broke. "Why are you crying?"

Mama looked away. "Your papa," she said, and fell silent.

"Papa what? *What?*"

Uncle Shurik took Olesya's hands, looked her in the eyes. "This is going to be hard."

"What is it?"

"I want you to take a deep breath—"

"Just tell me!" she shrieked. "Can't you just tell me?"

They were silent.

"He promised." Olesya blinked, forcing tears down. "My first recital. He said—he said he'd be here—he said . . ." Tears spilled.

Uncle Shurik looked down. "He never broke his promises, did he?"

"Broke?"

"Your papa was killed by a train." Mama's voice was flat.

Olesya shrunk. "What?"

"He's dead, Olesya. Dead."

"Dead?"

"He was hacking the ice off the last car," Mama said. Her eyes glinted strangely.

"Valya." Uncle Shurik touched her arm. "Valya, don't."

Mama swiped off his hand. "A freight train lost control and rode into him at full speed. Smashed three cars before it stopped. So you see, your papa . . . they had to scrape him off—"

"Valya!" Uncle Shurik cried, aghast.

She turned to him. "Don't tell me you're sorry."

"Valya, please."

"Scum." She was shaking.

He reached out, and she slapped his hand away.

"How could you?" Mama said.

"I know," Uncle Shurik said. "It's no excuse. But please, understand—"

"Whoops!" said Natasha's voice.

Olesya jumped.

A group of girls in winter coats had stopped a few doors away. Natasha whispered to Lena. Lena gasped. Natasha nodded. The other girls giggled and turned to stare at Olesya.

A sudden suspicion pricked her gut.

Natasha dangled out TUBE. "I was just bringing it to you," she said innocently. "Want it?"

Olesya started forward, and Natasha threw it behind her.

The girls ran past Olesya, squealing with laughter.

Olesya picked up TUBE and raced after them as she was, in her little swan costume.

She burst out the front door. Cold struck her like a fist. She leapt down the steps, slipped and fell and scrambled up in one breath, and ran, her pointe shoes slipping on the snow. There was no sign of the girls. The street was dark and busy in the evening rush hour. Hurried men and women swaddled up to their ears rushed past her, some knocked into her, some said something. Olesya didn't hear them.

She stopped and bent over, shaking, wheezing. Walked over to a streetlamp buried in a snowbank, watched her breath coil out of her mouth in white puffs. She was mad, so mad, *so mad* at Papa. She wanted to hurt him.

She couldn't.

She uttered a little wail and plunged TUBE deep into the virgin-white snow, pulled it out, plunged it in, and kept stabbing it until her arm went numb.

TURNING ON THE ENGINE

KHARKOV-ZAPOROZHYE

5 February 1989
21:45

TUBE bounced off the wall and fell to the floor, unscathed. Olesya snatched it and began to bash it against the table methodically, her face hot.

"What are you hiding?" she said. "What are you *hiding*?"

It infuriated her. Some kind of a family secret connected to TUBE that they were all covering up. And she couldn't remember it. She remembered nothing!

Olesya grunted, frustrated. It was maddening, not being able to remember, having to assemble bits and pieces like a jigsaw puzzle that didn't make any sense. Only one thing *did* make sense. She was certain of it.

Mama knew.

Because every mother knows.

Then what about Papa? If Mama knew, *he* knew. Nothing escaped him. And if he knew, Uncle Shurik knew. And Baba Zina knew. They all did.

But what did it have to do with a perfectly innocent game? It was a toy train, for God's sake, just a toy train. And all of Olesya's memories connected to it were happy. It was the best—the loveliest and the most exciting—time she'd had with her father. Then what on earth could compel her to hurt herself? What did they mean, those tracks on her legs? And why would she hide them from Papa? Was she afraid of his punishment? Clearly she was. But why would he punish her for drawing on her legs? Where was the crime in that?

And Mama . . . Why did she speak so evasively about it?

"You lied to me." Olesya trembled. "You all lied to me."

She set TUBE on the floor and stomped on it, hard, harder. It gave her satisfaction to watch its paint flake off, its headlamp crack, its wheels bend. She placed it in the doorway and smashed it with the door until it dented.

Fear seized her. What if she damaged it too much? What if it stopped working as a key? Stopped opening doors?

She went into the aisle.

Five more compartments.

She didn't have to see them all, did she?

"Yes, I do. If I want to remember, I do."

She stopped in front of compartment No. 4, listening.

Silence.

She took a deep breath, lifted her sweater. "I want to—"

There was no need to finish.

As though TUBE knew, it lit up. The tiny bulb shone through the broken plastic. The whistle blared. The bent wheels started spinning.

Olesya touched it to her stomach, and her belly button widened, stretched, grew. The pain was that of tearing tissue: skin, then muscle. She bit her lip, hard. Tears stood in her eyes. She watched with horror how the hole in her deepened, darkened, like a toy train tunnel lined with her own skin. No blood. At least there was no blood.

She clenched her jaws, pushed in TUBE, and turned.

Click. The door opened.

"Found you!" said a man's voice.

Olesya froze. "Papa?"

"How about some light?"

The light switched on in the compartment.

Olesya shut the door without looking, shaking all over.

She didn't want to remember this one. She didn't know why. It wasn't like she knew what was inside—she didn't—so how could she not want to remember it? It was beyond her, and this confusion was exhausting.

"Found you!" Papa had said. What was so scary about that? He sounded playful.

Then why did she close the door so quickly?

Her Papa. Her beloved Papa.

He always wanted a family. A wife. And a little girl. A daughter.

That's what Baba Zina told Olesya anyway. She said when Papa was a teenager he was shy and awkward, with his big, unwieldy head and puny body, but his eyes were striking, and he could spin a story that made the girls swoon. Baba Zina sewed dresses for them, wined and dined them, with the secret purpose of her favorite son marrying into a good family and staying close to her.

"All for nothing!" she complained to Olesya.

Because when Papa found out about her scheming, they had a big fight, and he left Alupka. "A hole in the middle of nowhere," he called it. A sleepy resort town on the Black Sea that had no future for him. He hopped on a train to Moscow to pursue an acting career. While on the train, he got a job as a car attendant and met Olesya's mother. They arrived, and he married her the next day.

"Not for love," Baba Zina said once, after she'd had too much vodka, "but for your mama's two-room apartment." She denied having said that later of course.

Olesya believed her.

So there was no love in her family, was there? Only secrets, unspoken truths, and lies.

Olesya felt sick. It didn't get her any closer to what happened, yet she knew—sensed it, almost tasted it as bitterness in her mouth—they were covering up something.

"How is this connected to playing TUBE?" She didn't realize she'd said it aloud, was startled by her own voice.

"Not how. *Why.*"

Olesya spun around.

Little Olesya stood in front of her, arms crossed. "You're wasting time."

"But—"

"Shut up and listen." She took TUBE from Olesya's hand. "You have to go in."

"Go in where?"

"Compartment number four. Where else?"

"And if I don't want to? What if I want to go see what's in the attendant's compartment? What are you doing in there with Papa? He's in there with you, isn't he?"

Little Olesya stared. "Don't you get it?"

"Don't I get what?"

"It's not *your* memory, stupid. You can only see yours."

Olesya blinked. "But how—"

"Don't act like you don't know. You're the one who did this, not me."

Sweat broke out on Olesya's forehead. "You mean . . . I locked you up?"

"You dumb goose!"

Olesya flinched.

Little Olesya poked her with TUBE. "You already lived through it. What's there to be afraid of?"

"But what . . . what was it that I lived through?"

"Go and see."

"Can't you just tell me?"

Little Olesya stuck out her lower lip. "You really *are* stupid."

"Stop it."

"Don't you remember?"

"No, I don't!" It came out as a shriek.

"Fine. I'll tell you. You locked me up in here because you didn't trust me. You trusted *them*"—Little Olesya waved at the doors—"but they lied to you, get it? I had to chew a hole through you, to get you to listen."

"So it was *you*?"

Little Olesya blew out air. "Who did you think, dummy?" She slipped TUBE under the hem of Olesya's sweater.

"Wait. Wait!" Olesya stepped back. "Why can't you just tell me?"

Little Olesya screwed up her face. "Coward." There was no malice in her voice, only grief. She handed Olesya TUBE, hung her head, and turned to walk.

"Where are you going?"

"Where you locked me up."

A bolt of recognition pierced Olesya. She felt what Little Olesya felt. Helplessness, fear, despair.

"Don't go there."

Little Olesya walked faster.

"Don't go there." Olesya ran after her. "Don't!"

The door to the attendant's compartment opened.

Olesya sidestepped Little Olesya to look in. It was pitch-black inside, as though the light from the aisle stopped at the threshold. She made to enter.

"No!" Little Olesya yelled.

The door shut in Olesya's face just as the door to compartment No. 4 opened.

"Found you!"

Olesya covered her ears, dashed up the aisle, and ran up the train, elbowing passengers out of her way, breathless, frantic, until she reached her car and collided with Yuri, who was carrying tea. The tray flew out of his hands. The tea glasses, holders, spoons, and sugar spilled all over the floor. A wet stain spread on Yuri's uniform.

"Devil take me!" he exclaimed.

"I'm sorry," Olesya said, panting. "I'm so sorry. I'm—" She burst into tears. Her knees buckled and she pitched forward.

Yuri caught her. "There, there."

She clutched the lapels of his jacket.

"I got you," he said. "I got you."

He held her.

She cried long and hard, gasping, sobbing, the way she hadn't allowed herself to cry for a long time. Yuri held her and rocked her. Once in a while he patted her on the back and said, "There, there."

23:11

"I saw it." Olesya sniffled, blew on the steaming tea, took a sip. "The hole."

"I knew you would." Yuri bit on a cookie.

"You did?"

"Of course I did." He shoved the rest of the cookie in his mouth and reached for another. "Go ahead, have some." He pushed the packet toward Olesya.

"But . . . how could you possibly know?"

Yuri slurped the rest of his tea, set the empty glass on the table. "Because you knew all along, didn't you? You knew all along."

Olesya took a cookie, twirled it in her hand. A buttery yellow rectangle, its name baked into it. YUBILEYNOYE—ANNIVERSARY.

"I guess I felt it," she said.

Yuri squinted at her. "And what did that feel like?"

"I don't know. Like something missing. Like . . ." She bit the cookie, chewed. "Like I was hollow inside? Like a part of me—"

"Was gone," Yuri finished for her.

"Yeah, like that."

He nodded.

"And something else. Like something was wrong with my body. Like there was something I needed to see, to know, to remember. But I couldn't figure out what or how to get there. It was like—like I had a hole. A hole in me." She looked at him, startled. The cookie dropped from her hand, broke in half.

"You've got guts, dorogusha." Yuri leaned over the table. "Most people don't dare to look. They get busy-busy-busy. They figure, if they're busy enough they're going somewhere, right? Doing something important? Only what's important is right under their noses. They never look there, do they? No, God forbid. It's too scary to look, so they patch up their holes any way they can—drink, whore, drug themselves. You name it. Anything they can do not to see, not to feel. A sorry existence if you ask me." He leaned back on the bunk.

Olesya picked up a piece of the cookie, put it in her mouth, chewed slowly. "I did it too," she said.

"Of course you did. Everyone does."

"Patched it up with ballet." She looked at him. "I worked myself to death. You know? Just so I couldn't feel anything. A workaholic. How is that different from drinking?"

"You wanted to forget, didn't you?"

"I did."

They sat in silence.

"It'll eat at you," Yuri said.

"It already has."

He rubbed his scar.

"Can you make it go away?" Olesya asked. "The hole? Can you close it?"

"Can you forget the pain once you've remembered it?"

"I don't know."

"Why do you think Raisa still visits me?"

"Your dead wife?"

"I can't let her go," Yuri said. "That's my weakness."

"So you're . . . stuck?"

He looked out the window, the passing lights throwing shadows on his face. "You've got to let go, dorogusha. The ghosts. The ones working on you, chewing at your hole. Until you do, they'll keep at it. You mind my words."

"Ghosts," Olesya said. "You know, in the haunted car, I saw myself when I was five. And she—the little me, Little Olesya—she told me she chewed a hole through me, to make me listen."

"She's dead inside you," Yuri said. "That's a heavy burden."

"Was that what you meant when you said I was lugging around 'dead weight'?"

"Sure did."

"I see."

Olesya fell quiet.

"How old are you?" Yuri asked.

"Twenty-one tomorrow." Olesya glanced at her watch. "In about half an hour."

"Goodness." He shook his head. "Lugging a dead child around for so long."

"What do you mean, *dead child*? She's not dead. I'm not dead."

"You know exactly what I mean." He peered into her eyes, his expression grim.

They sat for some time in silence.

"I quit ballet," Olesya said.

Yuri wrapped the leftover cookies in the package. "Did you?"

"Yes." Olesya stood. "And I'm getting off at the next station."

"Zaporozhye?" He gaped at her. "In the middle of the night?"

She nodded. "I'll wait for the next train to Moscow."

"That's a long wait."

"I don't care."

Yuri scratched his head. "Tell you what, dorogusha. Why don't you stay with me and Lidochka? Then you can go back to your Moscow. She'll be beyond herself, my Lidochka. To meet a real Bolshoi ballerina!"

"I'm not a ballerina anymore." Olesya gazed out the window at the flashing darkness, the passing snowfields, the distant lights. "Yuri." She looked at him. "You're the first person I don't have to explain anything to. You just . . . understand. Even though I don't understand this myself."

He watched her, waiting.

"Remember when I told you there was a man hurting his daughter?" She hesitated. "And then . . . we opened the compartment, and there was no one there? Well, there *is* someone there. Actually, I think I know who it is. It's the little me, Little Olesya, and . . . my father. I think. I think it's him. I heard his voice, and I'd recognize it anywhere. Only . . . how can that be? I mean, he's dead. He died a long time ago."

Yuri's expression didn't change. "How long ago? If you don't mind my asking."

"A little over ten years."

"Can I ask what happened?"

"Of course. He was killed."

"Killed?"

"Well, it was an accident. He was a car attendant. Just like you. He took me with him often on train trips. We sat in his compartment like you and I are now, drinking tea, talking. I miss talking to him, but I could never talk to him like I can talk to you. He never understood me the way you do, and you only met me today. Isn't that ironic?"

"How did he die?"

Olesya fingered her sweater. "Do you remember the train wreck by Simferopol? Ten years ago?"

Yuri whistled. "Christ Almighty. That was no train wreck, that was hell come to earth. A friend of mine was on that train. He said twelve people were killed, over a hundred injured. Your father was there?"

"Yeah. He was." She sighed. "He was hacking the ice off the last car. They told us he didn't hear the freight train approach. So he must've died quickly. We got a sealed coffin, you know, like Afghanistan soldiers."

"A zinc coffin."

Olesya nodded.

Yuri slumped in the seat. "That's an awful way to go. What was his name?"

"Grigory Vasilievich Bely."

"Huh, never heard of him. I'll ask Raisa. Maybe it's him who's haunting that car."

Olesya froze. "No. It can't be."

"How would you know?"

"You said that man killed himself. Papa would never do that."

"You sure?"

Olesya shifted uncomfortably under Yuri's gaze. "I better go."

Yuri got up. "You're not getting off this train in the middle of the night."

"But—"

"Listen here, dorogusha. Go back to that car and do what you have to do. I'll make sure no one bothers you." He opened the compartment door.

"But what if I don't want to?"

"Then we're done here, you and I."

"What do you mean?"

Yuri didn't answer, just stood there.

Olesya stalled, unsure. "What do you mean, Yuri?"

He crossed his arms. "You love that Dima of yours, don't you?"

She looked down.

"Well then. If you won't do it for yourself, will you do it for him?"

"Do what?"

Yuri shook his head.

"Yuri."

He stepped into his compartment.

"Yuri, wait."

He slid the door shut.

Olesya was stunned, her breath gone. "Yuri!"

Silence.

She glanced at her watch. It was almost midnight. She walked to her compartment, opened the door.

On her bunk lay Natasha, facedown.

Dima was on top of her, riding her hard.

6 February 1989
00:02

Happy twenty-first, Olesya thought. *You're not normal. And you'll never ever have sex.*

She stared at Natasha's naked back, at Dima's hands kneading her shoulders.

"A little harder," Natasha directed. "Yeah, like that. Yes, yes. That's good."

Dima panted. "I can't—I don't think I'm strong enough—"

"Yes, you can. Do it."

"Okay . . ."

Dima picked up speed.

Tears blurred Olesya's vision.

"Oh, this feels *good*," Natasha moaned.

Olesya could stand it no longer. She made a gasping noise. Stumbled back.

Dima turned around and saw her. "Olesya?" He slid off Natasha's back.

They gaped at each another.

"Sorry to interrupt," Olesya heard herself say. "I'll be going then. You guys can continue."

"Olesya, what . . . what happened to you? You look white as a ghost."

"Oh, nothing. Nothing." Olesya blinked away tears.

Natasha got off the bunk and stretched.

Olesya stared at her feet.

"You could've knocked," Natasha said. "You going to stand there all night?"

Olesya winced. "I came to say goodbye," she said. "I'm going back to Moscow."

"Okay. Goodbye."

There was silence.

"Is that all?" Natasha said.

"Olesya, you all right?" Dima said.

The irony of it. Olesya smirked. "Yeah, I'm fine. Fine. Just peachy."

"You don't sound fine."

How could he even talk to her? And so calmly?

"Why am I not surprised." Natasha walked up to Olesya. "Olesya Belaya," she said, "our porcelain doll. Cold and silent. You never cared to be a principal, did you? If it happened one day, fine. You'd be fine. If it didn't happen, fine! You'd also be fine. You're always fine. Nothing fazes you, not ever. I wonder—do you ever care about anything? Anything at all?"

Olesya's chest squeezed. She kept staring at the floor. "No, I don't. You're right. I have no feelings. I'm a porcelain doll, after all. And dolls can't feel, can they?"

"You asking me? How would I know?"

Dima shoved Natasha aside. "Damn you. Olesya, listen—"

Without looking up—seeing only his pants and feet and not wanting to see the rest—Olesya spun around and hurried off.

She quietly opened Yuri's compartment. He dozed on the bunk. His jacket hung by the door. She slipped her hand in the pocket, took out his keys, closed his door, and walked down the train, calm and empty.

How easy this was. Why didn't she think of it before? One step, and it would be all forgotten. Forgotten for good.

She reached the haunted car's vestibule, inserted the key in the exit door, and pushed it open.

The wind hit her. The wheels knocked in her ears, loudly. The distant lights danced.

She looked down at the smooth, rolling snow. What was it Papa used to tell her? "Stay away from the exit doors, Olesya. You don't want to step out to your death."

She smiled. "It's not death, Papa, just a leap offstage."

She lifted her leg.

"On the count of four. And one, and two, and three, and—"

00:34

The train whistle was sudden and shrill.

Olesya jerked back from the door. Her heart hammered. An oncoming freight train answered in a long blare. She covered her ears, watched the door slam against its frame. Closed it.

"I've tried this before," she said. "I've tried this before."

She did.

She now remembered.

They were on the train back to Moscow, returning from Baba Zina's funeral. It was summer, and it was very hot. Mama was napping with a wet towel over her face, fighting the heat. There was no air-conditioning, and the cars had poor ventilation. The open windows didn't help. The temperature was above thirty degrees Celsius. The passengers were bathed in sweat. Men smoked in the vestibules, shirtless. Women fanned themselves with newspapers. Children ran around naked.

Olesya had wandered off to the last car and discovered that the exit door was open.

She leaned out into the heat, looked at the running ground covered with sunburned grass. The wind washed over her, smelling of tar, and she dangled out one leg, retracted it, pulled out TUBE from her pocket, and crouched down, tensing to jump. Her movements were deliberate, as though she had thought it all through. She felt nothing. She watched the ground for a good spot to land and roll and roll into obscurity.

"Stay away from the exit doors," Papa used to say.

He told her stories. Stories of the accidents on the trains, how some people died, but some survived. How it was worse than death, to survive. She didn't want that. She wanted it to work, and so she had closed her eyes, getting ready to leap—

—when the train whistled.

Her heart jumped. She swayed back, shaking, and turned to run back up the train, thinking it was all TUBE's fault. If she threw it away, like Mama wanted, maybe she'd throw away—

The train jerked, screeched to a sudden stop, cutting off Olesya's memory.

She swayed back, clutched the handhold for balance.

There was faint scratching coming from below. She looked down.

TUBE scurried to her along the aisle. It bumped against her feet and stopped.

She picked it up.

"I wish you'd talk," she said. "I wish you'd tell me all that happened."

It was still.

"Do I have to? It hurts, you know. It hurts really bad."

TUBE waited.

Outside, soft snow fell, brushing the windows. The train whistled once and started and rolled, picking up speed.

"Okay," Olesya said. "All right. Let's play."

She lifted her sweater, and that was enough. No words needed. The hole opened. She pushed TUBE inside it, turned and—

MOSCOW, BELY APARTMENT

2 January 1978
18:19

—crawled up on her bed, nursing her bruised feet.

Ekaterina Petrovna had worked her like a horse in preparation for the recital. It was in four days, and Olesya was both thrilled and terrified. Her first performance in pointes! What if she botched it? What if something went wrong?

Papa's train arrived in Moscow at 18:23, and the recital started promptly at 19:00. He promised he'd rush over in a taxi. Promised he wouldn't be late.

The door cracked open.

"Olesya?"

She hid under the blanket.

"Are you hiding from me?"

Footsteps. The blanket lifted.

"Found you!" Papa said. "How about some light?"

The light switch clicked.

Olesya shielded her eyes. "I'm sleeping, Papa."

"At dinner time?"

"Yeah."

He sat on the edge of the bed and patted her legs. "What's wrong, my little ballerina?"

"I *said*, I'm sleeping."

"I call bull."

"Stop."

He tickled her.

"Stop it. Stop!"

"There's a smile." He kissed the top of her head.

He was already dressed in his navy attendant uniform. His train wasn't leaving until the next morning, but he had to report to the station the night before, with the other attendants, to be assigned a car and to get it ready for the trip. He had to take out the trash, to wash the restrooms, and to fire up the boiler. But most importantly, he had to stow empty cardboard boxes under his bunk. Olesya knew the drill. She wasn't to mention the boxes to anyone, and she never did.

She was good at keeping secrets.

Even when Uncle Shurik asked her about them one time, she said nothing—until he said not to be afraid. He knew. The boxes were for the imported goods smuggled in from abroad. Illegally. Which made Papa a criminal.

"Don't you have ballet class tonight?" Papa asked with good humor.

"My feet." Olesya pointed.

"What about them?"

"Bruised. Ekaterina Petrovna . . ."

The good humor vanished from Papa's eyes. "I'll have a talk with her."

"No no no. Please. It's nothing." Olesya got up on her elbows. "You're coming, aren't you? You said you would."

"Of course I am." He smiled, his eyes shining. "Why do you think I wouldn't?"

"I just . . . I don't know. What if something went wrong?"

"Like what?"

"Like . . . the train was late, or—"

"Olesya," he said. "Look at me."

She looked.

"I'll be there. I promise. Alive or dead, but I'll be there. Do you believe me?"

She nodded.

"There you go. That's my little ballerina." He ruffled her hair. "Want to play TUBE before I leave? It'll make you forget your hurting feet."

Olesya sat up. "Right now?"

Papa glanced at his watch. "Well, I need to leave in twenty minutes, so . . ."

"Is Mama home?"

"She left for school, you know that. Teacher's meeting."

"But . . ."

"But what?"

Olesya was silent.

"You used to beg me to play when you were little, remember?"

"Yeah . . ."

He waited. "I really don't have much time."

"Okay." Olesya sighed. "All right. Let's play."

Papa brightened. He got down on all fours by her bed, pulled out the train set box from underneath, and took out the cars one by one. "This could land me in jail," he said.

Olesya nodded.

"Remember not to tell anyone."

She nodded again.

"One quick little game."

"All right." She slid off the bed.

She was puzzled by Papa's need to hop around her room like a little boy with TUBE in hand, making tooting noises and jumping with glee when the train entered the tunnel they made from her blanket. Like it was a miracle for the red engine to emerge from the other side, its headlamp bright.

Olesya was not to tell Mama about their games. Papa said she wouldn't understand. That she'd killed the little girl inside of her. That made Olesya afraid. *Mama killed someone?* "It's a metaphor," Papa had explained. Olesya didn't know what a metaphor was, but she didn't dare ask. Papa got irritated when she asked too many questions.

She knew he'd wanted to be an actor. It never came to be, and so he became a car attendant instead. "A good, stable government job," Baba Zina said. Olesya guessed Papa needed an outlet, an acting practice. Perhaps this was one of them, playing a little boy. Another one, she knew, was ballet. Dance. Performance. Since Papa himself couldn't be onstage, he'd dreamed of Olesya becoming a ballerina. She didn't remember if it was his idea or her own. She knew only one thing.

Ballet was her life.

Papa and Mama fought about it quite often. Mama hated ballet. She thought dancing was a frivolous occupation for a girl. She wanted Olesya to be a teacher. An accountant. A lawyer. She didn't like Papa encouraging Olesya, spoiling her with gifts Mama condemned as illegal—pretty imported clothes, sticks of bubblegum that were the envy of kids at school, markers of so many colors, Olesya didn't know that many colors existed.

And so she was torn: pleasing Mama, pleasing Papa. She didn't want them to fight. She loved them both, and she thought it was her fault. They'd tell her things about one another, and she'd keep them as secrets.

Playing TUBE with Papa was one such secret.

Olesya joined him on the floor. They set up the tracks, the switches, connected the cables, coupled the cars to TUBE, and switched it on. It whistled happily and raced around the room—by Olesya's bed, by her desk, to the blanket folded over the tracks. It entered the tunnel. The blanket collapsed, and Papa lifted it, to help TUBE through.

"An accident," he said. "Let's do away with it." He flung the blanket aside and froze.

Olesya looked up.

Mama stood in the door. "What are you two doing here?" she asked, her lips moving separately from the rest of her face.

"Playing TUBE," Papa said matter-of-factly. "I thought you were at your meeting?"

"I forgot my notes," Mama said.

Silence.

The clock ticked off seconds.

Mama looked at Olesya.

Olesya got up from the floor, crawled onto her bed, and curled up. She wanted them to leave, wanted the light to be off. She was sore and tired, and she wanted to sleep and forget it all and—

The door slammed.

Olesya sat up with a start.

Mama was banging pots in the kitchen.

Papa was gathering the train set pieces, tossing them into the box.

"I have to go now," he said. "Give me a kiss."

Olesya turned to the wall, picked at the bit of wallpaper, tore off a strip.

"Aren't you going to kiss me goodbye?"

"I wish you'd get into an accident," she said quietly.

"I can't hear you."

"I wish your train would blow up." She turned. "I wish you'd burn with it!"

He paled. His eye grew huge. "What? What did you say?"

"I'm sorry." Olesya grabbed his arm. "I'm sorry I'm sorry I'm sorry. I didn't mean it."

He smiled. "So you're going to kiss your Papa?"

She climbed down from the bed, stood on tiptoes and kissed his rough cheek.

He kissed the top of her head. "Papa loves you. You know Papa loves you, don't you?"

"Yes."

"Never forget it."

"I won't."

He smiled. "Will you miss me?"

"Yes."

"Say, 'I'll miss you, Papa.' "

"I'll miss you, Papa."

"That's my girl." He tousled her hair. "My little ballerina. Play with TUBE while I'm gone. Then you won't miss me as much."

"I will."

He walked into the hall and put on his winter boots and coat, took his briefcase, and opened the door to the landing. Olesya ran out after him, watched him enter the elevator, listened to it whine and creak, heard it stop on the first floor, heard him open the doors and bang them shut.

"Olesya."

She turned around.

Mama gave her the trash can. "Take it out."

Olesya skipped down the steps, flung open the trash chute, and was about to dump the garbage when she saw something red. She pushed aside the potato peelings and pulled out TUBE. It was covered with slime. She set it on the steps and rummaged through the garbage. Every piece of her train set was there. She picked out car after car, hands shaking, eyes hot, tears spilling down her cheeks.

This was Mama's secret. Whatever she didn't like, she threw away. On the sly. Without Papa knowing. When he discovered it—if he discovered it—she denied it, and Olesya listened to them hurl insults at each other, the secret eating at her, the shame for Mama, the fear, the guilt.

"I hate you," Olesya said. "I hate you both. I wish you'd drop dead. I wish . . ."

ZAPOROZHYE-MELITOPOL

6 February 1989
01:07

Olesya staggered out of the compartment.

"My God," she said, "what a mean little creature I was. Wanted Papa dead, and that's what happened. I wanted Mama dead too. Why? *Why?*"

She watched her breath come out in little white puffs. She was cold. Very cold. She wrapped her coat tighter around her and paced up and down the dark aisle.

Kissing.

Kissing Papa bothered her the most.

Not the memory. Not the secrets it held—whatever they were. No.

It was Papa kissing the top of her head. She couldn't understand. It was a gesture of love, was it not?

This is so confusing.

She pressed her forehead against the window and closed her eyes. Her bruise smarted and her head cleared.

What did it mean? And how was it related to playing TUBE? The hole in her stomach? The dead weight? The dead *child*, rather, as Yuri had called it. What did he mean by that—dead Little Olesya? But how was it possible when she wasn't blood and flesh? She was part of her, wasn't she? She was Olesya's memory. Her past self.

Or was she?

Someone tapped her shoulder.

Olesya nearly screamed.

"Don't do that again," Yuri said.

"Yuri?"

He stretched out his hand, waiting.

She handed the keys to him. "I won't. Promise."

"Good." He pocketed the keys. "And no more jumping off the train."

"What? But how did you know?"

"My Raisa told me."

Olesya shrunk away.

"She did?"

"Boy, it's freezing in here." Yuri rubbed his hands. "How about a hot cup of tea?"

"I'm sorry. I can't." Olesya nodded at the compartments.

"You can't?" He followed her gaze. "Is there more to see?"

"Yes, there is."

"Well then, we can always have tea later, can't we? I'll keep the water hot for you, in case you change your mind." His smile faltered. "And don't you worry about the keys. It's not your time yet. Raisa said . . ." He hesitated.

"What?"

Yuri scratched his scar.

"What?" Olesya's heart beat faster.

"He's coming for you, that's what."

"Who?"

"The ghost, who." Yuri crossed himself.

"Oh God." Olesya's legs quivered. She held on to the wall. "Did she say who he is?"

"You know who he is."

She hesitated. "Papa?"

Yuri averted his eyes. "She said something else too. Said you've got something of his. Said he wants it back. You better give it back to him, dorogusha. I tell you, it's no good playing games with the dead."

Olesya pulled TUBE from her pocket. "This? Is this what he wants?"

Yuri squinted at it. "Is that the toy you lost?"

"Is this what he wants, Yuri?"

"What do you think?"

"I don't know what to think. Is there something you're not telling me?"

He looked her straight in the eyes, his expression blank.

"Yuri, what do you know? What is it?"

He blinked and was back to his cheery self. "Well, I'll be going then," he said.

"Wait. Why did you close the door on me? What does this all mean? Do you know something I don't?"

He turned around and looked at her. "May I give you some advice?"

"Yuri, please!"

"Never help those who don't ask for help," he said. "They won't take it."

"Who . . . I'm not trying to help anyone. Am I?"

He shook his head. "Just like my Lidochka. Always asking questions. Why don't you trust yourself?"

"Trust myself with what?"

"You know what."

"Stop it, Yuri! Tell me! *Please!*"

"Listen, dorogusha." He sounded stern. "I can't give you the answers. You know what you have to do. So do it. Open the doors. See what's inside."

Her gut squeezed. "You mean what's inside the compartments?"

"Inside of *you*," he said. "The hole in you. What do you think it's for? It's for looking."

"For looking," Olesya repeated. "But I did look."

"There you go. You've got more to see."

"But Yuri . . . it hurts."

"Of course it does. You think it wouldn't?"

"I think I'm doomed, that's what I think."

"Doomed?"

"Broken."

"You're not broken. You're afraid is all." He lowered his voice. "Don't be afraid of the dead, be afraid of the living. It's the living—" His eyes widened. He put a finger to his lips.

Olesya stopped breathing. Her throat tickled.

There was a soft rustling noise behind her, as though someone shifted from foot to foot.

She spun around, staring at the empty aisle and the door to the attendant's compartment. She was sure the noise was coming from there. Someone was on the other side of the door, an ear pressed to it, catching their every word.

She turned back to Yuri.

He was pale. "Devil take me, he's here. I better get going."

Olesya shook her head. "Please. Stay."

"I can't, dorogusha. You've got to face him alone."

"But I'm scared. I'm so scared, Yuri!"

"I know." He patted her shoulder. "Not as scared as when you were little, though, are you? Not as scared. Look at me."

She did.

"You're not a little girl anymore."

"I'm not?"

"You can fight him. And you can win."

"How can you be so sure?"

"Trust yourself. Can you trust yourself?"

The sound of the door opening, right behind her.

The hairs on the back of Olesya's neck lifted. She felt a presence, steps away, listening to them. Dead.

It was Papa, and he'd come back for TUBE.

"You can't run forever, can you?" Yuri said.

Then he was gone. Olesya hadn't seen him move this fast before. One moment he was in front of her, and another she was alone in the aisle.

No, not alone. Not alone at all.

Cold terror washed over her and traced her spine with its frozen finger. Olesya heard the steps behind her. Then she felt eyes on her back, and she forgot everything Yuri told her. She forgot her resolve. She forgot her need. She could think of only one thing.

Survival.

She ran.

01:32

How Olesya made it to the dining car and ended up sitting across the table from Dima, she couldn't remember. Had he been waiting for her here? Did Yuri tell him to wait for her here? Was Dima on his way to the haunted car, and she simply ran into him? And who opened the restaurant car for them? But the details didn't matter. What mattered was she escaped.

It was well past midnight. The restaurant was dark, illuminated only by the passing lights. Olesya looked at Dima. She could barely see his face.

"Hey," he said.

"Hey."

They were silent.

"I don't know how to say this," Dima said.

She was only half listening.

Was that a creak of the floor? No, it was the car's movement. Was that a draft coming from an open door? No, it was the wind buffeting the outside of the car. Were those footsteps?

Dima tapped his palm against the table. Olesya stared at it, willing herself not to glance behind her. Not to panic. Papa wouldn't dare face her in the company of someone living, would he? But he did when Yuri was there. He did. He could.

"Olesya."

"Yeah?"

Dima got up, walked around the table, and lowered to his knees in front of her. "It's not what you thought it was. I know what it looked like, but I was just . . . I was giving her a massage, Olesya. That's all. She asked for it, and like a fool I agreed. I was so worried about you, I had to distract myself somehow. I knew you probably wouldn't want to see me, so . . ."

"Yeah, sure." She listened hard for the footsteps.

"Nothing happened, I promise. You must've thought . . . Yuri told me you were on the verge . . . Olesya, I'm so sorry. I didn't think—"

"Shh!" She grabbed his arm. Her heart jumped to her throat. "Did you hear that?"

"Hear what?"

"Listen."

They listened.

Nothing.

"Will you forgive me?"

"Yeah. Okay," she said automatically.

"Okay?"

She looked at him, seeing and not seeing. "Dima—"

"I'm an idiot," he said.

"Dima, what if I told you—"

"Really, I am. Durak. That's what I am. You see, the thing is . . ." He picked up her hand, then the other. He searched her eyes. "I love you, Olesya."

"What?" She heard him and didn't, her attention split, her heart drumming.

"Please, hear me out. I'll do anything for you—"

"I know." She gripped his hands, hard.

"You know?"

"Dima."

He moved back a little. "Is this a bad time? Do you want me to go?"

"There is something—"

"Do you want me to leave you alone?"

"No. No no no no." She pulled him closer. "Please. Stay."

He studied her. The lights flashed across his face.

The rhythm of the wheels suddenly hiccupped, skipped a beat.

Olesya started. "Did you hear that?"

"Hear what?"

"The wheels."

He frowned. "Sure. What about them?"

Olesya teetered on the edge of telling him. Then she decided against it. Yuri said she had to do this alone. It was her fight. And she couldn't risk involving Dima.

"Nothing," she said, swallowing tears, happy it was dark. He couldn't see her face. He wouldn't guess. She hated lying. Every time she did, her face turned beet-red.

"Listen," she said. "This is very hard for me to say."

"Okay." He moved closer.

Olesya felt her eyes burn.

"I'm . . . I can't—" She looked down at their hands. "Something happened, and . . ." It was harder than she thought. She took a deep breath, let it all out. "I can't be with you, Dima. You were right when you called me a porcelain doll. I am a porcelain doll. Only she's me and not me . . . and I need to break her. Smash her to bits, you know?"

"What are you saying?"

"I'm saying . . . maybe it's better if—if you go out with Natasha. She'll be good for you. She can help your career, and you can— I mean, you won't be as frustrated, and—"

The tears gushed freely now. She turned her face away.

He let go of her hands. "Are you breaking up with me?"

"I am. I guess."

"You guess?"

There was pain in his voice. It racked her with guilt. Did she have to be more firm? Harsh? Cruel, maybe?

She grasped the edge of the table. "I'm breaking up with you. It's over. *Over.*"

There was no answer.

At last, he said, "All right. If it'll make you happy."

"Make me happy?"

"Breaking up with me."

It was all Olesya could do not to throw herself on him and tell him she loved him. She didn't know she did, not until this very moment. Didn't know she *could.* Didn't know it felt like this—searing pain, in her gut, chest, lungs, in her throat that couldn't draw a breath. It was bad. The timing. This feeling. It made her weak. She couldn't afford to be weak, not with Papa waiting for her in the haunted car, not with those memories left to see.

Or she could hide. Wait it out. Once they got to Simferopol, it'd be over. She'd be off the train, and she'd make herself forget. Yes, she could.

She was good at forgetting.

Dima said something.

"What?"

"Are you okay?"

"Yeah."

"You sure?"

She nodded.

"Hey, guess what day it is." He sounded strained, like he tried very hard to sound happy.

"What day is it?"

"Here." He reached into his pocket. "I know you don't like presents, but I thought you might like this." He gave her a jar of raspberry jam. "Happy birthday, Olesya. Happy twenty-one."

"Oh." She caught her breath. "I forgot."

"Of course you did." He nodded. "That's what I love about you."

"What?"

"Nothing." He shook his head. "Try it."

She twisted the lid. It opened with a *pop*.

"Go ahead," Dima encouraged.

Olesya dipped in a finger, licked it. "It's magnificent." The sweetness spread on her tongue, and her skin tingled. She scooped out some more. "Thank you."

"You're welcome." He extended his hand. "Friends?"

Olesya hesitated, then took it. "Friends."

"That's good enough for me." His face grew serious. "So, can I ask you a question?"

She closed the jar and nodded.

"Did you see more? I mean . . . the little you. Did you see that little girl again?"

"Yeah, I did."

"And?"

Olesya glanced at the closed door swallowed by darkness, at the bare tables glistening in the passing lights, at the curtains on the windows. "You won't believe me if I tell you."

"Come on. I thought we were past this."

"Well." She dropped her voice to a whisper. "My Papa is here. He came back. He came back for this." She placed TUBE on the table.

"For TUBE?"

"Yes."

"How do you know?"

"It's too long to explain. I just do. And there is more. It means something. TUBE. The toy itself and the game we were playing. I'm not sure exactly what, but . . . it's something bad. Something bad happened. And it made me hurt myself. I'm not sure what it was. But I've got to remember, I've got to *know*. Or it'll drive me crazy, not knowing. That's why I've got to go and see more."

"See more of what?"

"Memories." Olesya exhaled. "My forgotten memories. You see, TUBE works like a key. And the compartments—in that empty car, in the haunted car—they hold my memories, the ones I forgot. I've seen about half by now, I think. There is another half, and it seems that with each memory I'm getting closer to what happened. Only . . ."

"Only what?"

"Only now I'm not sure."

"Not sure you want to do it," he said. It wasn't a question.

"Yeah."

"You're scared."

"I am." She looked at him. "I'm terrified."

He was silent. "Can I ask you a favor?"

"What is it?"

"I've been thinking." Dima sighed. "I want to help you. In any way I can."

"Why?"

"Because I think I know. Not what happened to you. No, more like . . . the feeling of it. My dad was very violent, and—"

Olesya made to protest.

Dima caught her hand. "I don't mean to say that your dad was violent—I mean, whenever there is something you can't remember, it means it hurt a lot. As a kid, you don't really know how to hurt yourself, unless you see someone else do it. You know what I mean? That's how we learn. From adults around us. And I think—I think whatever happened—it wasn't you. At least not initially. Like in my family, it was my mom. She was the scapegoat. My dad would come home drunk, lock me up in my room, and beat her bloody. The next day they acted like nothing happened. Except for the bruises on her face. For some reason he never beat me. Slapped me, smacked me. But never really beat me. Not like the way he beat her." Dima looked down. "But after she died, he did. He started beating me bloody."

"I'm so sorry," Olesya said. "I didn't know."

"It's okay. It was a long time ago. What I mean is, you must've seen something. Witnessed something. Then you repeated it. Because . . . I used to cut myself. I felt nothing, no pain at all, when he beat me. It'd drive him mad, and he'd beat me harder. So when he was done, I'd cut myself. To feel something."

"Oh God. Dima. Oh God."

He moved back. "You do what you need to do, okay? Just know that I'm here for you if you need help."

"Okay." She didn't know what else to say. "Thank you. And thank you for the jam."

"Of course."

She glanced at her watch. Almost two in the morning.

"Be careful, all right?" he said.

"I will."

"Promise?"

"Promise."

Dima got up, turned around and walked out.

Olesya sat still for a long time, swaying with the car and watching the door where Dima went, waiting for him to return, to come back to her, to call for her.

Then the train whistled, braked and started slowing.

The loudspeaker squawked, announcing their next stop.

Olesya broke from her trance and walked out of the dining car.

In the vestibule, she collided with a man.

"Watch it!" he barked.

"Sorry."

He spat on the floor.

She recognized him. It was the father of the little girl in the heavy coat. There she stood, bundled up to her nose, eyes wet. The girl looked up at Olesya, blinking at the lights.

Olesya took the jar from her pocket.

The girl's eyes lit up. "Is that jam?" Her voice was thick with sleep. "I like jam."

"Hush," her father snapped. "Empty chatterbox. Always bothering people."

The girl's eyes turned dull.

"She's not bothering me," Olesya said.

A sleepy attendant woman in a crumpled jacket entered the vestibule and unlocked the exit door without a word. The train brakes screeched against the rails. The train came to a full stop. The man climbed down onto the snowy platform with his suitcase, and when he turned away to set it at his feet, Olesya slipped the jar into the girl's coat pocket and helped her down the steps.

"She can do it herself," the man grumbled.

The girl looked up at Olesya and waved. Olesya waved back and watched them walk away, their footsteps crunching on the snow, their two figures receding in the glow of lights.

"You getting off or what?" the attendant woman said.

It was tempting. Just hop off the train and be done with it all.

"No," Olesya said. "No, I'm not. I'm riding till the end."

WATCHING IT ROLL

MELITOPOL–SIMFEROPOL
02:15

Olesya looked through the door window to the haunted car. She squeezed TUBE so hard her fingers cramped, but she kept squeezing, staring out into the dark aisle where he stood.

The man.

The ghost.

Papa.

He was looking out the window, rocking on the balls of his feet, his hands in his pockets. His profile was uncertain in the flashing lights, and he didn't look dead, just suffering from insomnia. Yet he was too thin somehow, as though he'd lost a lot of weight. His jacket hung on him, loose, and his big head looked screwed on, as if at any moment it would fall off and roll and roll until it stopped at her feet. The image made Olesya recoil. It was her own head she saw, fallen from her neck. It was from him that she got her "ideal ballet body," as Alla Borisovna called it—long neck, short torso, and long legs.

She let out a breath. "Papa?"

He turned to look at her.

She didn't want to believe it. Naked terror gripped her.

His eyes.

They were perfectly round, larger than when he was alive, and they shone with electric light. He moved to her, machine-like, with sure, quick steps, his shining eyes never leaving her face. He stopped just on the other side of the door, the glass between them.

"There she is," he said. "My little ballerina."

Olesya's mouth went dry. Spots danced in her vision.

"Happy birthday," he said. "Did you miss me? Did you miss your Papa?"

His voice sounded harsh and metallic. It was shrill enough to penetrate the drone of the train, to penetrate the glass between them. Olesya thought that any moment he'd smash through it and seize her by the neck and shake TUBE out of her. What an idiot she was. She should've hidden it somewhere.

Hang on, she thought. *Hang on just a moment. Didn't I think this before? Just recently? No—in a memory. Was it with Mama? When she told me to throw TUBE into the dumpster, weren't those my exact same thoughts? But why? Why would I want to hide it from Papa? I loved playing with him—*(Did I? Did I?)*—loved it above all else.*

He seemed to have read her mind. "How about we play TUBE?" he said. "Just one little game, for old times' sake. What do you say?"

She opened her mouth and closed it, feeling helpless, useless. Dumb. She wanted to tell him no.

But why? she thought, incredulous. *Why don't I want to play it?* (Because this game—because—) *Because why?*

The knowledge flashed through her mind for a moment, and then it was gone. It escaped her. She felt her entire body screaming. It yelled at her, mutely. It hollered at her to run away. To hide. To protect herself.

It made her feel as though Papa was danger.

(Danger? Why *danger*?)

Olesya steeled herself and held his eyes. They were big and round—just the way she remembered them. And then she remembered something else. Something she'd forgotten. His eyes terrified her—into submission.

(Submission to *what*?)

But it was too late. The memory was gone, evaporated from her mind, and Olesya was a little girl again, eager to please.

It wasn't wise to keep Papa waiting. She had to say something. Anything. Quick! She could ask him a question— her favorite stalling tactic—(Stalling for what? *What*?)—but it did no good. He always won. (Won *what*?) He was bigger, stronger, meaner. (Mean? Papa was *never* mean!) All she could do was pretend it didn't hurt—(Hurt? Where did it *hurt*?)—pretend he was dead, dead—

He was.

No! Olesya thought. *Stop it! Wait! You're going too fast. I can't remember. I can't remember! I can't—please—*

(Do you really want to *stop* it?)

The thought doused Olesya like ice water. What was it that Yuri said? She wasn't a little girl anymore. She could fight him and she could win. All she needed was to trust herself. Because she couldn't keep running forever, could she?

"I'd like to, Papa," Olesya heard herself say. "I'd like that very much."

"That's my girl." He smiled.

She watched him.

"Go on then. Get TUBE."

"Oh." She pouted her lips. "I don't have it anymore."

"What do you mean?"

"Well. Mama threw it away after we . . . buried you."

She unclenched her fingers from around TUBE.

His eyes slipped to her pocket. "And you let her?"

"Of course I did. What else was I supposed to do?"

"I see."

There was an edge to his voice. Olesya shivered and glanced down to hide her discomfort. She looked at her watch. 02:36. Two and a half hours until Simferopol. She could still walk away. She could turn around, right now, and exit through the gangway—

Cold air wafted toward her.

She looked up to see that Papa had opened the door.

He stood across from her, an arm's length away, his head tipped to the side, his eyes shining.

"I think you're lying," he said.

His voice ripped into Olesya's ears. She took a step back. Papa moved forward.

Her back hit the wall. She gripped TUBE compulsively, breathing hard.

"Can we sit down?" She nodded back to the compartments. "It's been a long night, and I'm tired."

"Where is it?" Papa said sharply.

"I don't know," Olesya said.

He stepped closer. "You don't know, or you don't want to tell me?"

"I . . ." She pressed her back into the wall. "I'm sorry I let Mama throw it away. I should've stopped her. I'm sorry."

He searched her eyes.

"I missed you, Papa, I missed you so much. I want to talk to you."

"Isn't that what we're doing right now?"

He seemed to be back to his good humor, and she relaxed a little.

"Come." He opened his arms. "Give Papa a kiss."

Olesya stopped breathing.

"What's the matter? Don't you want to kiss me?"

"I do."

"Well?"

She willed herself to move, but her muscles seemed to have atrophied, and she felt herself slipping down the wall.

"I'm waiting."

A flash of movement behind Papa. Olesya glanced over his shoulder.

Little Olesya.

She stood in the aisle, holding on to the handrail with one arm lifted, her leg extended behind her in an arabesque. Their eyes met, and she let go and backed off quickly, quietly.

Olesya understood. "You promised," she said. "You never delivered on your promise. So . . . I'll kiss you after you do what you promised me."

Papa stood taller. She could see he knew what she meant. He prided himself at never breaking his promises.

"I did my best to be there," he said.

"I know."

"No, you don't."

They stood in silence.

"I was devastated," she said. "My first pointe recital, Papa. My first! It was so important to me."

"You can dance for me now." His eyes brightened.

"Yes, I can," she said, faint with relief. "Where though?"

"Baggage car?" He said it too quickly, like he knew she'd offer.

"Okay. Can I change first?"

"Go ahead. Here, let me take your coat."

Olesya nodded, grateful. She started shrugging out of her coat when she heard Little Olesya yell, "Idiot!" She was running at them. "Don't give him the coat!"

TUBE was in the pocket! Olesya jerked it back. Papa's hands closed on empty air.

Papa turned just as Little Olesya rammed into him. They toppled to the floor.

He flipped her around like a doll. "You think you're so clever?"

She thrashed in his hold, glaring at him.

He put his hands around her throat and choked her. "Coat," he told Olesya.

"Please—"

"Coat!"

Little Olesya's eyes watered. She gasped for breath.

"Here." Olesya offered the coat.

Papa released one hand to take it. Little Olesya twisted out of his grip, bent her head, and bit him. He roared. She drove her head into his stomach. He doubled over and sat down.

"Quick!" she cried. "Go! *Go!*"

Papa seized Little Olesya from behind and clamped his hand over her mouth.

"Let her go," Olesya said.

"Give me what's mine."

"No."

"Olesya."

"It's not yours. You gave it to me as a present. You—"

He squeezed Little Olesya's throat. She made a weak sound, clawed at his hand.

"Now," he said.

Olesya reached into the coat pocket. She met Little Olesya's pleading eyes, and understood. She had to do it quickly. Her hand closed on TUBE.

"Here you go," she said.

In one move she took TUBE out, dropped her coat, lifted her sweater, touched TUBE to her belly, and—

"No!" Papa roared, tossing Little Olesya aside and lunging forward.

Anticipating it, dizzy with pain, Olesya ducked and ran alongside the aisle wall as Little Olesya got up, clamped her arms around Papa's legs and dropped him.

"You bitch!" he yelled, and hit her.

Olesya flinched but kept running, counting the doors.

(He never called me *bitch*. He called Mama *bitch*. He—)

Compartment No. 5.

TUBE deep in her stomach, she turned it, saw the door open and fell inside. And as her memory took off, like a gliding train disappearing into a tunnel of darkness, in the compartment doorway she saw Papa's face. Twisted with hatred. His arm reached in.

Then it all receded, and the memory consumed her.

MOSCOW, GORKY PARK

28 August 1976
19:14

Whoops. Whistles. Shouts.

Papa pulled Olesya roughly by the arm through a thick crowd. The noise deafened her: the screams of the roller-coaster riders, the calls of the onlookers, the blaring music from the loudspeakers. It was too much. Too *much*. And it was dark, and hot, and muggy. Her dress was damp with her sweat, and it stuck to her back. Papa's grip was starting to hurt. And yet . . . Olesya smiled. She didn't mind. Because she was excited.

Earlier today she played TUBE with Papa, and now she was getting her reward.

An amusement ride.

He said she could pick any ride she wanted, any at all.

And Papa never broke his promises.

Olesya was giddy with choices, looking around at the glowing lights of the carousels and the bumper cars and the swings. The music ended. The loudspeakers poured out the beginning of Tchaikovsky's *Swan Lake*.

Olesya sucked in her breath. "Prince Siegfried."

She was in love with him. She was his Swan Princess. She'd watched the ballet so many times on TV she knew it by heart. So what if Mama said at eight she was too young to be in love. Mama didn't understand. Olesya knew—she just *knew* and didn't care why or how—that one day she'd meet him. The love of her life. A boy who was out there, somewhere, loving her as she loved him, waiting to meet her. Her Prince. Her beloved Prince. They'd love each other and tell that to each other every day. And they'd never fight. Not once. Not like Mama and Papa. Never ever *ever*. They'd spend their time talking and dancing around the lake, just like in the ballet, and they'd die one day, together.

Olesya sighed, content.

They broke out of the crowd, and she saw what she wanted.

"A kiddie train! Papa, I want to go on the kiddie train!"

She wrested her arm from his grip and ran up to the fence. A red engine and three cars puttered around in a circle. The children beamed from the windows; some leaned out and waved.

Olesya waved back.

"Olesya!" Papa grabbed her by the arm. "How many times do I have to tell you? Don't run away from me like that. You could've gotten lost."

"But Papa!" she said breathlessly. "I picked a ride. I picked it. I want this one."

"A kiddie train?" His eyes darkened. "Why? I can give you a ride on a real train any time you want."

"But you promised."

"Come on, Olesya, you're too old for this. Look at them. Babies."

He motioned to the kids who were climbing out of the cars. Olesya looked. They were about three or four or five years old, not older. Then she saw a girl who looked older than her, ten, maybe even eleven. "Papa, look!"

"Let's go." He tugged on her arm. "How about a Ferris wheel? You've never been on a Ferris wheel. Isn't that exciting? We'll look at the evening Moscow, at the Moskva River, at the lights reflecting in the water." He sounded dreamy. "I'll buy you ice cream after we get off. What do you say?"

Olesya pushed out her lower lip. "You *promised*."

He laughed uneasily. "Well, how was I to know you'd pick a kiddie train? I'd look ridiculous sitting in one of those tiny cars."

"You?" Olesya stared at him. "But why would you want to come with me? You said it's for babies. Are you a baby?" She snickered at her joke.

Papa's eyes bulged out. "I said no."

"But—"

He dragged her away from the fence and jerked her along, walking fast. "Stubborn like your mother. Always thinking about yourself. Only yourself."

Olesya stumbled after him, blinking back tears. It wasn't fair. Papa promised. *Promised.* He never broke his promises. Never ever. Or did he? Was this the first time? The wish to get on the kiddie train overwhelmed Olesya. It didn't matter that she didn't want it that bad. It didn't matter that in truth she'd probably have as much fun—or more—riding the Ferris wheel. It was a matter of principle. Papa promised she could pick any ride, and she picked the kiddie train, and on the kiddie train she'd go.

Her arm was going numb from his hold. She knew it was no good trying to wiggle out. The only way to make him let her go was to trick him.

They walked by an ice cream kiosk. A fat saleswoman in a starched white cap leaned on the counter, looking bored.

"Papa?" Olesya said in her sweetest voice.

He glanced at her and continued walking.

"Can we take ice cream with us? On the Ferris wheel? Please?" She smiled. What was it that he said about the lights? "We could eat ice cream *and* watch the lights reflect in the water. Wouldn't that be fun?"

He stopped.

She gave him a big smile.

"You'll go on the Ferris wheel?"

"Yes."

"No more kiddie train?"

"No." She shook her head. "You were right. It's for babies."

Papa brightened. "That's my girl. All right. Ice cream it is. Which one do you want?"

"Lakomka." It was her favorite. A chocolate tube filled with cream.

He let go of her arm, pulled out his wallet. Olesya watched him shake out coins and count them on his palm. He leaned on the counter, slapped the coins down. "Two Lakomkas, please."

The moment was perfect.

Olesya spun around and sprinted.

"Olesya!"

But she was already lost in the crowd, her strong legs carrying her without effort. She ran up to the fence around the kiddie train ride, climbed over it, and in two leaps reached the tracks.

Her eyes opened wide. The train was moving right at her. It wasn't going very fast, walking-speed at the most, but it scared her all the same. She stood rooted to the tracks, mesmerized by its size. It was so much bigger than TUBE, but not as big as the real train. Would it stop if it hit her? Or would it run over her and kill her like Papa said trains killed people who jumped in front of them? Was it big enough to do that?

"Hey, you there! Girl! Get off the tracks!" shouted the ticket lady.

The little boy in the driver's seat gaped at Olesya with his mouth open.

She stood still. It was a contest of wills. Who would win, her or the train? From the corner of her eye she saw Papa shove the ticket lady aside and bolt in her direction. He snatched her by the waist just as the train puttered by, the kids leaning out of the windows, staring.

"What"—he panted, his face deathly pale—"what did I tell you—about going on the tracks?"

"But it's not a real train, Papa. It's just a kiddie train. I would've jumped away."

"I told you." He was livid. "I told you not to go on the tracks." He shook her. Her head lolled back and forth.

"Hey, comrade!" the ticket lady called. "Stop shaking her, you hear? Or I'll call militia."

Papa recoiled as if smacked. The rage drained from him. "No need for militia. We were just leaving." He set Olesya down and led her out, ignoring the stares.

"Last ride!" the ticket lady called. "Who has the tickets for the last ride? Pick a seat."

Olesya's heart dropped. Tomorrow Papa was leaving for Simferopol and wouldn't be back for four days, and on Wednesday it was September first, the first day of school. The summer break would be over. She'd be so busy with homework and ballet classes, who knew when there'd be time to go to Gorky Park again.

She was devastated.

Papa had broken his promise.

They turned into an alley and walked to a bench under a tall, spreading tree. Its canopy blocked the light from the streetlamp, and the bench was sunk in shade. Papa sat down, pulled Olesya into his lap. Her skin pricked with gooseflesh. It was getting chilly.

"You tricked me," he said.

She was silent, fuming.

"What do you think you deserve for punishment?" He waited. "You're not talking to me now?"

She shrugged.

His demeanor softened. "Oh, come now, Olesya. Papa loves you. You know that, don't you?" He stroked her hair and kissed it. "I promise you, when I'm back we'll ride as many kiddie trains as you want. Honest Pioneer Word. How about another game? What do you say?" He smiled.

Olesya looked at him, aghast. "What, here? In the park?"

"Why not? I brought it with me." He pulled TUBE from his pocket.

She fidgeted. She didn't want to play. She was tired and sore, and she wanted to go home. "I don't want to ride a kiddie train anymore," she said. "And I don't want any more promises." She tried slipping off, but he held her fast.

"Now, now. What's the matter? Just one game."

He pushed TUBE at her. She swatted it off and twisted out of his hold and jumped away.

"Olesya. Don't make me repeat myself." He came at her, TUBE in hand.

She circled the bench, watching him from behind it.

"What's this now? What's going on?"

"I don't want to play TUBE anymore," she said, her voice shaking.

He stopped moving. "Well, then you won't get any more new clothes, or gum sticks, or markers."

Olesya gasped—she loved the special imported things Papa brought her—but she was determined. "I don't care," she said.

"Yes, you do."

"I don't."

"Olesya."

"I want to go home."

Papa watched her warily. "All right, we'll go home. Give me your hand."

Olesya felt a sudden suspicion. "No."

"I said, give me your hand."

She edged away. He sprung around the bench and grabbed her. She screamed. At the other end of the alley a couple stopped and looked in their direction, then resumed their strolling.

"Shh." Papa clapped a hand over her mouth. "Keep quiet."

She struggled.

"I said, quiet. I'm letting go on the count of three, and I don't want a peep out of you. Understood?"

She nodded.

"Okay. One. Two. Three." He let go.

Olesya hung her head.

He slipped TUBE back into his pocket and led her out of the park. By the time they reached the gate, he seemed to have cheered up. He stopped, sat on his haunches in front of her, lifted her face and said, "Remember your promise?"

She wanted to scream in his face, *But you broke yours!* Some instinct told her it wasn't wise. "Yes, Papa," she said.

"You won't tell Mama?"

"No."

"Good. Now that's my girl. That's my little ballerina."

He ruffled her hair, picked her up like when she was little and carried her all the way to their white Zhiguli, parked on a side street by an apartment building.

When Olesya slipped into the backseat, she unclenched her hand that was folded into a fig—her thumb between her index and middle fingers. "Fig tebe," she whispered. "I'll tell Mama. Yes, I will. I'll tell her *everything*."

MELITOPOL–SIMFEROPOL

6 February 1989

03:01

" 'I'll tell her *everything*,' " Olesya repeated, stunned.

She sat in the empty compartment, looking out the window, watching the snowy darkness slide by. The darkness around her bled into it, cold and heavy.

"Papa," she said, her breath white. "Papa."

Her lungs contracted painfully.

"What was our game about? What were we *really* playing?"

Dima was right. She had to have seen something. At first. Then she was part of it. Papa made her do it. A game. A game they called TUBE. She must've remembered what it was. And she must've fought him. Only what chance did she have? A little girl against a grown man? So of course she lost.

But she won in other ways.

She had created this cold, unfeeling porcelain doll, and she hid inside it. She buried herself as deep as she could. Then she threw herself into her work. Work, work, work. Where was life in that? There wasn't. So that meant she was dead. Alive and dead.

No. No. No.

She dropped her head into her hands.

What she lived until now was one big, fat lie. It was fake, just as her doll façade was fake. Her family. Mama. Papa. Uncle Shurik. Baba Zina. They were all part of it. They knew it, and they chose to ignore it. Like it didn't exist.

Why?

Olesya knew why. She'd done it herself.

It was easier this way. Easier to believe the lie than to be burned by the truth.

Because the truth is always ugly, she thought, *like your reflection in a mirror. Until you see it's you, really you, and there is nowhere to hide. And you know you must take it. Take it. Accept it. To continue living. It's all part of you, whether you like it or not. Not many people can do this, can they? They escape.*

"Oh, sweet escape . . ."

Olesya took a shuddering breath. She realized she was talking out loud. It sounded eerie in the emptiness around her, the silence, the stillness. The drone of the wheels that used to put her to sleep now kept her awake.

What was she going to do? She didn't know. Didn't want to know. Couldn't think.

The weight of betrayal crushed her.

What did he do to her?

What was it that he did?

She wanted to remember and she didn't. She was confused and frightened and mad. Mad at all of them. Mama walking in on them and doing nothing. Uncle Shurik giving that stupid speech at Papa's funeral, not letting Olesya talk. Even Baba Zina. He was her son after all. How could she not know?

Olesya felt sick.

She wanted to talk to someone, anyone. Ask them.

She shook her head. She'd already tried asking Mama. There was no way to reach Uncle Shurik—she didn't know where he was. That left . . . what?

Compartments. Memories.

A shudder of horror passed through her body, shook her. The pain in her belly, when she inserted TUBE. Could she endure it? Could she do more?

"Let's play TUBE," Papa would say, and she always agreed.

What choice did she have? Could she have stopped him? *I've endured this before, and I was little, so little* . . .

She looked at TUBE in her lap, at its shiny, metal body.

Fathers didn't hurt their daughters, did they? They were supposed to love them, to protect them. They weren't supposed to . . . to *what*? She didn't know. Didn't want to know. Couldn't name it.

"TUBE."

That was the name of it.

Hate welled inside her. Hot, all-consuming hate.

If he were alive, she would kill him. She wanted to do it herself, and she wanted to watch him die. She wanted to kill Mama. With Papa it was too late, he was already dead, but with Mama—

Olesya sat up straight. She suddenly understood her meanness, her wish, her—what was it that she said? When she was taking out the trash? "I hate you. I hate you both. I wish you'd drop dead."

Did she ever tell them? Tell anyone? *Tried* telling? At the funeral . . . what did she want to say? And when did he start? How old was she?

"Five. I was five."

Somehow she knew this. Little Olesya was five. She was five.

She was five when it started.

The thought pained her.

That look in Mama's eyes, when she told Olesya about how Papa's remains had to be scraped off. And Mama dismissing Olesya on the phone, outright dismissing. Why? He was gone, dead. Then why?

Well, it only made sense. It'd disrupt Mama's life—her safe, orderly life. Admitting to it.

"You have a hole in you too," Olesya said, "and it's eating you from inside out, Mama. Isn't it? It's eating you just like it's eating me."

She looked at TUBE.

"I'm glad you came back," she said. "Glad you found me."

TUBE glinted at her mutely.

An oncoming train blared its horn. Olesya looked out the window at the barreling, rushing mass. The windows flashed at her with their yellow light—bright, shining—and suddenly Olesya wished for him to find her.

What was he waiting for? Here she sat, unprotected, with the door open.

Olesya got up and peeked out the door, TUBE held aloft in front of her like a weapon.

The aisle was empty. The passing train was gone, and in the momentary silence that followed she heard crying. It was coming from the attendant's compartment. All this time she was sitting there, thinking, remembering, all this time—

"No. No!"

Her face burned with guilt, shame, horror.

Never taking her eyes off the door, she backed away, slowly, feeling her way with her hand, stopped by compartment No. 6, lifted her sweater. TUBE lit up, whistled shrilly.

The crying stopped.

"Olesya?" Papa's voice called.

The breath rasped out of Olesya's mouth.

The attendant's compartment door opened.

Papa stepped out, his shining eyes at once spotting TUBE in her hand.

She plunged it deep inside her and turned.

And just as he reached for her, lunged for her, the door opened. The car swayed around the bend, and they toppled in, Olesya and Papa both.

SIMFEROPOL RAILWAY STATION

4 June 1974

11:13

"Never go on the tracks." Papa's voice was shaking. *"Never. Do you understand?"*

Olesya nodded.

They were sitting on a bench, on a platform of Simferopol railway station. It was a hot, sunny day. The tracks glistened white in the sun, and the air was humid, ringing with the voices of travelers, the rattle of luggage carts, the creaking of the trains.

"I didn't hear you."

"Yes, Papa."

"Yes, Papa, what?"

"I won't go on the tracks."

"That's not good enough. Say, 'I'll *never* go on the tracks.' Say it."

"I'll *never* go on the tracks," she said louder. She wanted to please him. It was important to do exactly what he said, to make him forget about punishing her. "I promise." She looked up at him. "I'll *never* go on the tracks, Papa. Never. Never ever *ever*."

"That's my girl." He patted her on the head. "That's my little ballerina."

Olesya smiled. It wasn't so bad after all.

"I want you to remember something." He leaned over to her and lifted her face. "When it's between you and the machine, the machine always wins. Remember that."

"Okay."

"Good."

Olesya didn't understand what he meant. What machine? What would be between them?

"Let's go," he said.

There was an urgency to his voice, and Olesya shrank, scared. She didn't want him to hurt her like he did yesterday, on the train. She was sore and aching, and her eyes were swollen from crying.

When they arrived in Simferopol, and when after a long taxi ride they finally made it to Alupka and entered the house to Baba Zina's bone-crushing hugs and wet kisses, Papa explained to them all that Olesya was upset because she wet herself. It wasn't true, and Olesya cried when Papa said it. When Baba Zina scolded her, Olesya cried even harder.

She was embarrassed and mad at herself. And she was mad at Papa for lying and scared to say anything—anything at all—which made her cry harder yet, hiccupping and gasping. Papa said she should stop crying like that. She wasn't a baby anymore. She was a big girl. This September she was starting first grade, one year early.

That helped a little.

Olesya felt proud of herself. She wiped her tears.

Kids didn't start school until they turned seven, but Olesya wanted to go to school so badly that this winter, when she turned five, she hounded Mama to buy her a school bag. She said she was big enough. It took a few weeks. Mama finally bought her one just to stop her from nagging. Olesya was very happy. She slept with it under her pillow and would take it on their trip to Baba Zina, but Mama put her foot down. Enough was enough. It was too early for the first grade anyway. Olesya needed at least another year. At least until she turned six! Yes, she knew how to read and how to count, and yes, she was very diligent, disciplined, and quiet, but that wasn't the point.

"She's too young," Mama told Papa. "Too young!"

Papa wasn't convinced. "So what if she's only five when she starts?"

Olesya agreed with Papa.

But that was before their train trip. Before he made her cry.

Now she wasn't so sure anymore. Maybe Mama was right. Maybe she was too young. Maybe—

"Come on, Olesya." Papa took her hand.

Olesya slipped off the bench, wishing she'd stayed home with Baba Zina and Mama. They got up early this morning to make all the special dishes for dinner—to celebrate their arrival and Papa's raise. He was promoted from the coach car attendant to the sleeping car attendant, and the luxe car attendant wasn't far from that. Then it was chief car attendant, and then the whole train manager—"train boss." Baba Zina had asked Papa to buy dill, cucumbers, and tomatoes for the salad. Papa volunteered to go all the way to Simferopol. He had to meet one of his "business acquaintances" anyway, he explained, and he offered to take Olesya with him so she wouldn't get under everybody's feet.

Baba Zina thought it was a splendid idea. Mama only nodded.

So off they went on yet another long and bumpy taxi ride, for which Papa rewarded her as he always did—by buying her sweets. He got her a rooster lollipop from a babushka at the station. While he talked to a fat, balding man who stunk of sweat, Olesya sat on a bench and unwrapped her prize. It was golden in color, and it smelled so sweet! Olesya smiled, bit off the rooster's head, then she bit off its tail, then she crunched the rest—it was gone in no time. She tossed the stick and discovered that her hands were sticky. She tried cleaning them by licking her fingers. That got boring quickly, so she rubbed the mosquito bites on her legs, counting them, and that's when she saw a group of kids skip across the tracks. It looked like fun. She decided to join them.

Papa snatched her right out from in front of the moving train, his face white, eyes huge. Olesya's heart beat so fast she thought it'd explode in her chest. She wasn't scared of the train—it was moving slowly, and she'd planned to jump out of the way anyway. She was afraid because she had displeased Papa. That meant punishment.

But Papa simply held her for a long time, rocking her, stroking her hair. Then he bought her another lollipop, waited until she finished, and offered to play a counting game—how many cars in the train?

They'd never played this game before. Olesya got excited.

Papa hoisted her up, held her tight against him, and walked to the end of the platform, where he stopped, turned around, and said, "Go!"

Olesya clutched his neck and counted as he walked. "One, two, three, four . . ."

When they got to the engine, it blasted a throaty horn and startled her. Warm wind washed over her face. It smelled of tar and metal.

"Well?" Papa asked.

"Twenty," she said.

"You sure? I think it's twenty-one."

She sighed in exasperation. "The engine doesn't count, Papa. You know that."

"Aren't you a smart one for a first grader?" He set her down on the ground.

"I'm not a first grader *yet*." It bothered Olesya when Papa wasn't exact. "I'll be a first grader next year, on September first. It's August now."

"Goodness. Always so precise." He smiled at her. "When we're back, I'll talk to the school director. They'll accept you, you'll see."

"But Mama said—"

Papa's eyes darkened. "Mama said this, Mama said that. It doesn't matter what she said. I'm telling you, you're going to school, and that's final. So don't argue with me. Understand?"

"Yes, Papa."

"Yes, Papa, what?"

"Yes, I understand."

"Good. Now come on." He gripped her by the arm and led her away from the train.

Olesya's stomach flipped. She'd done it. She'd displeased him.

"Mama said we shouldn't take too long," she tried, half running to match his big strides. "She said—"

"I don't want to hear another word." His grip tightened. "What does your Mama know? Listen to what Papa tells you. Papa knows better. I want you to be educated, not empty-headed like your Mama. All she cares about is looking pretty." He spat on the platform.

Olesya watched his saliva hit the asphalt. "But Mama's not empty-headed," she said quietly, and bit her tongue.

Papa didn't seem to hear her. He pushed through the station doors.

Cool air touched her face, and she breathed in relief. Maybe they were leaving. Maybe he wasn't going to punish her after all. Maybe—

"Do you need to do number one?" he asked. His voice was quiet.

Dread circled Olesya's neck. "No," she squeaked, and immediately she needed to pee so bad she had to press her legs together.

Papa noticed. "Yes, you do. Come on."

He banged open the door to the men's restroom. It was empty. It stank. Olesya held her breath. She'd never been in the men's restroom before. It looked odd. The urinals were fixed right to the wall, and there were only two stalls. Papa stopped in front of one, opened the door. Squat toilet. Olesya shuddered. She hated those. She had to hitch up her dress and hover over the pan, afraid she'd miss it and pee all over her shoes.

Papa led her in and closed the door.

"Come on," he said.

Olesya looked at the bulge in his pocket. TUBE.

She closed her eyes, shaking. Why did she have to run in front of the train? Why did she have to mention Mama? She was so stupid. She deserved to be punished.

"Do you need help?"

"I don't need to pee, Papa. I really don't. I *promise*."

"Stand still." He reached under her dress and pulled down her panties, white cotton with blue dots—Mama picked them out this morning to match her blue dress.

Tears burned Olesya's eyes. She blinked.

"Come on," he said. "Help me."

He lifted her leg and struggled to free her foot. The sandal got caught. He yanked, and the fabric ripped. Papa swore under his breath, pulled her other foot through, and tossed her panties aside. His hands were shaking, his breath rapid. He stood Olesya to the wall and pulled out TUBE. She stared at it, at its angry red color, groping in her mind for something, anything, to stop him. Her buttocks goosed from brushing cold tiles, and the words formed in her mouth before she knew she'd spoken them.

"I need to do number two," she said.

"What?"

"I need to poop!"

The restroom door banged open. Heavy footfalls.

Papa clamped his hand over Olesya's mouth. They stood still, listening.

The sound of a buckle, a zipper. A stream hitting the urinal.

As soon as the man left, Papa stepped out. "Do it quickly," he said through the door.

Olesya squatted and peed, her mind racing. She was trapped. Her only hope was to pretend it was taking her a while and wait for someone else to come in, then rush out. Papa would be too afraid to drag her back in with some man looking on, wouldn't he? That man could call militia, and Papa was afraid of militia, Olesya knew that much. When he had fights with Mama, she'd threatened to call militia, and it got Papa quiet.

The restroom door slammed open, and the air suddenly filled with noises.

"Is that stall taken?" asked a rough voice.

"My kid's in there," Papa answered.

The voice grumbled.

Kid. Olesya smiled. Papa was afraid. It gave her courage. There was no toilet paper, so she dried herself with the hem of her skirt. She looked down at her torn panties. They'd be no good. She'd have to do without. She pushed at the door. It wouldn't open. He held it shut from the outside. Olesya pushed harder. No use. Despair washed over her, and she cried, "I'm done, Papa! I'm done!"

"Did you wipe your bottom?" he asked.

"I did! I'm done!"

"You sure?"

"My son is the same way, the scoundrel," said the rough voice. "Don't know how many times I told him. 'Wipe your ass, Vanya. You stink.' " The voice chuckled. "What can you do? He's only seven. How old is your boy?"

"Mind your own business," Papa snapped.

"Just asking."

The restroom door closed, and Papa tugged on the stall door. Olesya hung on the handle with all her weight.

"Open the door, Olesya." He sounded dangerous.

She grimly held on.

"I said, open the door." A pause, then right in her ear, "Found you!"

She startled, turned, and there was Papa with her in the stall.

"How about some light?" he said.

His eyes lit up with a strange, electric glow. He reached for Olesya. She screamed, let go of the door, fell out on the cold tile floor, and hit her head hard. As Papa stepped out, she sprang up and rammed the door shut in his face and—

MELITOPOL–SIMFEROPOL
6 February 1989
03:38

—it jerked and shook and rattled. Olesya gripped the latch with both hands, her breath white, around her the cold darkness of the haunted car. She was in the aisle, and Papa was inside compartment No. 6. Inside her memory.

Interrupted.

He got in with her, must've lost her and found her and . . . what?

"You don't want me to see it," she said.

The jerking stopped.

"That's it. That's what it is. You don't want me to remember. Even now, even after all these years. Even though you're *dead*."

Her anger was swift. It set her blood to boiling. It sang in her head, wiping away her fear.

"Even *dead* you won't leave me alone."

Silence.

"Even *dead* you're interrupting my living. I almost killed myself twice, Papa, did you know that? No, of course you don't. You don't care."

Breathing.

"You hurt me. You hurt me bad, didn't you? What a hero. Taking out your anger on a five-year-old girl. It was easy, wasn't it. God, you're such a coward. And here I thought I was the one in the wrong. I can't—I can't even— What did you do? What did you do to me? Can you tell me?"

No answer.

"You've nothing to say, do you? You're too scared—too scared to admit it. To face it. What was I to you? Not a daughter, that's for sure. Then, what, a little doll for your games? Yes, Papa? Yes. Yes, I was. All these years you stole from me, all these memories—I just . . . I don't understand. Why? Can you tell me *why*?"

She could hear him moving on the other side of the door. And she could sense his terror of her. It made her bolder.

"You didn't think I'd remember, did you?" she said. "I mean, what *did* you think, Papa? Anything at all? How—what kind of a man, what kind of a father—I don't—"

She stopped, her heart beating hard in her ears.

"You knew. You pathetic excuse for a father. You knew I'd remember one day. You just didn't know when. So you tried to frighten me into silence. It worked. It worked pretty well, actually. You died almost a hero. And yet . . . you're restless. Is that why you're back? Because you wanted to stop me from remembering? But why should you care, Papa? What do you want from me? TUBE? What for?"

"Let me out." Little Olesya's voice.

Olesya started. "Olesya?"

"Please. He's hurting me."

"Oh God."

Her little self, still in the restroom stall—

Olesya rolled the door open.

"Quick—" The words froze in her mouth.

"My little ballerina." Papa's shining eyes fixed on her. "So easy to trick."

She tried closing the door. He wedged his foot in it and it bounced.

"What's with the sullen look? It's only fair."

Olesya backed off.

His eyes flicked to TUBE in her hand.

She took another step, and her back hit the wall.

They stood in front of each other, sizing each other up.

"You asked why I came," he said. "I don't want to spoil the surprise. You're sure you want to know?"

She said nothing.

"You've grown so much." He tilted his head. "How many years has it been?"

"Nine. No, ten," she answered automatically, and hated herself for it.

"Ten years. How much I have missed. Your face." He reached out.

She shrank away from his touch.

His hand slipped down to TUBE, and the revulsion she felt became intolerable. She opened her fingers before he touched her. *Could* he touch her? She didn't know, didn't care. In that moment, she wanted to be as far away from him as was possible.

TUBE dropped to the floor.

Papa picked it up. "Thank you for giving back what's mine."

Olesya watched him, stunned. How did she let this happen?

"Give it back," she said.

"Not so fast now."

"Give it back!"

She charged at him. He stepped back. She lost her balance and fell. He bent as though to hoist her up, and she scrambled away and stood, panting. He was playing with her, she realized. This was all a game.

"Remember what day it is?" he asked.

"Yes."

"It's your birthday."

"I know."

"My sweet birthday girl." He smiled. "I have a surprise for you."

Olesya stared. What was he planning now?

"Don't you want to celebrate? With tea and cake and presents?"

He retreated into the shadows, beckoning. She followed, her eyes never leaving TUBE. What a fool she was. What a damn dura. Her only chance was to snatch it out of his hand. She lurched forward, and he sidestepped her easily, as though he'd expected it.

Olesya got to her feet. When she did, the car swayed around the bend. She lost her balance again. Before she understood what was happening, Papa had wrestled Little Olesya out of his compartment and simply let Olesya fall in.

He stepped inside behind her and locked the door.

"That's better," he said.

Little Olesya pounded on the door. "Let me in! Let me in!"

"Shut up," he said, "or I'll hurt her."

The pounding ceased.

Olesya sat on the bunk, facing him.

"Take off your clothes," he said.

"What?"

"You heard me."

She stared.

"I want to see how you've changed. I hope the years haven't ruined your perfect little ballet body."

Olesya backed into the wall. There was nowhere else to retreat.

Could he force her to do it? Could he *touch* her? She needed to find out, yet she couldn't make herself. Her flesh crawled at the thought of it. What if he could?

Papa smiled at her. "Well?"

"Well, what?" She was buying more time, and she knew that he knew.

He smiled wider.

Had they played this game before?

"Take off your clothes," he said again, and his voice was steel.

"I don't—"

He pushed TUBE against her neck and pressed. Olesya couldn't breathe. She grabbed for TUBE, but Papa had moved it away already.

"Do you want to make it difficult? Or do you want to make it easy? It's your choice," he said.

"You can't touch me," Olesya wheezed.

"I can't," he agreed easily. "But TUBE can." And the smile he gave her chilled her blood.

Olesya rubbed her throat. Of course. It made sense.

"That's why you wanted it so bad?"

Papa switched on TUBE. It shot a beam of light at her, whistled merrily, and Olesya did what she must've done before—what her desperate little girl's mind conceived as the only way to fight the large and strong man who could easily break her. She twisted to the side, pulled her knees to her chest, and with all her strength slammed her feet into TUBE.

It flew out of his hand. Papa groaned. They both dove for it. Olesya caught it first, rolled on her back. He bent over her, and she stabbed him in his stomach.

She thought maybe her hand would go through him. He was a ghost, after all, and ghosts didn't have flesh, did they? But she hit something with TUBE—some resistance. Then

TUBE tore through it like a knife tears through a cloth. Papa's eyes bulged out. He doubled over and hollered.

The pounding on the door resumed. "Olesya, get out! Get out *now*!"

Olesya scrambled up, TUBE in her hand. At her feet Papa rolled into a ball and screamed, clutching his stomach. Olesya watched him, horrified.

"Out! Get out!"

"Yes. Yes, I'm coming."

She fumbled for the latch behind her, hands sweaty and shaking. Found it. Pulled it and stumbled out the door. Rolled it shut.

Papa roared in fury.

Little Olesya stood in the aisle, eyes wide.

"You hurt him," she said in awe.

"I guess I did."

"You hurt him the only way you could. How did you know?"

"I didn't."

Papa shrieked and slammed against the door. It rattled.

"Oh God," Olesya said.

"Hold it!" Little Olesya cried. "Hold it!"

Olesya gripped the door. It twitched and rattled in her hand. She wedged her hip against it and pushed at it with her entire weight. The door shook. Papa threw his body against it. Again and again. The paneling creaked. The door shuddered under a heavy blow, and the latch ripped out of Olesya's hold.

The door screeched open.

Olesya stepped back. Little Olesya hid behind her.

Olesya slipped TUBE into her pocket and spread out protective arms around the girl, like wings of a swan.

Papa looked at them, tilted his head.

"Go back," Olesya said. "Go back to where you came from."

"My little ballerina," Papa said softly.

The words cut her deep—deep into her gut. The yearning of a child rose up in her—every child feels it, the need to be loved. It was so strong . . . she swayed as though to fall into his arms, to feel him hug her, pat her head, hear him whisper to her how much he loved her. She could endure anything for this. Any hurt, any pain. It was worth it, this small, fleeting moment.

That's when she understood the power of his lies. How easy it was for him. And what an idiot she was to believe him. Little Olesya was right. She was stupid. A dumb goose.

"I'm not your *anything*," she said, fighting tears. "You hear me?"

"My sweet daughter."

"No."

"My dear little girl."

"Stop it."

"What's that, tears?" he said, and that hurt the worst. "Why are you crying, silly?"

He opened his arms.

It took all she had not to fall into them. Not to trust him.

"How could you," she said. "Papa, how *could* you?"

"Why are you hurting me?" he said.

He was so close she could see his lips move.

"Hurting you? *I'm* hurting you?" She stared at him, baffled.

"Your Papa came to visit you, to wish you a happy birthday. Is this any way to treat me? I brought you tea and cake, thought we'd sit down and talk, and you're attacking me like I'm some enemy. Where is this violence coming from?"

Olesya didn't know what to say. He had her, again. She knew it, and she didn't know how to fight against it. She could see in his eyes that he knew he'd won. At least for now.

"Come on," he said, and smiled.

Olesya felt movement. Little Olesya's hand crept to her pocket from behind. Olesya shifted her body sideways, to aid her.

"Okay," she said.

His eyes lit up with their strange, electric light. "That's my girl."

"What kind of cake?" She infused her voice with childlike wonder. He loved spoiling her with sweets, loved seeing her get giddy at the sight of them, watching her eat them. Then, after, he would always take care to wipe her lips and her sticky fingers with his handkerchief, first spitting on it to make it wet.

"Your favorite," he said. "Raspberry sponge cake."

"Oh!" Olesya felt weak.

She couldn't remember the last time she'd eaten cake. With her ballet work and her diet she rarely ate sweets anymore. The thought of tasting it—no, better, the thought of eating *a whole slice*—overwhelmed her.

To make it was a chore.

First, you had to mix the smooth, creamy batter. Then you had to bake the sponge cake layers (and make sure they didn't overbake to come out moist and springy!). Next, you had to soak the sponges with rum, just enough for the rich taste but not too much lest you make them soggy. Finally, you had to smear the layers with raspberry jam—preferably homemade, as the store-bought jam was too thick. You sandwiched the layers together and set the cake under a weight for about thirty minutes. Done. But if you wanted to add one more flourish—for special occasions like birthdays or holidays—you smothered the whole thing with sour cream frosting and more raspberry jam and sprinkled it with powdered sugar. If raspberries were in season, you'd set some on top in whatever quantity you liked.

There was no comparable cake to this one. You couldn't buy it at the store, as it was their family recipe, and it always took Baba Zina the better portion of the day to make it. Mama's version was passable. Olesya was glad to devour it even if it was burned. But after Papa died, Mama stopped baking. She stopped cooking altogether, in fact. They existed on sandwiches, precooked deli meats and canned food until Olesya was old enough to cook herself. She never attempted to recreate Baba Zina's "masterpiece," for fear of spoiling memories.

And now this special cake—her favorite raspberry sponge cake—malinovy tort—was here. On this train. Within reach.

(Was it? *Was* it?)

Olesya could almost taste it.

"Raspberry sponge cake," she said. Her mouth filled with saliva.

"Raspberry sponge cake," Papa echoed. "Your favorite."

"And I can . . . eat it?"

"You sure can."

"All of it?"

"If you wish."

"I do. I—oh, I haven't had it since—"

"Eat *this*!" Little Olesya shrieked.

Olesya whirled around.

The girl had TUBE in her hands. She raised her arms and rammed it straight into Papa's belly. "Run! *Run!*"

Olesya didn't need to be told twice. She turned and ran.

Papa bellowed. It was the cry of a predator caught off guard.

"Catch!"

TUBE clattered to the floor in front of Olesya. She swiped it up, turned and froze.

Papa had Little Olesya in his grip.

"Go!" she yelled.

"But—"

"You stupid goose. You've almost no time left! *Now!*"

Papa's hands closed on Little Olesya's throat. Her face twisted with strain, her skin ghostly in the moonlight that filtered through the frosted windows. Her hands went to Papa's, clawing at them, slapping, scratching. Her arms were so thin and white they looked like they were made from porcelain that could snap any moment. Her whole body looked doll-like, easy to break.

Olesya took a step forward.

Their eyes met, and in them she saw an iron will, the kind of stubbornness that had helped her survive, that couldn't be broken.

The girl nodded, then her eyes glazed over.

Olesya went.

ALUPKA

18 August 1973
14:41

Olesya was five. She stood in front of Baba Zina's china cabinet, gazing at her collection of porcelain ballerinas, thinking about the scary thing Papa did to her this morning.

Today was Baba Zina's sixtieth birthday. Papa and Uncle Shurik had moved her sewing desk and armchairs to the walls and set up the dining table in the middle of her room. Mama and Baba Zina had loaded it with dishes—it was going to be a big celebration—but at the moment everyone was gone and the room was quiet.

Olesya tried to come up with words to explain what Papa did to her. She was frightened and hurting. Desperate to understand what she did wrong so she'd never do it again, she'd tried to come up with words but couldn't. She remembered only pictures.

This morning, while Uncle Shurik slept and Mama and Baba Zina shopped at the market, Papa made Olesya play TUBE—because Mama "killed that premature brat." Olesya didn't understand what that meant and why *she* had to be punished for it and not Mama. The pain from their game was so bad she was afraid she'd die from it, but somehow she didn't.

Papa said he'd make her do it again if she told anyone.

He'd shoved her into the bathroom and ordered her to clean up her mess. She did her best and decided to tell Mama. Surely Mama wouldn't let him hurt her again, would she? But when Olesya got out of the bathroom and saw Mama and Baba Zina stomp in through the door, dragging in heavy grocery bags and discussing the cake, she got frightened.

What if Mama killed *her* too?

It all became confused in her mind—all the things Papa did. She was losing them, fast. Only her body still felt it. Maybe that's how she could tell her story—show it with her body, like ballerinas did onstage.

Olesya passed her eyes from one figurine to the next. They were from Germany, she knew. They were *imported*. Baba Zina told her countless times how she'd had to hide them on the train so the border guards wouldn't confiscate them. A German woman gave them to her after the war, as payment for dresses. They were expensive and very fragile, especially the lace of their tutus. They were not to be played with, only looked at. Olesya thought it was silly, to have dolls you couldn't play with. Why have them at all? She badly wanted to get her hands on one and touch it, especially the lace. How could it be so delicate and so hard at the same time? There were ten of them, not much taller than tea cups. Each held a different pose—arms stretched up or to the sides, one leg extended behind or bent sideways or pointed in front in a curtsy, their tutus painted light pink or light blue and decorated with miniature roses.

"Why aren't you outside? Go play!"

Olesya spun around. "Baba Zina."

Baba Zina was in a good mood. She was already tipsy. Olesya could tell by her dancing eyes and by her smudged lipstick. This was it. She'd try showing her story to Baba Zina right now, with her body. Olesya hopped onto Baba Zina's bed.

"What's this now? Get off. Get off! You'll rumple it. The guests are coming any minute."

"But Baba Zina, look." Olesya lifted her dress. She wanted to show Baba Zina the tracks.

"Get off, I said! Obstinate child. *Off!*"

Baba Zina raised her arm to swat her, but Olesya was quicker. She jumped to the cabinet and pressed her back to it, trembling.

"Oh, I know what you want." Baba Zina shook a finger at Olesya so vigorously, her ruby earrings swung around in circles. "But only today, hear me? Today is special, and I'm feeling generous." She slid open the glass panel.

Olesya held her breath.

Baba Zina moved the figurines aside. "Do you know why it's a special day?"

Olesya nodded. "It's your birthday."

"And how old am I?"

"Sixty."

"Wrong! I'm six*teen*. Remember that. If anyone asks, your Baba Zina is always sixteen. So, how old am I?"

"Sixteen."

"That's right!"

Baba Zina let out a laugh, reached in the back, and took out a figurine Olesya hadn't seen before. It was hidden by the others. She immediately knew why. It was blank, unpainted. The tutu was white and had no roses on it, and the face had no eyes and no mouth, but Olesya liked it right away. It stood on tippy toes, arms raised like the wings of a swan about to take off.

Olesya took the figurine and held it to her chest, hardly believing her luck.

"This is the cheapest one," Baba Zina said. "In case you break it. You better not, hear me? Or I'll box your ears!"

"I won't," Olesya squeaked. "I promise. Can I show you something?"

Baba Zina didn't answer. She straightened the festive green bed cover, repositioned the cushions, and went to the front door, her skirt swishing behind her.

The hallway rang with voices of the old ladies—her girlfriends and clients for whom she sewed brightly colored dresses that were supposed to make them look younger but aged them instead. They loved squeezing and kissing Olesya. She hated it. Now her way to the kitchen was cut off. That meant she couldn't show her story to Mama, who was in the kitchen decorating the raspberry sponge cake.

Maybe it was a good thing. Olesya was a little afraid of Mama's reaction. Would she understand it the right way? What if she got mad? Better not risk it.

Olesya sighed. She wished Uncle Shurik were here. He'd understand her story right away, and he'd tell her what to do. But he'd gone with Papa to the liquor store. They were gone a long time and should've been back by now. Baba Zina would be cross with them for being late.

Olesya went to the window and looked out.

Their steep, narrow cobble street led directly to the sea. Every hour of the day it was busy with sunburned vacationers hauling things to the beach—sacks of groceries, watermelons, colorful pool floats—their children buzzing around like mosquitoes. Olesya smelled the salt on the air and wished she could run away, down to the water, but she'd be scolded if she went alone, so she stayed put, scanning the faces.

There was no sign of Uncle Shurik or Papa. The thought of Papa's face frightened her. She withdrew from the window, sat on a chair, and winced. She was still sore, but at least she was clean. She wouldn't get in trouble again. And she wanted to play with the figurine before Baba Zina changed her mind and took it away.

Olesya flipped over her plate and set the ballerina on the base, humming *Swan Lake*, gliding her around, pretending the guests who came into the room were the theater audience who came to watch ballet.

"Where did you get this?" Mama's voice said to her right. The chair creaked as she sat down.

Olesya was reluctant to break her humming. It made her forget the pain, made her feel at peace.

"Who gave it to you? Baba Zina? Did you take it out yourself?"

Olesya shook her head.

"Olesya."

She hummed louder.

Mama shook her shoulder. "Olesya, answer me."

"Yes."

"Yes, what?"

"Baba Zina gave her to me. Her name is Olesya too. She wants to show you a story. Can she show you a story?"

Mama pressed her lips together. She looked tired. Her face had no makeup. Her blouse was creased. "This lace is very fragile. You know that, yes?"

"Yes, Baba Zina told me. But, Mama—"

"If you drop it, it'll break. Give it to me."

"No."

"I'll put it away while you eat. You can play with it later."

"No!" Olesya cradled the ballerina in her hands.

"Zinaida Yefimovna!" Mama called to Baba Zina. "Did you give this to Olesya?"

Baba Zina turned away from talking to a pudgy old lady. "Why? She broke it *already*?"

"No, no, she didn't break anything. I just wanted to make sure she's not inventing some story again."

"Oh, she'll invent one soon enough!" Baba Zina laughed and whispered something to the pudgy lady, who chuckled.

Mama turned to Olesya. "I better take it from you before you break it."

Olesya pushed out her lower lip. Why didn't Mama ever believe her? It was no use showing her the story. She'd think she made it up.

The front door slammed.

"We're back!" Uncle Shurik called from the hallway.

A moment later Papa poked in his head, his face glistening with perspiration.

Olesya's heart dropped. She stared at him, but he didn't seem to notice. His eyes swept the room, slipping over Olesya's chair as though it were empty, paused on Baba Zina's bed, and returned to the table.

"Aha!" he exclaimed. "I see the beauties have already assembled."

The old ladies giggled.

"You're always so gallant, Grisha," said the pudgy one. She mopped her sweaty face with a handkerchief. "Zinaida Yefimovna raised you well."

"Oh, stop it." Baba Zina shook her head in mock humility, her ruby earrings swinging. "You're making me blush like I'm a young girl. It's embarrassing."

"You *are* a young girl," Papa said, and produced a bouquet of roses from behind his back. "Every year getting younger and younger."

"Oh!" Baba Zina clasped her hands.

"Happy sixteen, Mamochka."

He pecked her on the cheek. She grabbed his head and smothered him with kisses, planting the last one on his lips. Papa wiped his mouth with the back of his hand.

The ladies *ooh*ed and *ahh*ed and commented that this was true mother's love and that her son deserved it: handsome, smart, a non-drinker with a good, solid family and a promising career in the transportation sector. What else could a mother wish for?

"What's that smell?" Uncle Shurik said. "Something burning?"

"The meat!" Mama jumped up and rushed to the kitchen. Uncle Shurik sat in her chair. He looked like a younger, softer version of Papa. Olesya was so happy he was finally here she wanted to cry.

"Who's this little girl I see?" he whispered into her ear, his breath smelling of alcohol. "Do I know her?"

"I'm Olesya," Olesya whispered back. "And this is Olesya too." She pointed to the figurine. "She wants to show you a story."

"I don't blame her," he said, and winked. "She must be bored out of her mind. Did I get that right?"

Olesya nodded. Uncle Shurik always understood her without her having to explain anything. She was flooded with relief.

"So what's the story?"

"She can't tell you, because it's very scary." Olesya looked in her lap. "But she can show you. Like a ballerina."

"All right. Let's see it."

Olesya laid the ballerina facedown on the plate, but it looked wrong. She couldn't bend her hard, porcelain legs. It wasn't going to work after all. Tears sprung to Olesya's eyes.

"She can't show it right," she whispered, frustrated.

"Why don't you just tell me?"

"I can't," Olesya shook her head. "If I do, Papa—" She bit her lip, terrified.

Uncle Shurik frowned. "What happened?"

Olesya sat still.

"Did he yell at you? He can be scary when he yells."

She shook her head.

"Did he *hit* you?"

Uncle Shurik waited for her to answer, but she didn't know if what happened was called hitting. Maybe it was, maybe it wasn't. She shrugged.

Uncle Shurik put an arm around her shoulder. "How about you draw it for me?"

"Draw?"

"Yes. Can you draw it for me?"

"No. It's not my story." Olesya clutched the figurine to her chest.

"I'm sorry. I mean . . . can *Olesya* draw it?" He pointed at the figurine.

Olesya thought about it. "She can't, but I can draw it for her."

"Okay." He turned around, took a pen and notepad from the telephone stand, and set them on the table. "Here you go."

She picked up the pen and froze. It was a mess in her mind again—a big mess of scary pictures. She didn't know which one to draw first.

"How about we play a game?" Uncle Shurik offered.

"What game?"

"Heads, Bodies, and Legs."

"Heads, bodies, and legs?"

"That's right. You know how to play it?"

She shook her head.

"Here, let me show you." He took the pen and the pad from her and flipped it to a clean sheet, which he ripped out. "You draw the head"—he drew a circle with dots for eyes and a squiggly line for a mouth—"then you fold the paper over so I can't see it, all right?" He folded the paper down. "Then you give it to me, because it's my turn. I draw the body, fold the paper down"—he drew a torso with circles for coat buttons and folded the paper over—"and then it's your turn again."

"Do I draw the legs?"

"You got it!"

"And then what?"

"Then we unfold it and laugh at it. It's usually pretty funny."

Olesya smiled. "Okay."

"What parts do you want to draw?"

"The head and the legs!"

She touched pen to paper and drew a big round head with two ears sticking out. In the middle of the face she drew two huge eyes. Then she drew a long thin neck and folded the paper over.

"Your turn!"

Uncle Shurik took the pen and cupped the paper with his hand. "No peeking."

Olesya shied back and giggled, the figurine held tightly in her sweaty fist. Her heart was racing. She knew exactly what to draw when Uncle Shurik was done. When he pushed over the paper she bent down, hard at work, oblivious to the voices talking over one another, the scrapes of forks and knives, the clinking of glasses . . .

It was important she show exactly what she saw in her head, exactly what happened. Olesya hated lying. She did her best to draw every detail. Her hand shook a little, and it took her longer than she thought.

When she was done, she looked over her drawing proudly. She did well. She was sure Uncle Shurik would praise her for it. She folded the paper and pushed it over to him—

But in his place sat Mama.

"Where's Uncle Shurik?" Olesya asked.

"What's this?"

Olesya hid the drawing behind her back. "Where is he?"

"In the bathroom. He'll be right back." Mama stretched out a hand. "Can I see?"

"It's for Uncle Shurik," Olesya said. If Mama saw it, she wouldn't understand.

"What's that you got there?" Papa asked Olesya from across the table.

The warmth drained out of her face. She felt cold all over.

"Are you playing Heads, Bodies, and Legs?" Papa asked.

"You two used to play it all the time when you were boys!" Baba Zina exclaimed, waving around a glass full of vodka. "My Grisha doted on Shurik, such a good older brother," she told the table. "They were close, very close." She moved her hands together to show how close they were, and the vodka spilled. She knocked it back, slammed it on the table and said, "Let me see."

Olesya shrank back.

"Come on, don't be shy. We won't laugh too hard. Right, girls?"

The ladies giggled.

The toilet flushed in the hallway. Olesya took a shuddering breath. Uncle Shurik was coming any minute. She was safe. She was—

Baba Zina leaned over the table and snatched the drawing from Olesya's hand.

"You all know this game?" she asked the table. "My boys played it all the time. They'd laugh until they cried. Let's see what we've got here." She unfolded the paper, pointing away from her and toward the table so everyone could see.

Just then Uncle Shurik walked in.

Everyone fell quiet and looked at the drawing, poised to laugh.

Then the silence stretched. Baba Zina turned it around, gasped, and flung it to the table, right at the cake. She clasped both hands over her mouth and made a strange noise. A whimper? A moan? Olesya didn't understand her reaction. As much as she was afraid, she was proud of what she drew, and she liked what Uncle Shurik drew—it was funny.

On the paper was Papa.

His big round head looked comical on his thin neck, but his face looked surprisingly accurate, especially the eyes. His body was that of a train, made up of segments like cars— Uncle Shurik drew that part. And below his waist, where his legs joined his torso, Olesya drew TUBE. The engine. It stuck out at a perpendicular angle. She copied it exactly: the long metal body, the eight wheels, the round headlamp. She also drew snow on its roof. It was melting, dripping down to Papa's feet in a puddle. By the puddle lay a little girl, her legs streaked with dark lines. They were tracks—train tracks—for TUBE to ride. But the cake spoiled them. The raspberry jam had soaked into this part of the drawing, and the girl was quickly disappearing into an ugly red stain.

Olesya stretched her arm to take the drawing, but Baba Zina was first. She snatched it and shook it, her face white.

"What is—what is this?" she stuttered. "What is this, I ask you? Who drew this? Who drew this filth?"

She passed her eyes from Olesya to Uncle Shurik.

He opened his mouth.

"I did!" Olesya piped up. She couldn't let Uncle Shurik lie for her. Lying was bad.

She searched the table for Papa, but he was up and slipping out of the room. Uncle Shurik caught him by the arm. Papa shook him off and walked out.

"What does this mean, Olesya?" Mama asked, her voice dangerously quiet.

"It's my story."

Olesya smiled. She did it. So what if she didn't know how to explain it with words. She did it with pictures! And she did it all on her own. Well, Uncle Shurik helped a little, but still— she did it herself. Olesya felt very proud.

Then why did Mama look at her so strangely?

"You dirty little girl," Baba Zina said. "I'll teach you. I'll teach you how to draw dirty pictures."

She walked around the table to Olesya, seized her ear, and twisted it.

Olesya cried out.

"Zinaida Yefimovna!" Mama jumped up.

Baba Zina let go of Olesya's ear and looked wildly about her, meeting watching eyes. Her hand twitched upward. Olesya cringed, knowing that if they were alone she'd hit the back of her head so hard it'd hurt for days. But there were guests, so instead of hitting her Baba Zina ripped the ballerina out of her hand and hurled it at the table. It hit a carafe filled with juice and smashed to bits that flew every which way—the legs, the arms, the lacy bits of the tutu.

And the head. It bounced up and plopped onto the cake, facing Olesya, staring at her with blank, unpainted eyes and screaming a silent scream with her mute, unpainted mouth.

MELITOPOL–SIMFEROPOL

6 February 1989
04:05

"My God . . . the tracks . . . they weren't tracks at all," Olesya said.

Papa smiled.

She looked at him, speechless.

They were sitting in the attendant's compartment, the table between them. On it sat a raspberry sponge cake with twenty-one candles.

Papa had found Olesya in compartment No. 6, passed out from shock. It didn't take much threatening to get her moving. In fact, all it took was the cake. He leaned over her with it, his face lit up with candle glow, and the smell of it got Olesya on her feet. The thought of asking him questions and learning what it meant to play TUBE—what he did to her—how he hurt her—(oh, but she already knew, she *knew*, yet she didn't want to believe it, couldn't accept it, no, no)—got her walking ahead of him without a fight.

Could she ask him? Would he answer?

She could try. And so she heard herself say, "What happened after?"

"We ate the cake," Papa said matter-of-factly.

"We ate the cake?"

"Yes."

"We ate the cake." She looked at it.

That was her family. They ate the cake.

"I remembered, Papa . . ." she said slowly.

"Yes."

"I remembered that it was—"

He waited.

"—it was *you*."

"Yes."

"You *hurt* me."

"Yes, yes."

Olesya stared at him, stunned. He simply admitted to it. It made no sense.

"How? What did you do to me?" She felt TUBE in her pocket. "What kind of game was it?"

(Why did she ask? *Why?*)

"TUBE," Papa said, and smiled again.

(No! No!)

"How *could* you?"

"Make a wish," he said, and motioned to the cake. "The candles are burning out."

Olesya was frozen. What was she supposed to say? What was she supposed to *do*? The shock of his admittance, of her remembering what she'd drawn—what it really was—made her cold, jittery, weak. And so she sat motionless, watching the candles burn, smelling the hot wax, and listening to the wheels beat their rhythm.

The cake taunted her. Olesya's stomach grumbled. Her mouth filled with saliva. She swooned at the sweet, nostalgic aroma, fighting the urge to reach out and swipe her finger across the surface and pop it into her mouth and lick it. Just like she did when she was little, no matter how many times Baba Zina scolded her.

Her favorite cake. There it was, only a touch away.

She gripped the edge of the bunk to stop herself from reaching out. There was no cake. There couldn't be. Papa was dead, and this was simply a very convincing illusion.

"Why are you here?" she said at last.

"The candles are burning out."

"You didn't answer my question."

"Come on, Olesya."

She gritted her teeth. "Where is Little Olesya? What did you do to her?"

"Make a wish," he said. "Look, the wax is ruining the cake."

Olesya forced herself to hold his gaze.

"Tell me exactly what you did to me, Papa. Can you tell me?"

(Don't! Don't! I don't want to *know*!)

He simply looked at her, smiling, waiting.

"Did you . . . did you use TUBE to—to—"

She couldn't say it, wouldn't say it. (Say it. *Say* it.) No! It sounded wrong, sick. She broke into a sweat. Tears burned her eyes. She didn't care if they spilled.

"Why, Papa? Why? And . . . *how*? I don't understand. Were you . . . I just . . . was Mama not enough? Did you . . . did you guys do it, or . . . did you lose interest? Or were you never interested? But then, how—I don't— *Please*, explain it to me. Do you like girls over women? Is that it? Is that—" She had to catch her breath. "What kind of a man would do something like this to his own daughter?"

A grimace of distaste passed over Papa's face. "I see you don't want to make a wish."

Olesya's temples pounded. Her hands trembled.

"I used to fall for this, you know," she said. "Every time I'd ask you something you didn't want to answer, you'd steer the conversation away. You'd simply pretend you didn't hear me. But not this time, Papa. Not this time. I'm not a little girl anymore for you to fool. You'll sit here and listen to what I have to say. So, let me recount what I think happened on the morning of Baba Zina's sixtieth birthday.

"I was going to have a sister or a brother. Except, Mama hated the idea of having another child with you—I understand that now—so she had an abortion. You were outraged when you found out. She shattered your dream of having a son—a boy—and not just some weakling girl like me. You think I don't know this? Uncle Shurik told me. You always wanted a boy, you never wanted a girl. In your eyes, Mama committed an unforgivable crime. She killed your future son, and you wanted to punish her, but she was too big and too strong for you. Not physically, no. You could kick her to death if you wanted to. The problem is . . . you're scared of women, aren't you? That's why you *hate* them.

"You're a coward. You did what all cowards do. You turned your rage on a child. After all, it's much easier to hurt a five-year-old than a twenty-five-year-old. Isn't that right, Papa?"

He was silent.

"What I don't understand is, why did you do it with a toy? Why with TUBE?"

"Well, I'll make your wish for you," Papa said, and blew out the sputtering candles. The bluish smoke coiled up to his face in the darkness, and when it drifted away, the cake was gone. "Come on. I have a birthday present for you—something special. I hope you like it."

He stood and went into the aisle, and Olesya followed him on wooden legs, TUBE held firmly in her hand, her eyes searching the darkness for Little Olesya. There was no sign of her.

Olesya stopped. She'd almost fallen for it again. Papa was luring her away from compartment No. 8, the last of her forgotten memories.

Or was he?

She watched him enter the attendant's compartment. He didn't seem to care. She had enough time to open the door and vanish.

Her hand hovered over her stomach. She hesitated, and then it was too late. Papa was walking back, in his hands a big box. He passed a window. The box glistened in the moonlight. Lacquered wood stamped with English letters:

TUBE

TRANS-URBAN BLITZ EXPRESS

Olesya's heart skipped a beat. Nostalgia raked at her. She was back to being a little girl, thrilled, wanting to grab her present, to open it, to play with it.

"How do you like it?" Papa asked with a radiant smile, and swung back the lid.

Inside sat all the parts as Olesya remembered them: the tracks, the cables, the speed dial, the ten shiny cars.

The engine slot was empty.

"It's a very special toy," Papa said. "Every Soviet child's envy. Want to play with it? We can set it up right here." He waved his hand along the aisle.

"It's missing the engine," Olesya piped up.

"No, it isn't. You have it right there." Papa pointed to her pocket. "Let's play with it. Just one game. I'll buy you as much candy as you want. Well?"

He reached for her hand, and Olesya stepped back.

I'll buy you as much candy as you want. The words slammed into her, jarred her memory. Her knees went weak, and she held on to the rail.

"That's what you told me that morning," she said quietly. "We were alone, and you took me to Baba Zina's room and said, 'I'll buy you as much candy as you want.' And I believed you because you always told the truth. You said lying was bad. So I told the truth, just like you taught me. I remember it now. After Baba Zina smashed the figurine, Mama asked me who it was in the picture. I said it was you.

"It was the truth. But you told everyone I was lying, you said it was Uncle Shurik. You said you caught us that morning, him showing me dirty pictures, filling my head with dirty ideas. You accused your own brother, in front of everyone, and they believed you. Only Mama doubted you. I could see it in her eyes.

"Because every mother knows.

"Always.

"That night Baba Zina belted me until I fainted. You weren't there to see it. You left to get drunk. You know what she told me? She said it was for my own good. She was beating the 'dirt' out of me, so I wouldn't turn into a whore. A five-year-old girl who tried to tell her family that her father hurt her was beaten for it and accused of lying. Only . . . it wasn't me who was a liar, it was you. I never made up any of my stories—you did. How afraid must you have been to hide behind the back of a little girl? My God, you're pathetic."

Papa's shining eyes blazed. He tossed the box to the floor. "Give me back what's mine, and I'll forgive you."

"Forgive me? *You* will forgive *me*?"

"You're trying my patience, Olesya."

"Go to hell."

He lunged at her.

Olesya flailed, caught off guard. Papa's shining eyes zeroed in on TUBE in her hand. He grabbed for it. She backed off, lost her balance and sat down hard, accidentally flipping the switch on the engine. Its headlamp lit up. It whistled. Its wheels started spinning. Papa roared in fury.

She rolled away from him as he came at her, turned around, threw all her weight behind her arm and stabbed him in the stomach. TUBE met resistance and stopped.

Olesya turned it.

This time Papa didn't scream. He made no noise at all.

It was the train that made the noise. It came to a sudden, screeching stop.

Olesya was thrown against the wall. Her head hit something hard and sharp, and her vision went black.

When she opened her eyes, there were people in the car, dressed in robes and pajamas, talking over one another.

"Is this Simferopol?"

"What's going on?"

"Why did we stop?"

"Let me through. Let me through!" A woman with a fur coat thrown over her nightgown elbowed passengers out of the way. "Attendant!"

She walked down the aisle. Olesya followed her, realizing that she no longer had TUBE, realizing that none of the passengers seemed to see her. The woman jumped out of the car and sank to her ankles in the snow. Olesya climbed down after her.

"Get back on the train! Get back!" the attendant yelled.

"Why did we stop?" the woman demanded.

"You're deaf or what? What did I tell you?"

He raised the iron rod he held, as though to strike her, and shone his flashlight straight in her face. She cowered and quickly climbed back inside, stomping off the snow and grumbling under her breath.

The attendant patted down his hat, turned up the collar of his coat, and tramped back toward the tail of the train, banging the rod on the wheels, knocking off the ice.

Olesya watched him, breathless.

"Papa," she said, and she knew where she was.

The train, stopped close to Simferopol . . . the unusually cold winter . . .

She had opened his memory—his last one.

39KM TO SIMFEROPOL
04:42

Olesya followed Papa at a safe distance, the length of a car between them. She didn't know if he'd be able to see her as she'd seen him in the restroom when he'd interrupted her memory. She assumed he could. Then again, she was not sure of the rules of this game. The snow was real enough, soft under her feet. The cold made her breath white, made her skin tingle.

Was this real?

If it was *his* memory, was she a ghost to him now?

Did she care?

She did not.

What she did care about was that TUBE had worked. If she wanted to, if she found a way, maybe she could see more of Papa's memories, maybe—

She stopped abruptly, cold with terror.

Did she want to see them? Did she *really* want to see them?

Olesya shook her head—(No. Yes. Maybe.)—and kept walking, her eyes on Papa's back, her feet kicking up white powder, her breath sharp.

He suddenly stopped, turned around, and swung up his flashlight. Olesya ducked and hopped closer to the train. Did he see her? She leaned on the car and pressed herself into it, closed her eyes.

Silence. Her erratic breathing. Then footsteps, receding.

He was walking away.

She followed him, feeling anger rise inside her. She wanted to see his face when it happened, wanted to watch his pain. She wanted to witness and to savor his destruction.

It was ironic, the way he died, Uncle Shurik had said. No. She disagreed. It was a punishment. He deserved it.

She sped up.

She wanted to be a part of it, was afraid to miss it. The distance closed between them. Papa walked in a steady gait, passing the pools of glow from the windows then melting back into the dark, the beam of his flashlight bobbing up and down.

When he got to the last car, he stopped. Olesya stopped too, out of breath, a few steps behind. Papa shone the light on the wheels caked with mud and slush that had frozen solid, and looked up and back. He shone the light along the tracks that disappeared around the bend, climbed up the slope, and set the flashlight on the ground. Legs planted wide apart, he began hacking at the ice.

Olesya watched his concentrated face lit up from the bottom, grotesque and yellow, his movements precise, and in that brief moment she loved him and wondered if he ever loved her too. If he worried about getting back to Moscow on time to see her first pointe recital. If he knew about the gripping hold of her childlike yearning—to be held, to be loved, to be cared for and acknowledged and reassured.

She took a step forward, another. "Papa."

He didn't hear her for the hacking noise.

"You have to get down from there."

He still didn't hear her.

"Papa. Get down."

She reached to him.

He adjusted his grip and resumed his hacking, snow spraying around him. She took another step—almost touched him—when the ground shook under her feet.

A second later a loud, low-throated horn tore through the silence. A freight train was barreling their way. The rails vibrated under its weight.

"Papa! Get down!"

She stepped on a patch of ice and slipped, crashed down to all fours, scrambled to haul herself up.

"Papa!"

He stopped hacking, alert, but instead of looking at her he faced the train.

All these years they wondered why he didn't get out of the way. Did he fail to hear it because his hat covered his ears? No—even a deaf person would hear it, through their feet. The ground shook under its weight. Then why? Was he caught in something that prevented him? Got stuck? No, not that either. He simply stood there, his arms lax, his posture erect.

A yellow eye rounded the bend, and with it came a great wall of sound. The train was going full speed, tons of it, loaded boxcars and cisterns. Olesya remembered reading about the accident in the newspapers. There were pictures— cars strewn against the white snow, looking like a toy train set kicked by an impatient child who didn't want to play with it anymore. They were never real to Olesya, those pictures, until now.

She screamed.

Her scream drowned in the screech of the locking brakes and the blaring horn.

Papa had seconds. He could drop and roll out of the way. He didn't. Instead, he tossed the rod and the flashlight and clasped his hands, his jaw set.

It happened too fast.

She saw the metal, flat face of the freight engine blaze its light at Papa's terrified face, his mouth open, his eyes bulging out of their sockets.

Then the train struck.

The shock wave threw Olesya in the air.

She expected to fall, to hit the ground and tumble, the snow stuffing her eyes and her mouth, her head ringing with the loud, twisting crack of the collision. She thought she'd hear the sounds of the groaning, breaking metal—all the creaking and the banging. She thought she'd smell the acrid smoke.

There was none of it. None of what she'd imagined for years.

Instead, she lay on something hard in hushed silence.

"Did you enjoy it?" Papa's voice asked.

Olesya opened her eyes. She was on the floor, in the aisle. He stood over her, TUBE in his hand.

She gasped. "TUBE!"

"It's time for our game," Papa said. "Get up. Hurry. We've got minutes left. I want every one of them to count."

He smiled, and Olesya did the only thing she could think of.

She got up and ran.

04:55

Olesya burst into the next car, the aisle full of children, luggage, sleepy passengers preparing to get off the train. She elbowed her way between them, dodging them, Papa's footfalls behind her.

"Why are you running?" he called.

She didn't dare slow down to see how close he was.

"Don't you want to play?"

A blow on her back made her stagger. He had struck her with TUBE.

"Come on now, just one last game. A few minutes and we'll be done. I promise."

She kept pushing through, kept shoving people out of her way, beginning to sweat, her boots and coat weighing her down.

"Why don't you answer me? Don't you want to talk to your Papa anymore? That's rude. I didn't raise you to be rude, Olesya. I raised you well-mannered."

Another blow, on the side of her head. She felt it cut her skin, felt the blood start to drip. She staggered out of the aisle into the vestibule and crashed through the gangway into the next car. And the next. And the next. Her pace was slowing.

"You can't outrun me," Papa said, just behind her. "You know that. So what's the point? The quicker we start, the faster it'll be over."

"No," she rasped. "Never. Never again."

She entered yet another vestibule and stopped short.

The dancers stood by the exit door, dressed and packed. There was Alla Borisovna, and Natasha, and Dima. They all looked at her. Olesya ignored Dima's calls, pushed through, into the next car, with more disembarking passengers, until she got to the door that was locked—the door to the engine.

There was nowhere else to run.

She spun around.

They were alone.

"Well," Papa said, "what did I tell you?"

He raised his arm and brought TUBE down on her forehead, right on the bruise.

The pain shot through her, and she howled.

As though in answer, the train whistled, started slowing.

They were arriving in Simferopol. Any minute it'd be over.

Any minute.

"Please. Please."

She had no strength to fight him. When he struck again, her legs buckled underneath her. She slid to the floor and covered her face, the wheels rattling in her ears, the brakes squealing and hissing, and then . . . silence.

She opened her eyes.

Cold air rushed in through the open doorway. Outside on the platform the loudspeakers announced their arrival.

"You drunk or what?"

Olesya looked up.

An attendant woman offered her a hand. "It's the last stop. You getting off?"

"Yes. Yes."

The woman helped her up. Olesya looked around.

Papa was gone, and with him TUBE.

It was too good to be true.

Olesya climbed down on the platform and stood there, lost, silent.

Dima who woke her from her trance. "Olesya?"

"Huh?"

He put a hand on her shoulder. "Are you okay? Your face."

She didn't answer.

"You're bleeding."

He pulled his sweater sleeve over his hand and dabbed at it. "What happened?"

Yuri walked up to them. "Oh, dorogusha. He went after you, didn't he?"

"Who?" Dima asked.

"The ghost, who," Yuri said.

Dima's face darkened.

"He won't stop now. You mark my words." Yuri crossed himself.

Olesya looked at the train. Was Papa still there? And Little Olesya? Where was she? Was the game over?

(It's not. It's *not*. It's just a little break. And she knew. Oh, she *knew*.)

"Better you know what you're up against. You don't want to mess with them ghosts." Yuri glanced at Dima as though it were somehow his fault.

"What did he do?" Dima asked.

"It's me who did it, not him," Olesya said slowly. Speaking was difficult. "I think . . . I think I saw his memory. Papa's memory. How he killed himself—I mean, how he let the freight train kill him. You were right, Yuri."

Yuri nodded.

They stood in silence, the three of them.

Olesya shivered. She wrapped her arms around herself and looked away, at the standing train and along the platform that was now nearly empty. The last of the passengers hauled their luggage toward the station building and beyond, to the parking lot with the buses, trolleybuses and taxis. The sounds of luggage carts, carrier's calls and loudspeaker announcements receded into the gray winter morning. She looked at the train windows, frosted with ice like the eyes of a blind man looking for her and not seeing her, looking, looking.

Dima sniffled. His nose was red and dripping. He wiped it on his sleeve.

"Why don't you kids go inside where it's warm?" Yuri said.

Olesya shrugged.

"Where are your things?"

She looked to the end of the train. "In the haunted car."

"I'll get them," Dima said quickly.

"You don't want to go in there, son," Yuri said. "I'll get them for you, dorogusha. Don't you worry."

"I don't mind, really. I want to help." Dima looked at Olesya.

She was silent.

"Are you . . . are you leaving right away, or . . . ?"

"I'm staying," she said. "For a while. In Baba Zina's house. That's where—" She stopped. Could she stomach going there? Could she stomach remembering? "Those memories, in the compartments, they're only memories. The real thing—"

Dima put a hand on her arm. "I get it. You don't need to say it."

"Thank you."

"Is that in Alupka?"

"Yeah."

"How will you get there?"

"I'll give you a ride," Yuri offered.

Olesya looked at him. "You will?"

"Sure."

"But that's a couple hours at least."

"I live there, dorogusha." He grinned. "In Alupka. Have lived there all my life."

"Oh. Okay. Thank you."

"Don't thank me yet. Thank me when we get there. I've got to clean up my car first. Collect dirty laundry. Report to the boss. Would you be willing to wait?"

"Sure." It was easier to agree.

Yuri beamed. "It'd be a treat for my Lidochka. She'd be beside herself to meet you. A real Bolshoi ballerina."

Olesya nodded and looked at Dima. "Good luck with *Swan Lake*."

"You're not coming to see it?"

"No, I don't think so. I don't think I can."

"But—"

"I need to be alone."

"All right." He hung his head. "I understand."

"No, really. Thank you . . . thank you for everything."

He looked at her and his eyes turned wet. He blinked, looked away, picked up his bags, and walked off without a word.

Olesya watched him go. Just as he entered the station building, she felt as though she were being watched herself. Papa was there. Behind one of the frosted windows, his eyes on her. She knew. She knew it in her gut. Knew it by the way her skin crawled. Was he going to get off the train? Could he? Would he? Would he chase her across the station like he'd chased her along the train?

The game wasn't over yet. They hadn't played TUBE. And it wasn't like Papa to leave things unfinished.

Olesya froze, scared. Of him, of Baba Zina's house. Of that room. That bed. But she was also oddly calm. She didn't need TUBE anymore, didn't need to open compartments. And she knew where to find Little Olesya. And Papa. She knew where they'd go. Or rather, where he'd force her to go.

"Yuri? How soon do you think you'll be done?"

"A couple hours. Why?"

"Just wondering."

"Wait for me in the restaurant. The food isn't all that bad, and the tea is good and strong."

Olesya barely heard him. How much time did she have?

"Well, see you later then." He ambled off.

Olesya walked to the restaurant in a daze.

She suddenly knew Papa's next move. And it scared her. It scared her so much she had to force her legs up the steps, force her hand out of the pocket and onto the door handle.

The station. That same station. The bench. The rooster lollipop.

Olesya walked inside.

PICKING UP SPEED

SIMFEROPOL STATION RESTAURANT

06:49

Someone tapped Olesya's shoulder.

She jerked up her head, blinking, disoriented.

But it was only Dima. She exhaled in relief, trying to quiet her heart.

She was in the station restaurant, sitting at a table, her hand clutching a fork, in front of her a clean plate that she vaguely remembered the waitress slopping with buckwheat kasha. She must've eaten it all and fallen asleep from the warmth.

She pushed the plate away.

"Hey," Dima said.

"Hey. You're still here?"

"Yeah. Sorry to wake you."

"It's okay. Not a good idea to sleep here anyway. What time is it?"

She still had the feeling of being watched and looked around. Half the tables were empty, another half occupied by harried passengers eating breakfast. No one she knew.

"Almost seven."

"Wow. I must've fallen asleep right after I ate."

"Yeah, you look pretty tired. May I join you?"

"Sure."

He set in front of her a steaming cup of tea and a red-and-gold package of Yubileynoye, pulled out a chair and sat down. "It's for you."

"Oh. Thank you."

She picked up the package, sniffed it, and opened it. Inside were two stacks of golden, buttery cookies. She took one out, bit into it, and closed her eyes. Then she took another one, dipped it into the tea, watched it soften. It was so easy to distract her with food. She shifted uncomfortably, eyeing a man as he slurped his coffee.

"Where did you get it?"

"What?"

"The cookies."

"Yuri gave them to me."

"Of course," she said without looking. She watched a woman stick a spoon into her kasha. "He knows I love them." A little girl swiped jam off the cake and popped her finger into her mouth. Her mother scolded her and the girl cried.

"I wanted to check on you," Dima said apologetically. "I hope you don't mind—"

A cold breeze brushed Olesya's back. She spun around, alert, heart pounding. Her eyes scanned the travelers. They were eating, carrying trays to their tables. She searched their faces, turned around and shook her head. She was being paranoid. It was just a cold draft, nothing more.

"You okay?"

"What?"

Dima was looking at her. "Are you okay? You don't look so well."

"I'm fine, thanks." She smoothed back her hair. "Why are you still here?"

"Our minibuses are late." He shrugged. "My guess is, the drivers are hungover from Sunday drinking. Or maybe they forgot about us. I don't know. We're in the lobby." He motioned toward the door. "Alla Borisovna has half the station workers running around trying to find us a ride. You know how she is—doesn't want to hear about taking the bus."

"Yeah, I know."

Olesya smiled, and Dima smiled back. She wanted to reach across the table, to touch his hair, to feel his lips. She wanted to kiss him.

He watched her, waiting. Did he feel the same?

"I'm sorry," she said.

"For what?"

"For . . . you know. For pushing you away." She sighed. "I'm really good at that, pushing people away. I know you wanted to help, I just . . . I don't know how to ask for help. I'm so used to doing it all on my own. Bottling it up."

"Burying it."

She nodded. "Burying it."

"I get it," he said. "No need to apologize. I'm the same way." He picked up a cookie, crumbled it, pushed it away. "I'm not trying to get back together or anything. In case you're wondering. I know you said you needed to do this alone, but—it's just that—I had time to kill, and then I saw Yuri and—"

"It's okay," she said. "I understand. Look." She picked up his hand. "You're a really bad liar, you know that?"

Dima glanced down.

"I hate it when you lie. I really do. Why don't you just tell me what's going on?"

He took his hand away. "Like I haven't tried."

"You watched me, didn't you?"

His face colored.

"You watched me eat and fall asleep, then you picked the right moment to wake me up. And you brought me cookies. Of course you did. You know my weakness. You know I can't resist sweets—especially now, since I quit ballet and can eat whatever the hell I want."

Dima squeezed his hand into a fist. "Here we go. You always turn it around on me."

"Turn what around?"

"How is this about me all of a sudden?"

"What are you talking about?"

"What do you want me to say, Olesya?"

"I don't want anything. I don't—" She stopped, confused. "I hate this, okay? I don't know how to talk to you."

"Then don't talk to me."

"I'm not! You're the one who found me. I told you I was done. It's done, Dima. Over."

"All right. I'll go." He stood up.

"Wait!"

He sat down.

She was fuming. "Can I ask you something?"

"What?"

"Can you please be honest with me?"

"I haven't been honest?'

"Please. You know what I mean. Promise me you'll tell me what's going on with you. Always."

"Okay. I promise."

"No, not like that. Look me in the eyes."

He did.

"Now say it."

"I promise."

They sat in silence, looking at each other, until Olesya felt like crying. She picked up her tea and took a sip. It was warm and strong.

"You're right," Dima said. "I lied. I'm sorry. I came here to give you this."

He pulled out a stack of rubles and set them next to Olesya.

She stared at the money—five pink ten-ruble banknotes. Half of Dima's salary.

"What's this for?"

"Just in case."

"In case of what?"

"If you need a taxi. It's a long ride to Alupka."

"But Yuri is giving me a ride."

"Yeah, about Yuri." Dima took out his jackknife and twirled it in his hand. "You just met him. He could be . . . I don't know, he could be anybody. Who knows what he's got on his mind? Maybe he's—"

"Stop. Stop right there." Olesya sat up straight. "I don't need your protection, Dima. I never asked for it. And, frankly, I'm tired of being seen as a weakling that needs to be protected. That's what my family did to me. I was this frail little girl who had to be fed and educated and raised properly so I'd obey them without question. They turned me into this quiet, well-mannered doll that did what she was told and felt nothing. Because she was trained not to. They thought disciplining was loving. That's why Papa—" She caught herself.

Dima waited.

"That's why he . . ." She couldn't bring herself to say it. "I can't . . ."

"You don't have to."

"No, no. I want to."

"Why?"

"Because I need to say it. To believe it. Don't you get that?"

Dima frowned.

Olesya exhaled in exasperation. "Never mind."

"No, what?"

"Never mind!"

"Please. I'm sorry, okay?"

She looked down. "My body," she said quietly. "You see, it's one hundred percent sure, but my mind . . . I've convinced myself for so long that I imagined it all, it just refuses to accept it. It's like . . . I feel like I'm going crazy. Like with Papa—he's dead, Dima. *Dead.* How can he possibly be here? But he's here. I saw him. I fought him. He choked me with TUBE."

Dima clenched his jaw. "Bastard."

"I know. But that's not the worst of it. You know the worst part?"

"What?"

"I called him. I was the one who called him back. It's my fault."

"It's not your fault. Nothing is your fault."

"Yes, it is. I should've told someone."

"Maybe you did and you don't remember."

"Dima—"

"Stop."

"—I did it. I—"

"No." He grabbed her hand. "You didn't do anything. You were a kid. A little girl."

"Then why? Why did he do it?" Her voice broke.

"Because some people do that. Some people exist to hurt other people. It brings them pleasure. They're not well, okay? Not all there." He knocked on his head.

"But he was normal."

"He *appeared* normal. They usually do. It's like a mask, like a . . . I don't know. To fit in. Have a job, a family. Look normal. Like what everyone expects of you. So you don't stick out."

"How do you know all this?"

It took him some time to answer. "My father. He's a high-functioning alcoholic. Nobody ever questioned my mother's suicide, but I know she killed herself because of him. So it was *him* who killed her. He belongs in jail."

"You hate him."

Dima nodded, his face white.

"Did you ever want to kill him?"

"Yes." Dima flicked open his jackknife. "Many times."

"I wished Papa dead," Olesya said. "And he died. I felt so guilty. I always thought it was my fault. Now I know it wasn't. He killed himself. He showed me. I mean, he didn't want me to see it. I saw it by accident. With TUBE." She leaned over the table and whispered, "He's got TUBE now, Dima. I'm afraid he's looking for me. I'm afraid he got off the train. And I know where he's headed."

"The house in Alupka? Is that why you're going there?"

She nodded.

"Don't."

"But I need to. Don't you understand?"

"Maybe."

She threw up her hands. "Why did you need to see your mother?"

"That's different."

"How is that different?"

"Olesya, please."

"See? This is why I didn't want to talk to you."

Dima's face drained of blood. "Why?"

"I don't need your help, okay? You're forcing it on me. I don't want it."

"I'm not *forcing* anything." His voice was shaking with anger. "I'm trying to save you."

"*Save* me?"

"I failed to save my mother. I'm not failing you." He stood up. "She never asked for help, and I could've helped her. I could've. If I did, she'd be alive. I failed her, Olesya. I failed because I was too scared." His eyes filled with tears. "I was just a kid, just a little boy. And then it was too late! I promised myself I'd never let that happen again. I'd never lose someone I love because they tell me to get lost." He stopped abruptly.

Olesya stared at him. "You love me?"

He averted his eyes. "I followed you."

"You *what*?"

"Every night, after ballet class, right to your house. To make sure you got home safe."

"Oh God." She recoiled from him.

He walked around the table, closer to her.

"That night we watched the snowflakes, remember?"

"Something like that," she said cautiously.

"I'd been with Bolshoi for about a month. I wanted to talk to you, was waiting for an opportune moment."

"But . . . I thought you were interested in Natasha."

"Never. She was interested in me, and I didn't know how to say no. I wanted to talk to you, but you never noticed me. You'd look right through me. Then, that night, we were the last ones to leave. I caught up to you at the door. You were putting on your mittens. It was snowing. You said the snowflakes reminded you of tiny ballerinas. It was late, after midnight, and it was so quiet. The street was white with snow. No cars, no people. That's when I knew I loved you, in that moment. It was stupid to follow you, I know. I felt like a damn dog, trailing after you, but I couldn't stop myself. So, ever since that night, I always walked you home and stood under your window."

"You stood under my window?"

"Every night. Until the light went out. Then I went home."

Olesya gaped at him. "But the Metro . . . it'd be closed by then."

Dima shrugged. "I'd catch a taxi. A couple times I chanced hitching a ride with a late driver, told him I was poor and in love."

She touched his arm. "I didn't know."

He took her hand in his. "It's all right. I—" He broke off, looking over her shoulder.

"What?"

"I think there's someone . . . never mind."

"No, what?"

"Some guy was staring at you. Pretty intensely."

The hairs rose on Olesya's neck. "What did he look like?"

"I don't know. Shortish. Large head. His ears were funny, sticking out."

Olesya's throat went dry. The noise of the restaurant receded into the background. "He got off then. Off the train."

"Who did?"

"Papa."

SIMFEROPOL RAILWAY STATION

07:34

"I'm going after him."

"Wait. Olesya!"

She bolted to the door, pushing people out of the way.

Papa was in the restroom. She was sure of it. There, or on his way there with Little Olesya in tow. It gave him pleasure to hurt her. Olesya understood why now. He'd never dared to face his pain, whatever it was. She was sure there was something—*something*—that made him a spineless, cowardly, violent man. Something that was the reason for his constant fights with Baba Zina and with Mama. Something that turned him on Olesya. He didn't have to fight her—she was a little girl, and she did as she was told.

How convenient.

Olesya's blood boiled.

Come on, run faster.

She darted into the lobby, past the wooden benches, where she nearly tripped over the dancers sprawled on the floor. Heads turned. Voices called her. She didn't slow down, didn't look. She passed the ticket booths, and suddenly there it was, the entrance archway, on its left the women's restroom, on its right the men's.

She steadied her breath and pushed through the door on the right.

The restroom was much smaller and shabbier than she remembered, but it stank all the same. A balding man in a tracksuit was pissing into a urinal. He turned, blinked and yelled, "Hey! The fuck is wrong with you?"

Olesya ignored him, marched straight to the last stall, and pushed the door open.

It was as she feared.

She was too late, but Papa had left her a sign. There it was, on the dirty floor tiles. Two lines of tracks drawn with red marker.

Olesya's vision went dark. She leaned on the wall, dizzy.

"Hey!" the man shouted behind her. "Hey, you bitch—"

She reeled around and shoved him in the chest. "Out of my way, old goat."

He staggered back, face red. He yelled insults after her, but she was already out the door, running. She had no time to waste. She had to find Yuri, had to convince him to drive her straight to Baba Zina's house. Because Papa was there.

Papa was there, and he was hurting Little Olesya.

He was waiting for her.

He knew she'd come.

What he didn't know was that she understood something else now. She'd go through with it, yes—his last little game—but then she'd find out the truth.

She'd expose his secret.

SIMFEROPOL STATION PLAZA

08:02

The winter sun spilled cold light over the station plaza. A couple of empty trolleybuses stood parked by the curb. The few cars in the parking lot were white with snow. Olesya scanned the plaza for Yuri.

A taxi approached. The driver rolled down the passenger window. "Hey, beautiful! Going somewhere?" His face soured. "You! You bitch. You—"

"Go fuck yourself."

The man choked on the insult.

Olesya sprinted to the parking lot. Her heart hammered. She'd never told a man off, never swore at a man—not once in her life. It felt good, and she felt no fear. It gave her immense satisfaction. The taxi crawled after her. The man shouted out the window, blared the horn. She pretended he wasn't there until he finally gave up.

She spotted Yuri.

"Olesya!" He waved from an old Zhiguli. He was sitting in the driver's seat, revving the engine. Coils of exhaust rose from the tailpipe. The engine coughed, sputtered and died. He cursed.

"Can I help you somehow?"

Yuri shook his head. "No, no need for that, dorogusha. Don't you worry, she'll make up her mind. Just being pesky is all. Mad I left her alone in the cold for so long without a cover."

"She?"

"My old lady here. Starushka." He patted the wheel. "You see, I promised her a cover last month, but they're late with my salary, so what can I do?" He looked at Olesya and at her stomach and grimaced. "Christ Almighty."

"What?"

"Your hole."

"What about it?" She looked down at herself.

"It got bigger. All the way to your heart."

Olesya shifted uneasily. "Did you get my luggage?"

"Sure did."

"Can I get inside?"

Yuri leaned over and opened the passenger door. She climbed in.

"Why didn't you wait for me in the restaurant?"

"Never mind. Can we go?"

Yuri peered at her. "Give me a minute."

He got out and walked around the car, checked the wheels, got back inside, and turned the key in the ignition. The engine choked on itself.

"Come on, Starushka." He tapped the wheel. "Don't you die on me."

The engine puttered, came to life.

"That's more like it."

Olesya expelled the air from her lungs and closed her eyes.

Yuri shifted gears. The car jerked and died.

Olesya's eyes flew open.

"Devil take you!" Yuri smacked the wheel.

"Should we ask one of the drivers to push us?"

"Not on my life." Yuri glared at her. "I'm not letting those punks put their filthy hands on my old girl. No way. She'll start on her own. Just have to give her time is all."

"I can't, Yuri," Olesya said. "I need to go *now*."

"What's with the hurry?"

"Papa, he . . . he got off the train."

"You're sure about that?"

"I'm sure."

Yuri's face went gray. He crossed himself.

"He's on his way to our old house," Olesya said. "I have to get there to, to—" She faltered. "To remember."

Yuri exhaled sharply. "I'm not leaving you."

"What do you mean?"

He smacked the wheel so hard Olesya jumped. "He'll kill you, that's what. Not on my watch. I'm not letting you in that house alone."

Olesya folded her hands in her lap. "Look. I really appreciate you trying to protect me," she said quietly, "but I'm kind of done with it, to be honest. I'm done with men doing things for me, doing things *to* me, doing things they decided to do . . . you know, without asking me. I want to do things myself. This is my fight, not yours. I have to face him alone. You said so yourself, remember?"

Yuri wasn't swayed. "I'm not letting you in that house alone, and that's that," he said stubbornly.

Olesya curled her hands into fists.

He turned to her. "Tell you what. Why don't we go to my house first? Lidochka would be beside herself to meet you. We'll have lunch, you'll rest, maybe catch a nap. Then you can go there."

Olesya looked at him. "You'll drive me to Alupka, but you won't let me inside my grandmother's house. Not unless you come with me. Did I get that right?"

"Listen—"

Olesya opened the door. "Is my luggage in the trunk?"

"Why, yes—"

She got out of the car.

A dirty minibus pulled up to the curb. Olesya watched the dancers crowd next to it and climb aboard. She could go with them to the city, ask Dima for that money he offered, take a taxi—

The engine revved, evened to a steady rumble.

Yuri emerged from the car, his expression grim. "Get in."

"No, thanks."

"Get in, I said. Go ahead and do it your way. I only ask for one thing."

"What's that?"

"I'm going to wait for you. Outside." He sighed. "Outside that house of yours."

Olesya clenched her teeth. She'd have to wiggle out of it later somehow.

"Okay. Thank you."

"Don't you thank me yet. Let's get there first."

Olesya got in.

SIMFEROPOL–ALUPKA
09:19

Yuri hunched over the wheel, eyes on the road, mouth pressed into a line.

They rode in silence. Every once in a while he stopped the car, wiped the fogged-up windshield and scraped clean the wipers. Then off they went again on the treacherous road that was wet one minute, another turned to snow, yet another turned to black ice. Olesya counted at least six cars off the road, smashed into one another, the passengers huddling around, waiting for help. Every time Yuri slowed to pass them, her stomach clenched. She looked away at the candlelike cypresses, at the gas stations, houses, and, beyond them, at the mountains and the Black Sea.

The heating vent blew hot air on her knees. It was warm in the car. At one point Olesya must've dozed off. The car jerked. She sat up with a start. They turned off the roadway and crawled down a narrow lane. Olesya recognized the streets, the low stone walls, the squat, whitewashed houses.

Alupka.

The car bumped over potholes. The sea came closer and got louder, foaming.

"Look at it," Yuri said. "Laps at the coast like it wants to swallow it. Beautiful."

"I've never seen it in the winter," Olesya said.

"Not once?"

"No. We only came here in the summer. The last time I was here was ten years ago."

"We can go to the beach. Take a little stroll."

She looked at him.

He grinned. "Later. If you want. My Lidochka knows every stone here. Been scouring these streets since she learned how to walk. I could barely keep up with her. Could never sit still, that girl. Still can't."

"I wasn't allowed to walk to the sea by myself," Olesya said.

Yuri nodded. "That's a pity."

They stopped at an intersection.

"Well? Which way?"

"Seaside Street. Number eight. It's up this way." She pointed. "And then to the left."

"You got it." Yuri shifted the gears.

They turned away from the sea and crawled up a narrow cobbled street white with snow. The cypresses on either side stood tall and white as if they had been dipped in wax. The car swayed and bumped over the cobbles. It was quiet, still, empty. The summer houses were closed off for the winter, their windows blinded with shutters, their doors locked. The gardens in front of them stood lifeless and bare.

Olesya took hold of the door handle.

"Don't even think about it," Yuri said without looking.

"Think about what?"

"You know what. Not going to work."

"I don't understand—"

"You know better than this."

She sighed. "I hate it that you can read my mind so easily."

"Don't need to." Yuri chuckled. "I can read it on your face."

"But you can't even *see* my face."

"I can see enough. Sitting there, scheming how to get rid of me."

Olesya felt her face grow hot. "Do you love your daughter?"

"Of course I do. What kind of question is that?"

"Well . . . would you do what she asked you to do? For her. Even if you disagreed. Even if you thought—"

"Not going to work, dorogusha."

They crested a hill. The tires skidded in the snow. The car came to a sliding stop by a stone wall.

Yuri pulled up the handbrake, turned off the ignition, and put his hands in his lap.

"Here's the deal. You're not my daughter."

Olesya's stomach shrank.

He faced her. "You're one of my passengers, and you could be lying through your teeth for all I know. Couldn't you? Only I know you're not. Because holes don't lie, and yours"—he nodded at it—"has nearly consumed you. I never told you how my wife died, did I? My Raisa. Well, I'll tell you now. Cancer took her. Ate her up in two months flat. There was nothing I could do to stop it. It drove me out of my mind, sitting there by her bed watching her fade away. But with you it's different. This, with you . . . I *can* do something, you hear?"

"No, you can't. You're only wasting your time." Olesya jerked at the door handle; it was locked. She pulled up the door lock and elbowed the door open. It hit the stone wall. "Let me out. I need to get out, Yuri. I'll be late."

"No such thing as being late when you meet the dead."

She slapped her knees. "Why are you doing this? Why?"

"Don't you get mad at me now," he said quietly. "I'm as scared as you are." He crossed himself. "Never been this scared in my life, you hear? That's the God's honest truth. But at least I'm in sound health. You . . . look at you. You've hardly eaten anything, hardly slept. You're exhausted. What's going to be left of you when he's done with you, huh? What's your plan?"

Olesya was silent.

"Freeze to death in that house? Wait for someone to find you? And who'd that be? Some old bag passing by in the spring, thinking she smelled something funny?"

Olesya covered her face with her hands. Yuri saw right through her.

"You think I plan to kill myself," she said.

"I don't think. I know."

She looked out the window, eyes burning.

They had parked on a street she remembered well. It led directly down to the sea. Just ahead was their turn, where the trash bins usually stood, always overflowing, always buzzing with flies, now empty and frozen.

Then she saw the footprints.

There were two sets, printed clearly in the virgin snow.

An adult's and a child's.

"They're here," she whispered.

Yuri nodded. "Now you notice."

"Wait. You can see them? The footprints?"

"Why'd you think I stopped?"

Olesya's heart pounded. She didn't have to face Papa alone. She didn't have to face him at all. She could accept Yuri's offer, go to his house, meet his daughter Lidochka, have lunch, nap. Stay with them. Then return to Moscow. She didn't have to visit Baba Zina's house. She could pretend none of this ever happened. She could *forget*. She was so good at forgetting—

It started snowing. The flakes twirled in the air like so many ballerinas, and for a moment Olesya forgot where she was. She felt happy. It was the happiness of a child who hasn't known pain. She was that child before . . . before Papa hurt her. Before she locked up Little Olesya inside herself. Before she told her to shut up.

Before she'd forgotten.

"I owe it to her," Olesya said.

"Say what?"

"I owe it—to that little girl inside me. Remember you said she's dead? You said I'm lugging a dead child around."

"Sure, I remember."

"Well, she's not dead. I can feel her heart beating. All my life I—" Olesya's voice caught, and she paused. Took a deep breath. "All my life I didn't trust her. Thought she told me lies. I thought . . . I thought if I locked her up somewhere, locked her up on that train, in that car, maybe—maybe she'd never come back. Maybe she'd leave me alone. But she didn't. She kept nagging at me, kept reminding me, and I'm glad. I'm glad she didn't leave me alone. I'm glad she found me." Hot tears welled up and spilled down Olesya's cheeks.

Yuri took her hand.

"You were right." She turned to him, her vision blurry. "I don't care much about my life. It's so easy for me to throw it away. But not hers. I can't do that to her. I can't. She's just a kid. Just a little—" She had to stop and wipe her face.

Yuri waited.

"She had to endure it alone, you know?"

"I know, dorogusha, I know." He patted her hand.

"There was no one to help her. No one. And she survived. Somehow she survived. Then she protected me— all these years she protected me from . . . from this pain, so I could live. So I could live my life. So I could *dance*." She took a shuddering breath. Tears dripped from her chin to her coat. She dropped her face into her hands and let go.

Yuri was quiet.

After some time Olesya spoke. "It's my turn now. To hurt."

"God help you."

He turned the key in the ignition and gave it gas. The engine revved. The wheels spun in the snow, caught on. The car moved forward.

Olesya's heart squeezed.

They turned into an alley. Yuri eased on the brakes. "Seaside Street, number eight."

She looked out the window.

The same two-story whitewashed house, only much smaller, darker, and shabbier than she remembered. It used to look so festive in the summer, with its red roof, red curtains in the windows, red door—Baba Zina loved red accents—but now the paint was cracked and peeling, brown with age. The bare apple trees in the yard, the path with two sets of footprints leading to the porch, the metal plate to the left of the door, the number eight—

"Oh dear God," Olesya said.

"Something wrong?"

"No. Nothing."

Her ears started ringing. She closed her eyes.

Compartment No. 8.

"Looks empty. Anyone live here?"

"My uncle. Uncle Shurik. He locks it up for the winter. Goes off on his expeditions. He's a geologist."

"Does he have a wife?"

"No. No wife. No kids."

"Then how do you aim to get in?"

"I know where he leaves the key."

TUBE

Olesya wasn't surprised when she saw Little Olesya crack the door open, nor when she peeked out and beckoned Olesya inside.

Someone yanked her back inside and shut the door.

Olesya got out.

ALUPKA, SEASIDE ST., NO. 8
09:31

By the time she opened the front gate and got to the porch, a whole minute had passed.

She grabbed the doorknob. It was locked.

She hooked her nails under the bottom lip of the number plate and tugged. It was frozen to the wood. She wiggled the rusty nail that held it to the wall and tried again. The plate scraped aside. Underneath, in a little hole, she felt for the key. There! She slid it out, her hand shaking. On the third try, she managed to insert it into the keyhole, but it was stuck. She jiggled it gently until it felt just right and then turned it.

The lock clicked.

She wrenched the door open.

A musty smell hit her nose. She sneezed and lurched inside, looking around wildly.

The house was dead quiet.

She was too late.

It was over.

09:49

Olesya ran through the house.

They were here somewhere, she knew it. It wasn't like Papa to just quit. He was waiting for her to find them—but *where?*

Baba Zina's room was empty. It had the look of a room that hadn't been lived in for years. Olesya glanced at the bed and the sewing desk and rushed out, slamming the door behind her. Ran into the kitchen. It was small and cramped but clean, the evidence of Uncle Shurik living a bachelor's life in one cup and one plate stacked by the sink.

Back to the hallway.

The bathroom.

Nothing.

She raced up the steps to the second floor, her heart pounding, stepped into the anteroom right off the staircase, and stopped.

Yawning black on either side of the room were the openings to the attic closets—long, dusty crawlspaces between the floor and the roof, stuffed with broken furniture and old junk. When she was small she liked hiding there, just sitting in the darkness and the silence and thinking. This was where she fled when she hurt.

Olesya peered inside one, another. Clean and empty. Uncle Shurik must've thrown everything out.

She stood quietly, listening.

"Little Olesya, where are you? Come on, give me a sign."

She took hold of the knob to Uncle Shurik's room—the room where the two brothers grew up and where later her family stayed when they visited Baba Zina. Uncle Shurik would sleep in the anteroom on the cot, and they slept on two beds pushed to opposite walls—Papa and Mama on the bigger one, Olesya on the smaller.

Her heart hammered in her chest. She pushed the door open.

No one here.

The room looked spartan but lived-in. The bigger bed was gone, but the smaller one stood where she remembered it, a wardrobe next to it, a desk and a chair by the window. She parted the curtains and looked out at the snowy street, at Yuri's car parked by the fence.

Something was wrong.

Olesya had hoped for a rush of memories, but there was nothing. Nothing at all.

She tried recalling all the times she stood by this window in the summer, watching cars rattle by, dogs run and bark, vacationers strut to the sea with their children.

Nothing.

She held her head, frustrated, then scanned the street below. Not a person in sight.

Olesya sat on the bed.

Was this the end? Did she make a mistake? What now? There was nowhere else to go. Nothing else to see, to trigger her memory. TUBE was gone. Papa and Little Olesya weren't here. And she was off the train. That only left going back to Moscow.

She sat up straight.

Back. She could go back, like Dima. Back to Baba Zina's room. Retrace the steps of that morning before the party. Her chest squeezed. The porcelain ballerinas. Were they still in the china cabinet? The broken one. Did Baba Zina glue it back together? Throw it out? Was the china cabinet even there, or did Uncle Shurik throw it out too?

She couldn't remember seeing it. Did she?

Olesya got to her feet, walked to the door, and froze.

The sound came from below—faint scratching.

It was the same scratching she'd heard from the attendant's compartment. Olesya held her breath, listening. All was quiet. Did she imagine it? She took a step down the stairs. The scratching came back.

Then she knew what it was. How could she forget?

On the bare parquet floor below, someone was assembling the train track sections.

10:18

Olesya put her hand on the wall, balanced on one leg, slipped off her boots one by one, and crept down the stairs in her socks, stepping on the planks that didn't creak.

The door to Baba Zina's room stood ajar.

She pushed it open.

INTO THE TUNNEL

ALUPKA, SEASIDE ST., NO. 8
18 August 1973
10:30

The clock showed 10:30 in the morning exactly.

Olesya smiled. She'd just learned how to tell the time, and she was proud of it.

Yesterday Mama went to see a friend. She said she'd be back by three but was gone all day. No one would tell Olesya what time it was.

Baba Zina shooed her out of the kitchen.

Papa snapped at her.

Then Uncle Shurik came home and explained that the short clock arms pointed at the hours and the long ones at the minutes. When they joined, it was the whole hour. So if they joined by number three, it was three o'clock. In the middle of his explanation, Uncle Shurik slumped and dozed off, right there on the floor, but Olesya figured out the rest by herself.

She knew every hour had sixty minutes, and every half hour thirty. She'd heard it on the radio in a children's program. That meant that if it was a whole hour when the clock arms joined, it must've been a half hour when they separated and cut the clock face in half, like cutting a cake. A raspberry sponge cake. Her favorite.

Olesya felt proud. She'd figured this out on her own, without anyone's help.

She already knew how to read and how to count, and now she could tell the time!

Next year, when she turned six and started school, she'd be smarter than the other girls. Papa said all girls were stupid. He didn't want her to grow up stupid; he wanted her to grow up educated. And here she was, educating herself. Papa would approve.

Olesya yawned deliciously and rubbed her eyes. She'd slept in this morning, and she was wearing only her panties. Papa, Mama, and Baba Zina left early to get groceries for the party—she had heard the gate slam and spied them walk away from the window—and Uncle Shurik was snoring on the cot in the anteroom. She was alone. The whole house belonged to her.

She could do anything she wanted.

I know, I know! she thought. *I'll get ready to play TUBE with Papa!*

Yesterday he promised he'd play with her tomorrow if only she'd stop pestering him. And today *was* tomorrow, and she *did* stop pestering him. That meant they could play when he got back.

Olesya got to work.

First she examined the floor. Baba Zina had washed and polished it the night before. It shone like a mirror. Papa and Uncle Shurik had moved the heavy sewing desk and the armchairs against the wall, then brought in the dinner table and the chairs to set up later, so the middle of the room was empty.

"Perfect," Olesya whispered.

She had played TUBE with Papa as often as she could since winter—since he gave it to her on her fifth birthday. She was in awe of it. She'd never seen a toy train like that in her life—not in stores, not in daycare, not on television. She was convinced it was real, only miniature. She imagined herself a ballerina, like one of Baba Zina's figurines, riding it across the fields and the woods and the mountains, racing along the bridges over the rivers, passing through dark tunnels.

She crept upstairs, tiptoed past snoring Uncle Shurik, slipped the box from under her bed, then stole back, careful not to step on the creaking floorboards. She set the box on the floor, swung back the lid, and took out all the parts: the tracks, the cables, the speed dial, the ten cars, and, finally, the shiny red engine stamped with black letters.

TUBE
TRANS-URBAN BLITZ EXPRESS

She weighed it in her hand. It was pleasantly heavy. She carefully set it on the floor. Next she pulled the rubber bands off the tracks and loosely arranged them in figure eight. Her hair fell over her face, and she impatiently tucked it behind her ears. Her hands moved swiftly—grabbing, fitting, snapping. Within minutes the track was assembled. She placed TUBE at the intersection, attached the cars to it, connected the cables, and turned up the speed dial.

TUBE's headlamp lit up. It whistled, its wheels starting to spin. It took off, pulling the cars behind it.

Olesya crossed her legs, propped her chin on her hands, and watched it go round and round and round. Soon it wasn't a toy anymore—it was real.

She was standing by the tracks, the wind whipping her hair. The magnificent train rumbled by in all its shiny splendor. The car windows opened, and the passengers hung out of them and waved to Olesya, shouting something. They were shouting in English! She squinted against the wind to see them better, their smiling faces, their smoothed-back hair, their fancy clothes. They were dancers! They were on tour, and they were dressed in costumes! Olesya held her breath, waited for the train to return. The next time it went by, she saw that the women wore white leotards and sparkling tutus, and the men wore tights and velvet jackets with puffy sleeves. Music trailed from the windows. Tchaikovsky's *Swan Lake*, her favorite ballet. She was so enthralled she lost caution and stepped closer. The wind snatched her up and whirled her high in the air. Many hands reached out, caught her and pulled her inside the car. One of the dancers, tall and handsome—Prince Siegfried!—reached behind her and slammed the door shut.

Olesya jumped.

She was back in Baba Zina's room.

In the door stood Papa. He was breathing hard as though he had been running. His eyes bulged out of their sockets, and right away Olesya knew he was mad.

She turned down the speed dial. TUBE stopped.

In the sudden silence the clock was ticking.

"What's this?" Papa said.

Olesya froze, frantically thinking what she could've done wrong. But she could think of nothing.

"It's TUBE," she said. "Yesterday you promised—"

"Why are you naked?"

She looked down at herself. "I'm not naked. I got my panties on."

"Take them off."

"What?"

"Do as I say."

"But, Papa—"

258

"Don't you get smart with me." He unbuckled his belt and slid it out of his trousers.

She stared at it. He was going to belt her on her naked butt, just like Baba Zina did last week when she caught her peeing in the yard. *That* Olesya understood. *That* was punishment.

But this was unfair. She did nothing wrong. Papa promised they'd play, and she got everything ready. She didn't break anything, didn't get anything dirty. In her excitement, she forgot to get dressed, but she didn't understand how that was wrong. When they went to the beach she wore only her panties, as did all the other children—some were even naked—but Papa never said anything about it. He liked rubbing her back and her belly and tickling her, making her roll on the towel until she choked with laughter and begged him to stop.

Olesya stood and crossed her arms.

"Don't *you* get smart with *me*," she said, echoing his words as she heard Baba Zina do when they were fighting. After that Papa always fell quiet. She hoped it would work.

It did. Papa halted midstep. "What did you say?"

He was pretending he hadn't heard her. Olesya hated it when he did that because right after it he would say something mean.

"You *promised*. You said we'd play tomorrow, and today *is* tomorrow. And I didn't pester you. And—" She searched her mind for other things Baba Zina yelled at him. It came to her in a flash of inspiration. "You better do it, Papa. You better do it, or I'll box your ears!"

Papa's face turned white.

Immediately Olesya knew she'd gone too far. She backed off, but his hand was already closing on her arm. He picked her up and threw her on Baba Zina's bed. She was suddenly frightened. She turned around to ask what she did wrong and swallowed her words.

Papa looked scary. There was a hateful gleam in his eyes . . . and something else. Something she'd never seen before. He was looking at her like he wanted to hurt her.

He raised his hand and slapped her.

She fell back, her cheek stinging. Her eyes welled up with tears.

"You spoiled little brat," he said. "What did I tell you about talking back to me? What did I *tell* you?"

He folded the belt, put a knee on the bed, and his trousers slipped down. His briefs were white cotton, just like Olesya's, but they looked wrong, all bunched up. Olesya gasped. Something *lived* there. It was long and hard, and it moved. Her fear receded, replaced by curiosity.

"What's that?" She reached out and touched it. It shifted under her fingers, surprisingly warm. She pulled on it, but it didn't come out as she thought it would.

Papa made a strange noise, clasped her arm, and twisted it.

"Ow!" She tried pulling away, but his grip was strong. "It hurts. It hurts, Papa. Let go."

"Why, you're a little whore in the making, aren't you? Blyad. Just like your mother. Whores, all of you." He shoved her back on the pillow, ripped off her panties. "A whore and a killer, that's who your mother is."

Olesya stared at him. *Whore* was a bad word. Papa yelled it at Mama and Baba Zina when they fought. Mama later told Olesya to never say this word. When Olesya asked why Papa called her that, she shushed her and promised her that if she said it again her tongue would turn black and fall out. Olesya had been very upset at this. She'd heard Mishka, the boy in their daycare, yell "Whore!" at their nanny, for which he was beaten with a wet towel, but his tongue was fine and never fell out. That meant Mama was lying. Olesya concluded it was something worse than *dura*. And now Papa called her Mama not just a whore but also a killer.

"Mama didn't kill anyone," she said cautiously, and made to sit up.

Papa pushed her back. "Oh, she didn't? And how do you know that?"

"I don't know."

"You don't know."

"Mama said—"

The gleam in Papa's eyes flared. Olesya bit her tongue.

"How many times did I tell you to not listen to what Mama is saying? How many times?"

Olesya was paralyzed. She didn't remember. She couldn't count in her head and give him a number, and that meant punishment, and that—

"Your mama was *lying*."

That Olesya agreed with. Mama had lied to her before.

"Where do you think she went yesterday?"

"I don't know."

He shook her. "Where?"

"I-I-I don't know," she stammered.

"Want me to tell you?" His face was so close to hers she saw blood vessels fan out in red lines from his irises, huge and dark.

"Yes," she squeaked.

"Say, 'Yes, Papa.' "

"Yes, Papa."

"All right. I'll tell you." He smiled in a strange way, as though there were a mask on his face and he stretched its lips. "She went to kill the premature brat she got with that darky scum from the market. The bitch. Was afraid I'd find out she cheated on me. Asked for a divorce. Well, she isn't going anywhere, and neither are you. Understand? I won't let her corrupt you."

"What's a . . . what's 'premature brat'?"

Papa lifted her chin. "Look at this. Just look at your eyes. I can already see it—always shifting, always looking for a man to twist around your finger. I should've known better than to marry a whore. Must be in her genes. Well, I'll beat this out of you, you'll see. One day you'll thank me."

He pushed Olesya back again, his breath rapid.

She had a sudden urge to pee. "I have to go to the bathroom."

"You're not going anywhere."

"But I have to—I—I . . ."

She squeezed her legs together. The urge was unbearable. She started to cry.

It was like she'd flipped a switch in Papa. His expression changed to something giddy, something so excited it gave him the look of a crazed, nightmarish puppet. Olesya saw a puppet like that once when Mama took her to the Puppet Theater for a play. Instead of amusing her, it frightened her, the jerky, animated doll that swiveled its head like it wasn't truly attached to its body. Olesya had thought it would roll off any moment, and that's what Papa looked like right now. He wasn't her Papa at all. He was a puppet. A doll. He was one of Baba Zina's figurines come alive, tired of sitting in the china cabinet behind the glass. And he was hungry—oh yes, he was very hungry—he was hungry to hurt Olesya, and hurt her he did, with his strong, pinching fingers.

He shoved them inside her.

Olesya cried out.

"Be quiet."

"Oooooooow!"

"*Quiet*, I said."

She hollered.

"Shut up. Shut *up!*"

He clapped his hand over her mouth. She tried breathing through her nose. It was stuffed. Snot shot out of her nostrils.

Then she saw it.

It slipped out of Papa's briefs and aimed its head at her, red and angry, glaring at her with one empty eye. *The headlamp,* Olesya thought, and, incredibly, giggled. Any moment it would light up. Any moment. Then it would whistle, its wheels would start spinning, and—

"It's TUBE!" she said. "Why were you hiding TUBE in your panties?"

"Shh." Papa flipped her around. "Stand on all fours."

She did. She felt TUBE poke her. It wanted to ride through her like through a tunnel, didn't it? Olesya thought it was silly. She giggled again. She didn't have a tunnel inside her! She needed to tell Papa. But then she thought better of it. It wasn't her Papa, was it? It was a puppet, a mechanical doll. TUBE was part of it. Or maybe TUBE lived inside it? Like in a train depot? Papa took her to a train depot once, and—

TUBE broke through.

It felt like she had a door to her tunnel, and when TUBE couldn't open it, it simply smashed it. She understood. TUBE was mad at her because she didn't have a tunnel, so it was going to make one, ride it, and come out the other end, through her mouth.

It was going to kill her.

Olesya flopped down on her stomach, pressed her face into the pillow. She couldn't breathe. The burning, pounding pain in her belly reached up higher and higher. Now it touched her stomach. Now her lungs. Now her throat.

She closed her eyes.

TUBE burst out of her mouth—hot and slimy. She retched, turned her head and looked behind her. And she saw a terrible face of someone she didn't know.

It wasn't her Papa. No. It was a monster.

"Please . . ." she said. "Please—"

Then she died.

6 February 1989
12:30

Olesya stood by Baba Zina's bed, cold all over. She felt her fingers lose blood, felt her flesh crawl up and shrink. The skin on her body turned to paper. It was about to rip.

She didn't know how long she'd been standing here in this shocked stupor.

Her eyes swiveled up to the clock. It was half past twelve.

Two hours. She'd stood here for two hours.

I split in half, she thought. *Me and Little Olesya. She's the one who died. For me. So I could continue living.*

She was both of them, alive and dead. Like Baba Zina's figurine, inanimate yet animated. A heavy weight to lug around. A stone that slowed down her life.

A dead child.

Olesya put her hands on her stomach and felt them sink inside, sink into nothing. Into a hole. There was no need for TUBE. She turned her hands. The rest of the memory played out.

Papa warning Little Olesya not to tell anyone.

Papa hauling her off the bed.

Papa shoving her into the bathroom, telling her to clean up her mess and slamming the door shut. And Little Olesya—

Olesya shuddered.

—Little Olesya thinking it was all a game. Of course it was. Papa would never hurt her. Little Olesya thinking it wasn't blood trickling down her legs, it was train tracks, drawn in red marker. Little Olesya hearing Uncle Shurik come downstairs and ask what was wrong. Little Olesya hearing them argue, hearing Papa threaten to expose their secret. Little Olesya deciding Papa must've played TUBE with Uncle Shurik, too, when he was little—

Oh God. Oh dear God. Olesya swayed.

She couldn't stand any more of this. Could she?

She could. She would. She had to. For that little girl.

It was her turn to hurt. Her turn to be dead.

She understood everything. Mama calling Uncle Shurik scum. Uncle Shurik not letting Olesya tell her story at Papa's funeral. The games he played with his little brother. With her. And Uncle Shurik . . . Uncle Shurik always being nice to her. The only adult in the family who listened to her stories, who never doubted her.

Because he *related*.

And she understood the worst.

There was never any TUBE.

There was—the actual toy train engine—but it wasn't connected to—

She had made the connection herself. To cope. To make it bearable. To survive.

Olesya sat down on Baba Zina's bed. A strange noise escaped her throat. A kind of a keening. The price she paid. The price for her family's secret.

"Of course," she said, and her voice surprised her. It was calm. It was the voice of knowledge. All those memories she'd seen. They were true. They happened.

In the men's restroom at Simferopol railway station.

On the bench in Gorky Park.

On that January night when Papa left for his job—hours away from his death—when Mama walked in on them because she suspected.

And at Baba Zina's birthday party.

The day it began.

Her family's shameful, unspeakable secret.

But no, it didn't start that day. It started earlier, with Uncle Shurik. And maybe even earlier than that. The most protected secrets had the longest lives.

When Papa died, it got buried with him. What a relief for all of them. They wanted it gone. It was too painful to remember. It was better to forget.

"Of course," Olesya said again, and her voice hissed with anger.

Where was Mama?

She must've known from the start, must've seen the obvious, physical evidence on Olesya's body. Seen the change in her, noticed she'd started wetting the bed, started having nightmares, stopped talking, stopped eating. But no, Mama conveniently closed her eyes. She left her five-year-old kid— *five years old!*—alone with a grown, violent man who was clearly mentally unstable, prone to sadistic outbursts, and with no sense of shame or guilt or remorse. Why? Because Mama couldn't stand the idea of confronting him, divorcing him, and kicking him out of her apartment. So Olesya got the brunt of it. Little, pig-tailed Olesya in a summer dress Baba Zina made for her from one of Papa's old shirts. The dress that clung to her skin like poison. The dress that reminded her she was never alone, never in control of her body, never her own person. How convenient it was for Mama to misplace her guilt at Uncle Shurik when she learned Papa was killed. How convenient it was that he stayed silent, that Baba Zina died shortly after, that Olesya forgot it all when she was older. And when she was younger, *how convenient* it was to call her stories lies.

"How could you, all of you?" Olesya asked incredulously. "How *could* you?"

The truth was always there, just under the surface, waiting to break through. Mama's hate of Papa's things. Baba Zina's mockery. Uncle Shurik's absence. And above all of it, Papa's ghost, his hands on their throats to keep them silent even after his death.

Olesya boiled with anger.

She wanted to kill him.

But it was impossible. He was already dead.

No, he wasn't. He was back. She could feel his presence.

"Papa?"

Breathing.

"I want to play TUBE," she said.

And there he was, TUBE in his hand, his eyes shining.

"My little ballerina," he said. "Took you long enough. I was starting to get worried. Did I hear you right? You want to play TUBE one more time?"

Olesya smiled. "Let's do it."

12:41

"Take off your clothes," Olesya said.

"What?"

"You heard me."

She saw a flicker of terror in Papa's eyes. Good.

She walked to him, smiling wider. "What's with the sullen look, *Grisha*? Take them off. Now. Or I'll *box your ears*."

A moment of hesitation was all she needed. Papa tensed to back off, and she lunged at him and snatched TUBE from his hold.

"You bitch," he said, in awe.

"Not anymore. Now you'll be my bitch. How about it?"

His eyes widened. "I knew it."

"You knew what?"

"I knew it'd come to this," he said. "Something like this, at any rate. The moment you were born—that red, squealing thing—I knew you'd be the death of me."

She couldn't believe her ears. "The death of you. Really?"

"You made me do this. Look what you did. You turned me into a monster."

Olesya's mouth opened. "*I* turned you into a monster?"

"That and more. You made me hate myself. You made me take my life!" His voice rose to a shriek. *"You bitch! You stinking, whoring bitch! Look at those slutty eyes of yours! Look—"*

Olesya slapped him with TUBE. It struck his head. He went stumbling backward.

"Liar," she hissed.

He looked up at her, grinning. "Did you like that?"

"You lied to me . . . all my life. You—"

"Did you like hitting me?"

Olesya shook. It was all she could do not to raise her hand and drive TUBE into his sickening, hideous smile.

"You told me you loved me," she said. "You used it— used my trust, my . . . my need to be cared for, to be held, to— I was a kid, just a *kid*, and I'd have done anything to make you pleased, make you utter those words. That moment, when you'd kiss the top of my head, right after, when I was hurt and crying, you'd say, 'Why are you crying, silly? Papa loves you.' That moment . . . I'd have died for it. I didn't care what price I had to pay, I was ready to die. Who does that to their own child, can you tell me? Who? Or . . . *what?* What are you? I don't have a word for you. Not a monster, no. That's too large somehow. You're much smaller than that. A pitiful little thing. A mean little boy. Yeah, that's what you are. A mean, cowardly, lying little boy."

She felt a new wave of anger wash over her, shake her breathing.

"You know lying is bad, don't you, Grisha? You know what happens to boys who lie? They get punished."

She passed TUBE from one hand to another, watched his eyes follow it greedily.

He looked up at her, and she saw strange excitement in his face.

"Well, how about it," he said. "My little girl grew up."

"Don't call me—"

"This is the daughter I raised. This is the Olesya Belaya I wanted to see onstage, to take command of it. It's good to hear you talk with authority for once. I must say, it was worth dying to hear."

There was pride in his voice. Olesya felt a prickle of yearning. She forced it out of her mind. No, no. She couldn't listen to him. He was lying. *Lying!*

"It's a relief to talk as equals," he continued. "No more of this whining or crying or begging. It drove me up the wall, the sound of it. You knew it, and you used it, so don't tell me these sob stories of yours. You were always good at stories, always managed to wiggle your way out of things by wagging that restless little tongue. I must say, perhaps you turned out not as empty-headed as your mother after all."

He looked her straight in the eyes and she saw that he meant every word.

She fought to keep her voice steady. "I would've preferred that, you know? Living life empty-headed. It would've been so much easier. I'm glad I didn't take after your line of the family, especially Baba Zina. Why, she never had a thought in her head except how to look pretty."

A muscle twitched in Papa's carefully composed face.

Olesya knew she'd hit the mark. "She didn't care much for you, did she? She told you to shut your trap. That was her love. She boxed your ears, belted you. Do you think she liked it, Papa? Did *you* like it? I wonder. Did you misbehave on purpose?"

Papa's lips curled inward. "Don't you dare insult my mother."

"Or what?"

He made a sudden grab for TUBE, but Olesya was ready. She jumped back and brought it down on his head. He ducked. Her blow only grazed his cheek. He threw himself at her. Olesya sidestepped him.

"You're not here, you're not here," she panted. "You're *dead*."

"You're the one who called me."

"You wanted me to call you, didn't you? Admit it."

Papa stopped, his eyes on TUBE.

"It was a sick game you played with me," Olesya said. "Sick."

"Was it?" He smiled.

She aimed TUBE at his stomach.

"You're enjoying this," Papa said, and his eyes lit up.

"No, I'm not."

"You want more, don't you?"

"I just want you to know what it felt like."

"You think I don't?"

The way he said it gave Olesya chills. She faltered. "What do you mean?"

"You think I don't know?"

He watched her, amused. But the laughter in his eyes was fake. Something hid behind it. Something like pain.

Olesya waited. "I don't understand."

"Of course you don't. How could you? My little ballerina."

The light in his eyes dimmed for a breath. His attention slipped. He glanced away from TUBE, away and through it, at something only he could see.

Olesya crouched.

Now.

She charged, arm outstretched, TUBE clenched in her fingers, eyes on Papa. But instead of avoiding her like before, he took a step toward her. Surprised, she weakened her hold.

Papa took TUBE from her easily. Looked at it for a moment. Then he did the strangest thing. He stuck it deep inside him, in his belly, and turned it. There was an audible scrape. Papa made a noise like that of an intake of air.

Olesya watched him, horrified.

"I'll show you," he said. There were tears in his eyes.

"No." She understood too late. "No."

"Yes, my little ballerina. You wanted to know. Come with me."

The light in his eyes went out with a *click* like someone turned it off.

"No." Olesya shook her head. "No no no no no. Not this. I changed my mind, Papa—I—"

"This way." He beckoned to her, his eyes extinguished, two dark holes, vacant and dead. "One last ride, my little ballerina. Never mind the others. This is a real one."

"No."

The door opened.

"No!"

The room tilted, and she fell into darkness.

She heard a man's voice. So familiar yet new. "Where are you?" it said. "You silly thing. Get back in here."

Then a child's voice: "I'm coming! I'm coming!"

SIMFEROPOL TRAIN DEPOT

23 December 1950
15:26

Olesya's eyes adjusted to the semidarkness.

She was inside an attendant's compartment.

The train wasn't moving.

Through the window filtered in weak electric light. In that light Olesya saw two figures on the lower bunk. They kneeled in a kind of forced embrace—a boy of eight or nine, naked, and a middle-aged, heavyset man. His shirt was unbuttoned. His pants were pulled down and cinched around his ankles. With one hand he gripped the table, the other the boy's hip.

The man's buttocks clenched and unclenched, white in the shadows.

The boy was silent.

The only noise was that of skin-on-skin slapping and the man's laborious, gasping grunts.

Olesya closed her eyes. "I can't. I can't—"

The boy whimpered.

Her eyes flew open.

The boy turned his head, and she saw his face. It was like looking in the mirror. Same big eyes, same nose, same curl of the lips. Only his ears were different—sticking out. For a second she thought he saw her, then he blinked and turned away. His head dropped down. It lolled to the rising rhythm.

Olesya felt sick. That look she saw in his eyes. The look of helplessness and resignation. She knew it so well, felt it so often herself.

"Papa," she called. "Grisha. Grisha!"

Grisha didn't hear her. He was silent. The only sign of distress was his hands clenched in fists, his knuckles white.

Olesya took a step forward, not knowing why she did it, until she saw her arm rise up to do . . . what? She wasn't sure.

(Yes, she was. She *was*.)

How satisfying it would be. How deserving.

She wanted to kill this man.

She wanted to circle her hands around his thick, repulsive neck and squeeze and squeeze until his ugly face turned purple.

She wanted to look him in the eyes so that in his last living moments he saw her face and he was sorry, so very sorry for what he did to this little boy. To little Grisha.

To Papa.

Olesya dropped her arm. There was nothing she could do. It was a memory. It already happened. And yet, if she could . . . if she could stop it . . . how different would her father's life have been?

And her own?

The man moved faster. He came to a shuddering, sudden stop, grunted, and pushed Grisha away.

"Get dressed. Be quick about it."

That same voice. It was the voice she'd heard coming from the attendant's compartment. In the haunted car. Her stomach dropped. She recognized the man. His flat, brutal face—the face that so often gazed at her from the photographs in Baba Zina's house.

Matvey Larionovich, she thought. *Papa's stepfather.*

Matvey Larionovich was Baba Zina's third husband. He worked as a baggage handler at Simferopol railway station and he died before Olesya was born, having drunk himself to death. Papa never talked of him. All Olesya knew about him she'd heard from Baba Zina. She never wondered why that was. Until now.

She shrank away from the bunk.

Grisha picked up his clothes from the floor and started dressing.

Matvey smacked his head. "Move a little faster, will you?" He grabbed his coat and put it on, then smacked Grisha again. "I asked you a question."

"Yes," Grisha said.

"Yes, what?"

"Yes, I'll move a little faster."

"Go on, then! Don't just stand there flopping your eyes at me. Remember what I told you?"

Grisha's hands stopped on the button.

"Answer me."

"I won't tell Mama," Grisha said mechanically, as though he'd said it many times before.

"What else?"

"I won't disobey Mama. I won't play with her dolls. I won't—" He stopped.

"Go on."

"I won't—" He dragged in a shuddering breath.

Matvey peered at him. "What's that? Crying? Are we crying again? Goddamn you, you little son of a bitch. Stop it, will you? Stop it! I'm sick of your crying. What do I have to do to put you out of your misery, huh? Smash your face in? *What?*"

Grisha shook, silent.

"Go on then, boy. Don't try my patience. What else?"

The air whooshed out of Grisha. "I won't dance."

Olesya caught her breath.

"That's right," Matvey nodded. "Dancing is for sissies. You hear me?" He grabbed Grisha's chin, jerked up his head and said, "For little girls and for *sissies*."

He abruptly let go. Grisha lost his balance and plopped on the bunk.

"Repeat what I said."

"Dancing is for sissies," Grisha repeated. When he looked up, his eyes were different. There was no fear in them, no hate, no resignation. Only a strange, calm serenity—and something else too. Olesya couldn't put her finger on it. They were . . . shining.

"When I grow up," Grisha said, "I'll work on trains like you, Matvey Larionovich. Like a *real man*. I promise."

Matvey smiled. "Good. Good. Now remember what I said. If you tell your mother, if you so much as breathe a word—"

"I won't, Matvey Larionovich! I pro—"

Matvey smacked him. "Don't interrupt me. As I was saying, if you so much as breathe a word to her, you're dead, pansy. I'll kill you, you hear me? With these very hands." He spread his fingers and put them close to Grisha's face then grabbed his throat, squeezed it playfully and let go. "Do you believe me?"

Grisha stared at him.

"Do you?"

"Yes."

"Good. Let's go." He threw a coat at Grisha.

Grisha put it on, his eyes never leaving Matvey.

"And don't you pester your mother when we get to the hospital, you hear me?"

"Yes, Matvey Larionovich."

"She's in no condition to deal with you. She just gave me a son." Matvey's face transformed. It glowed with pride. "I'll make sure he grows up into a *real man*. Not like you, pansy."

He slapped Grisha's butt. Grisha flinched and jumped. Matvey laughed.

"Can't you take a joke? I'm teasing you. Grisha-Shisha. *Ptu!*" He spat. "What kind of a name is that? More fitting for an old woman. I'll call my son Alexander, like Alexander the Great. Now *that* has a ring to it, don't you think?"

A flicker of hatred flashed through Grisha's eyes. Then they were shining again with that strange, empty light. "Yes, Matvey Larionovich," he said automatically.

"Yes, Matvey Larionovich. Yes, Matvey Larionovich," Matvey copied him. "Is that all you've got to say? You little cocksucker. Look at me when I'm talking to you!"

Grisha looked.

"Aren't you happy you got a baby brother? You could at least smile. Don't you ever smile?" He smacked him.

Grisha stretched his lips. "I can't wait for my baby brother to come home. I'll take good care of him, I promise. I'll play with him every day."

Olesya saw what he meant by it. She saw the malice and the envy and the gleeful anticipation that rippled over Grisha's face like a wave over dark water. Then it was gone just as fast as it came.

"Good. Good," Matvey said, satisfied. "Out you go."

The compartment door rolled open.

Olesya followed them out into the dark, cold aisle of the empty car.

The empty car, she thought. *The attendant's compartment. You couldn't part with them even in death, could you, Papa? The pull was too strong. I understand it now, and I wish I didn't. God, how I wish I didn't. I wish I'd never seen what you showed me. I wish.*

Matvey unlocked the exit door and climbed down the stairs. He glanced from side to side, beckoned to Grisha. "Hurry."

Grisha took one step down, then suddenly turned around and looked right at Olesya. The illusion of him being aware of her presence was too strong. Olesya recoiled. Grisha leaned toward her, as though he wanted her to hear him.

"Alexander the Great," he whispered, and smiled.

The skin on Olesya's scalp shrank.

"Let's see how great you are, baby brother," Grisha said, looking at Olesya and through her. "I bet you'll cry like a little girl when I pinch your butt."

He hopped off the train.

ALUPKA, SEASIDE ST., NO. 8
6 February 1989
13:05

TUBE trembled in Papa's hand.

He truly looked like a ghost now. His face was gray, his figure indistinct, as though the memory had carved him out and left him an empty shell.

Olesya watched Papa dispassionately, from a faraway distance—the distance of knowledge.

She did nothing wrong.

She'd punished herself all her life for the horror that wasn't her own. The horror that was so sickening and wrong that as a little girl she couldn't comprehend it. It was beyond her understanding of life, beyond her simple daily existence. Little things like waking up, eating breakfast, going to school, coming home, eating dinner, brushing teeth, going to bed, day after day the same, comforting pattern.

So when that pattern got broken—violently, with a secret purpose—her mind couldn't cope with it. And she split herself in two. One Olesya believed that her parents loved her and did all the things parents did for their children. Another Olesya wanted to kill them.

"It wasn't me," Olesya said.

Papa looked at her.

"It wasn't me you were hurting. It was you all along. I was just a substitute, wasn't I? But that was later. First it was Uncle Shurik. Your little brother. Alexander the Great. You watched the pain on his face and it was like looking in the mirror. Then he got older, strong enough to resist you, so you had to stop. Then you met Mama. A young, naïve Moscow girl with both parents dead. Very convenient. No one to complain to. Even better, they left her a two-room apartment, so you wasted no time. You knocked her up. You got married. I guess she loved you, at first, until I was born, until she saw . . . until she really *saw* you for the first time, who you really were, and she got scared. Maybe she resisted you at first, but you shut her up quickly. Divorce would've been bad for your careers, so she chose her career over me, closed her eyes and pretended . . . pretended for years that it wasn't happening. Couldn't be. As if the less she thought about it, the better chance it would simply disappear. Go away. Vanish.

"Only she knew. And Baba Zina knew it too. Or suspected. The women of our family protected you, and you . . . you did as you pleased. You used me for your games. I looked a lot like you, and it gave you a certain pleasure. You were in control for once. It must've felt addicting, didn't it? You couldn't stop. Stopping would've meant to face your pain, and you were scared of it. Scared you'd cry like a little girl. Like a sissy, a pansy. You had to be a 'real man.'

"And so you were. Or at least you tried your best. But in the end . . . that monstrous thing you did, it came back for you, and it took your life."

She waited for him to say something.

Papa was silent.

She stepped closer, looked him in the face.

"We're so much alike," she said, "it scares me. When I look in the mirror . . . when I want to see *me*, I see *you*, and I hate it. I hate it so much I hate myself. I came close to killing myself for that very reason. You know what stopped me? Love for you. There is a part of me—a child in me—who will always love you. No matter what you do to her, no matter how much you hurt her—she'll love you with that . . . with that abandon that only children are capable of. Children and pets." She smiled in spite of herself.

His mouth twitched, as though he were trying to smile with her.

Olesya moved closer still.

"Grisha, little Grisha. I'm devastated by what happened to you. I can relate, you know?"

She laughed, bitterly. The sound surprised and frightened her. Was she losing her mind?

"Can I ask you a question?" she said.

He simply looked at her.

"Why me, Papa? I mean . . . didn't you feel anything toward me? At least some affection? Nothing? Nothing at all? Why? Tell me. Why your own daughter?"

"Why not?" he said.

Olesya recoiled. "You really *are* a monster."

He smiled. Like Little Grisha smiled not too long ago. His lips stretched up and out and away from his teeth. It was a leer of a predator, ready to bite a chunk out of her.

Olesya took a step back, suddenly aware of the darkness in the corridor, the coldness of the unheated house, the presence of her dead father in front of her.

She was alone with him. Alone. *Alone.*

"Why—" She choked on her words. "Why didn't you tell someone?"

He knocked his head back and laughed. "You think I haven't tried?"

"Have you?"

He took a step forward. "My mother boxed my ears when I told her."

Olesya moved back, hit the wall and stopped.

Papa took another step. "The first time it happened, I ran to her, crying. I was seven. She said boys didn't cry, said to *man up*. I had bloody diarrhea, my sweet little girl. He tore me up, the bastard. The blood wouldn't stop, so Mama took me to the hospital. You know what the doctor said? He said I must've eaten something off the street—like a *stray dog*. Gave Mama a valid excuse for punishment. She washed my mouth with soap, said that'd teach me a lesson. Teach me how to eat filth. Then she belted me. I couldn't sit for days."

He smiled that smile again.

Olesya's heart flew to her mouth. "How often . . . how often did he—"

"That's enough," Papa said sharply.

"But—"

"I said, enough." He bristled. "I want you to thank me."

"Thank you?"

"I did you good. I made sure your pretty little head wasn't worried about boys so you could focus on your career. So you could focus on ballet."

She gaped. "Is that what you think you did? You did me *good*?"

"That and more. I made sure your mother didn't interfere. Made sure there was enough money for you to continue. In case something happened to me."

"You mean, in case you killed yourself sooner than later."

"You ungrateful little bitch," he spat.

It was strange, what she felt. Not anger. Not shame. It was his hurt. His need to bite her before he was bitten. His old and childlike fear that made him small and weak. He didn't like it, she knew, so he carefully hid it behind his attacks.

It was up to her to end it, she realized. To end his pain. If she did it—if she succeeded—he'd never return. He'd leave her in peace.

"Where did he do it?" she asked. "Matvey Larionovich. The first time, I mean."

Papa's leer became a grimace of fury. His eyes bulged out of his sockets. "You—" he choked out, "you—"

"Your mother's bed," Olesya said. It wasn't a question.

Papa gasped for breath.

"She knew it, didn't she? Of course she did. She was your mother. And you knew that she knew, and she did nothing to help you. *Nothing*. She closed her eyes on it. It was safer that way, safer for her. How you hated her for it. I can imagine. You must've hated her more than your step-father. You hated her so much for letting him do this to you that you wanted to kill her. Dreamed about it. Schemed. Planned. Came close to it, maybe. Maybe snuck into her room one night, watched her sleep, a kitchen knife in your sweaty hand. But you were too scared to go through with it. You were just a kid after all. Just Little Grisha. Did I get this right, Papa? Did I come close?"

The shape in front of her—was it Papa?—crumpled.

It was like watching something dry and dead slough off something smaller underneath. And there he stood, Little Grisha, his hands curled in fists, his face streaked with tears.

"I hate you! I hate you!" His voice rose to a shriek. "*I hate you!*"

"Grisha?"

"Shut up!"

"Grisha!"

He spun around and rushed upstairs.

"Wait!" Olesya ran after him. "Papa! *Papa!*"

She found him curled up in the attic closet, face in his hands, shoulders shaking. He was crying.

She crouched next to him. "I'm sorry," she said. "Sorry it happened to you. I—"

"Go away," he said.

"I just wanted—"

"Go away!" he yelled. "Leave me alone! *Leave me alone!*"

He jumped to his feet and advanced, his fists ready.

She backed out of the closet. "I only wanted—"

"Shut up!" he screamed. "Why won't you shut up?"

She sucked in her breath. "I want to help you."

"I don't need your help, you stupid bitch! Did I ever ask for it? No!"

"Yes, you did."

He stared at her. "When?"

"When we . . . when we played TUBE for the very first time."

Grisha's face turned vicious in the way children's faces get—twisted with an overwhelming, helpless rage. He swiped a fist at her, his eyes blazing.

Olesya ducked and skipped down the stairs to the first floor.

"I can help you get rid of it," she said. "Your pain."

He halted. "Liar."

"I think I know the way."

"Liar!"

"Come on, I'll show you." She backed into Baba Zina's room.

He followed.

She offered him TUBE.

He took it. His eyes widened with excitement. "You want to play with me?"

She sat on the bed. "Yes. One last game."

Grisha whooped.

They played.

13:32

Olesya sat on Baba Zina's bed, naked. She held TUBE in her hand—it was wet and sticky. There were red streaks on her thighs, already drying. She stared at them until her eyes watered, then tossed TUBE aside and got up.

"Happy twenty-first," she said. "You're normal. You had sex."

The laughter that came out of her was that of a loony. A wild and hysteric cackle. She felt sanity slip away from her, sat back down and gasped.

The pain.

The pain was real and sharp. Olesya smiled at it—grinned, more like. For once it was where it belonged, not in some hole in her stomach. It was real, it was raw, and it hurt like hell. She squeezed her legs together, afraid it would vanish.

"I'm proud of you. You figured it out *all by yourself*."

Olesya raised her eyes.

Little Olesya stood by the china cabinet, her head inclined, as though she'd been watching Olesya for quite some time.

"Oh God. You're here. You're . . . I thought you left me."

"I couldn't leave you if I wanted to, you dummy."

Olesya smiled. "I'm so glad, *so glad* you're here."

Little Olesya was silent. She was waiting for her something.

"Wait, what do you mean?" Olesya said. "What is it that I figured out all by myself?"

"The tracks on your legs. The red marker." Little Olesya pointed. "You get what they are now." It wasn't a question.

Olesya looked down at her legs. "Blood," she said quietly.

"Blood," Little Olesya repeated.

"I had to pretend it was something else," Olesya said. "So I pretended . . . I pretended I drew them with a red marker. One of the markers Papa gave me. Because in my mind it made perfect sense. I was the tunnel for the train. For TUBE. But it had to ride on something, didn't it? It had to have train tracks. And there they were. Very convenient. It . . . it followed a pattern. The pattern of the game. It made sense. And it wasn't scary, all of a sudden. Or painful. It was fun. It was our special game with Papa." She looked up at Little Olesya.

The girl was smiling. "You're not so dumb after all."

"That's sick," Olesya said. "That's just sick."

"It's not sick," Little Olesya said. "It's how you won. How you beat him. Come. I want to show you something." She walked out of the room.

"Wait!" Olesya draped the blanket over her shoulders, tiptoed out into the corridor and up the stairs. Little Olesya stood by the door to Uncle Shurik's room. She pressed a finger across her lips and pushed the door open.

On the floor sat Little Grisha. He hummed a tune under his breath. In front of him stood a dozen porcelain ballerinas in a semicircle. He moved them to the center one by one, twirling them, lifting them up and setting them down gently, imitating jumps. Olesya thought she recognized the tune he was humming.

"It's from *Swan Lake*."

"Shh!" Little Olesya motioned her out.

They crept downstairs, back into Baba Zina's room, to the china cabinet. There they were, the ballerinas, a layer of dust on them, as though no one had touched them for years.

The plain ballerina. Olesya caught her breath. It was missing. Of course, it was. Baba Zina smashed it against the carafe. She probably swept up the pieces and threw them away.

"He looked so happy there," Olesya said. "Do you think he's happy?"

Little Olesya shrugged. "Do you want him to be?"

"Yeah. I think so."

"Then he probably is." She looked down. "Are we done now?"

"Done?"

"Will you let me out?"

"Out? Oh. Yes, of course. But . . . how do I do it?"

"Are you playing dumb again?" Little Olesya crossed her arms. She tried giving Olesya a mean stare, but she looked close to tears. "I'm tired," she said.

"I'm sorry."

"No, you're not. You want to see it until the end. All of it."

"All of it?"

"Will you stop playing stupid?"

Olesya sat next to Little Olesya and tried putting her arm around her, but the girl moved away from her before she could.

"You try it, okay?" Little Olesya said. "You try it and see how long you last."

"I don't—"

"If you tell me you don't understand, I'm going to scream!"

Olesya sighed. "You're right."

"Of course I am."

"I just . . . I need to know. To remember. All of it. Wouldn't you? The times, the days, the weather . . . everything I can recall. What he said, what he did, where and how and—"

"No, you don't," Little Olesya cut her off.

"But I need to be sure."

"Why?"

"Because . . . it drives me crazy not to remember. Because it makes me think I'm crazy. And maybe I am. It's debilitating."

Little Olesya scoffed. "Tell me something I don't know."

"But you do. You *do* know!"

"Would you stop screaming?"

"I'm not!"

"Yes, you are."

Olesya breathed hard. "What am I going to tell Mama?"

"Yeah, what *are* you going to tell her?"

"I don't know."

"That's very funny." The girl smiled sadly.

"What did *you* tell her? Or . . . try telling her?"

She looked Olesya straight in the face. "Chicken. You're still afraid you'd be accused of making up stories, aren't you? Well, here's the truth for you. You want to know? I'll tell you. You'll *never* remember. Get it? You'll never be sure." Her lips trembled. "It's like the tracks, like the red marker. It's not real. It's confusing. And it's never the same. It always changes. You'll never know exactly what happened. *Never*. No matter how hard you try."

Olesya was stunned. "So this was all for nothing?"

Little Olesya spun around, her eyes black with fury. "I hate you."

Olesya moved to her.

She shrank back. "Don't touch me."

She sounded so much like Grisha. Olesya was struck by how similar they looked, and spoke, and behaved. How much of him she carried in her, how much of him she was, whether she wanted to or not. He was part of her.

He lived in her.

"I'm sorry I did this to you," she said. "I didn't—didn't realize—" She looked down. "I missed you."

There was silence.

"I missed you too. But you're still mean, and stubborn, and stupid." Little Olesya shot Olesya an angry look from under her furrowed brow, her arms crossed.

Olesya mimicked her—furrowed her brow and crossed her arms. The girl giggled, then burst into laughter. Olesya joined her. Tears sprang from her eyes. She doubled over, held on to her stomach, and laughed and laughed with an abandon she hadn't felt in years.

When it was over, she let the blanket drop from her shoulders and opened her arms.

"To hell with it, with the truth. I don't need it."

"Really?"

"Really. It's *you* that I need. I need you back, Little Olesya. Please?"

Little Olesya tilted her head, eyes cautious. "You won't lock me up again?"

"Do you need to be sure?"

The girl smiled, and at that moment she looked like a happy five-year-old kid. She took a deep breath and leaned in. Olesya wrapped her arms around her, felt her breath and her heart going fast as a bird's, and she knew this was happiness, *this*—sitting alone in the cold, unheated house, hurting, naked, a dusty blanket at her feet, but whole.

She was whole.

She was whole.

13:54

Olesya found it in the attic closet.

It lay hidden under a loose board, wrapped in her old summer dress.

The plain ballerina.

It was chipped and crisscrossed with crack lines but intact, painstakingly glued back together bit by bit.

Olesya carefully unwrapped it, traced the scars on her body.

She remembered how she stole down to the kitchen, after everyone fell asleep, her butt still smarting from Baba Zina's belt. She picked out the bits from the trash can and right there on the floor, by the light of the moon, painted them with clear nail polish she'd taken earlier from Mama's purse. She pressed the bits together. It worked. The figurine held.

The next morning Olesya got her revenge by hiding in the attic closet. The entire family looked for her all over the house. She gleefully listened to their shouts, sitting cramped in the hot, dusty dark, picking at the floorboards, when one of them gave. She lifted it, felt inside, and on a whim wiggled out of her dress, wrapped it around the ballerina, and hid her.

And so she lay there all these years.

Olesya brought the dress to her face, breathed in. It smelled of mold and dampness. She looked at it. It was nothing special, just a child's button-up dress sewn from a man's shirt, blue in color. She looked at the figurine and saw how crudely she'd fixed her—the head was stuck on sideways, the tutu bits mashed together, the legs cracked.

"But I made you whole," she said. "I did the best I could."

She looked down at herself, half expecting to see the same scars, and simply stood there for a long time, unaware of the cold, her skin turning to gooseflesh, her feet icy.

"I never loved you, did I?" she told her body. "I'm sorry. I'll make it up to you, okay?"

It was strange yet somehow perfectly normal to stand alone in the house of her dead grandmother, stark naked like the day she was born, talking to her body as though it could hear her. And it could. It did.

It was alive.

An overwhelming desire to touch it washed over Olesya. Her face grew hot. Her heartbeat quickened. She raced downstairs to Baba Zina's room, put the figurine on the bed, and was putting on her panties when there was a knock at the door.

Olesya froze. "Who is it? Uncle Shurik?" She hopped on one leg, trying to step into the panty hole, but missed and fell to the floor, flat on her butt. "Shit."

The door shook under heavy blows.

She grabbed the blanket, wrapped it around her shoulders.

"Hang on! I'm coming!"

The door crashed open.

14:31

Yuri stomped in, his breath rolling off him in a white cloud. He closed the door and took a few steps inside before he saw Olesya. "Oh, thank goodness. You're alive."

"Yuri."

Olesya was mortified. She'd forgotten about him.

"I dozed off. Would you believe it? Dozed off!" He smacked his forehead. "Old fool. Had my Starushka running, keeping her warm for you—" He glanced around, took off his hat, and said quietly, "Never mind that. You all right?" And then, quieter still: "Where is he?"

"Who, Papa? He's gone."

"*Gone?*"

"Yeah."

"Gone for good?"

"I think so."

"Gone," Yuri repeated, and nodded. He looked around once more, crossed himself, and saw Olesya's bare feet.

"Oh, I—" she began, and stopped herself.

How many times had she done this? Explained to others what she didn't need to explain. Out of guilt that she didn't need to feel. Out of shame that wasn't hers. Out of obligation and submission and groveling that Papa taught her. No, *trained* her. Successfully. She was such an obliging pupil.

What could she say instead? Olesya shivered, and she knew.

"I'm cold," she said. So simple. So hard. It was new to her, to say what she wanted. "I want some hot tea."

Yuri grinned. His golden teeth glittered in the semidarkness. He clapped his hands. "Some hot tea, eh? Sounds good to me. Is there tea in this ice bucket? A stove or something to get the fire going?"

She pointed to the kitchen. "Should be some in the cupboards. Tea, sugar. The wood is in the shed in the backyard. If Uncle Shurik stored any."

Yuri sprang to action.

Olesya followed him like a hungry kid about to be fed by a parent. Her mouth filled with saliva in anticipation. Her stomach clamored for food. She watched him open the cupboards, slam them shut, mutter under his breath.

"Buckwheat . . . sunflower oil . . . salt, pepper . . . tell you what." He turned around, holding up the paper bag of buckwheat with triumph. "I'll make you kasha. Hot kasha ought to warm you up."

"Yes, please," she said without thinking. The prospect of eating homemade food—cooked just for her—made her swoon. She couldn't remember the last time someone fed her. Not like this. Not like a parent feeds a hungry child.

Yuri set the bag on the counter, opened it, and scooped out the grains with a spoon. "Go on," he said without looking. "Do what you need to do."

"But I don't know if the shed—"

"No buts. I'll find my way around. Go. Get out of here. *Shoo!*"

He shook the spoon at her.

Olesya walked out, grinning.

She had put on her sweater and was reaching for her pants when the door to Baba Zina's room burst open. Cold air washed over the backs of her legs.

She spun around.

"Dima?"

Dima stood swaying in the door. His coat was unbuttoned. His ears were bright red from the cold. His eyes were bloodshot, fixed on Olesya's legs.

"Dima?" she repeated. "What are you doing here? How . . . how did you find me?"

He looked at the crumpled blanket on the bed then out the window. His expression changed from shock to hostility.

Olesya followed his eyes.

In the backyard Yuri came out of the shed with a bundle of wood in his arms, smiling.

Dima's eyes darkened.

"Sorry to interrupt," he said, his words slurring. "I'll leave you two alone."

Olesya's face grew hot. "You're drunk."

He smirked. "Am I? A nice nest you made here." He nodded at the bed.

"What?" Olesya turned to look. "What do you suggest—"

"Oh, you know what," he snapped, his jaw pulsing.

"Dima—"

"You could've told me."

"Listen to me." Her voice was harsh, low with anger.

"You could've told me," he repeated. "Would've saved me a trip."

"Would you shut up and *listen to me*, please?"

"Oh yeah? Why? What are you going to say that I don't already know?"

They stared at each other.

He belched.

Olesya said quietly, so quietly she barely heard herself, "Get the fuck out."

"Huh?" There was confusion in his eyes.

"The door is behind you."

She calmly put on her pants, tucked her hair behind her ears, picked up the ballerina figurine from the bed, and put it back in its place in the china cabinet. Her movements were smooth and unhurried, but inside she was boiling.

She put her hands in her pockets. "Waiting for something?"

Dima's mouth twitched. "You didn't mean that."

"Yes, I did."

"You want me to leave."

"Yes, I want you to leave. You were going anyway, weren't you?"

His nostrils flared, and he swayed on his feet. "You don't get it—"

"No, *you* don't get it!" She stuck a finger at his chest. "I'm tired of this, okay? Sick sick *sick!* I'm not your property—"

"I never said—"

"You don't have to. You behave like I am. Don't you see?"

He leaned closer. His alcohol breath made her recoil.

"Get out," she said. "Get out, before—"

Heavy footsteps walked up the porch and entered the hall.

"Why did you leave the door open?" Yuri's voice called. "You're letting out all the warm air, dorogusha."

Dima smirked. "Dorogusha?"

"Don't. Don't even . . ." Olesya shook, unable to speak, a metallic taste in her mouth.

"That was some piece of work, that shed!" Yuri called. "Thought I'd never get the damn door open. Got frozen shut in the frame."

There was a clatter of wood on the floor.

Dima's cheeks colored a blotchy red. He put his hand in his pocket, turned around, and strode toward Yuri.

In an instant Olesya understood his intent.

"Dima, no. *No!*"

The floor shuddered under a fallen body.

Olesya ran out into the hall.

Yuri lay sprawled on top of the scattered wood, his arms raised over his head. Dima sat astride him, in his hand a jackknife.

"Stop! Stop it! Get off him!"

He didn't hear her. He raised his arm.

Everything hushed.

Olesya saw them both with perfect clarity. Two men on top of each other, one to kill and one to die for the wrong reasons. Or perhaps not wrong. Perhaps she should let them do it. She was suddenly so tired, so bone-weary, so exhausted.

She was tired of caring and worrying and wanting to please others. But not herself. Never herself. It occurred to her that maybe that's why Little Olesya was mad at her. Of course she was. Anyone would be.

She stood and watched them in that terrible, frozen moment.

Beyond them, in the yard, snow fell and settled on the bare trees, on the gate, on Yuri's car. And suddenly none of this mattered anymore—memories, Papa, Little Olesya, TUBE. Life was just one big coincidence of random events and people, some luckier than others, some not so much. There was no reason for any of it, no explanation, only the outcome. Life or death. This strangely comforted Olesya. Her body relaxed. She felt like running out into the snow and catching snowflakes on her tongue.

Just for the fun of it.

To feel alive.

It only lasted a breath, this feeling.

Then she felt the cold floor under her feet. Saw Dima's hand tremble. Saw Yuri move his hands away from his face. Heard him suck in air. Heard Dima utter a strangled, keening whine. The jackknife slipped from his fingers, clattered to the floor. He rose and staggered on unsteady feet, pitched forward, held on to the wall. His head hung, and he dissolved in great, shuddering sobs.

"I'm sorry. I'm sorry. I'm so sorry . . ."

He clutched his face.

Yuri dragged himself up by the wall.

The three of them stood motionless in the dark hall.

Then Yuri picked up his hat and pushed it down on his head. "Well, I'll be going then," he said.

"Wait. Yuri!"

But he was already in the yard, walking to the gate. He opened it and closed it behind him, got in the car, started it on the first try, and rolled off into the snowy silence.

14:54

Olesya looked at Dima. "Say something."

He shook his head.

Her irritation climbed. "Are you just going to stand there?"

He shrugged.

"Whatever." She walked into Baba Zina's room, sat on the bed, wrapped the blanket around herself, and propped her chin on her knees.

Dima came in and sat down next to her.

The clock ticked off minutes.

A car puttered by in the street, then all was quiet again.

"It felt like death," Olesya said finally.

Dima studied her, silent.

"I thought . . ." She fingered the blanket. "I thought I was going to die, thought it would kill me. I thought it would bore a tunnel right through me and kill me."

He said nothing.

Olesya sighed. "Do you think it was worth it?"

He shrugged.

"Why are you quiet?"

"I'm afraid—" He cleared his throat. "Afraid to say anything."

"Why?"

"I'm afraid to say something wrong."

"I'm sorry."

"No no no. It's not your fault. It's mine." He reached for her hand and stopped. "I must disgust you," he said.

"No, you don't."

"Yes. I'm disgusting. Just like my dad. I disgust myself." They were silent again.

After some time Olesya spoke. "It was always there, you know? Always with me. I just refused to see it. You know what I mean?"

"Yeah," Dima said. "You weren't ready."

"Like you weren't ready to see your mom?"

"Something like that."

"Okay. But—" She cut herself off.

"But what?"

"Nothing."

"No, please."

"Well . . . how could I forget something . . . something so horrible? I would've remembered for sure, wouldn't I? I mean—"

"Don't." He put his hands on hers. "Don't doubt yourself, Olesya."

"But—" She felt tears coming.

"I'm so sorry," he said. "I'm so very sorry. For everything. I shouldn't have followed you. I shouldn't have . . . with Yuri, it was just . . . I thought, I thought for sure—"

"It's okay."

"No, it's not. I—"

"Dima." She looked at him. "Really, I don't care."

"You don't?"

He held her hand in both of his. They were warm. They were always warm. Olesya loved it. Her skin tingled.

"Look, the worst is over," she said. "Or at least I think it is. And all the other things . . . you know, they just kind of lost importance. Like they're so small and so stupid. All these worries for nothing." She leaned her head on his shoulder.

"So . . . can I ask you . . . ?"

"Ask me what?"

"What happened?"

Olesya thought about it.

Dima stroked her hair.

"I'm whole now," she said.

"Whole?"

"Yeah. *Whole*."

"Okay."

"Okay," she agreed.

He held her and rocked her.

"He's not coming back," she whispered. "He's not—"

"Shh."

She looked up.

"Dance with me," Dima said.

"What?"

He looked at her with a strange intensity. "Dance with me."

"What, right now?"

"Yeah. And later."

"Later?"

"Come back."

"Come back? What do you mean?"

Dima glanced at the clock. "It's only four. We've got two hours."

"You mean, dance *Swan Lake*?" Olesya gaped at him. "But—Alla Borisovna—Natasha—"

"Is that a yes?"

"Are you crazy? What are we going to do, just show up?"

"Something like that." His eyes glittered with excitement.

Olesya smiled. "You'll lose your job, you idiot."

"I don't care."

She looked at him for some time.

And then she felt a stupid, happy grin spread across her face.

"Okay. I'm in. Let's do it."

RIDE OVER

SIMFEROPOL THEATRE OF DRAMA AND MUSICAL COMEDY

16:55

Simferopol's theater was nothing more than a block of cement with a red banner stretched along the roof: FEBRUARY 23RD—GLORY TO SOVIET ARMED FORCES!

"I'm not going in," Olesya said.

"What? Why not?"

"Sorry. I changed my mind." She watched the slush spray over the curb from the passing cars.

Dima stopped, a bewildered look on his face. "Hang on. Hang on a moment. I thought you said you're in."

"I know. I'm sorry, I just . . . I can't. I can't explain."

She unbuttoned her coat.

It was getting warm, as though the winter had finally decided it had taken the wrong turn. A drop of water hit her head. She looked up. The icicles on the wires were dripping.

"You'll be late. Go." She gave Dima a nudge.

He said nothing, only nodded, looking forlorn with his hands in his pockets.

"Oh God. Fine. *Fine.*" Olesya sighed. "I'll go in with you. But just to look, okay? I don't want to run into Alla Borisovna or, you know—" She cut herself off.

"Yeah, I understand," he said quickly. "Just to look."

He took her hand.

They jogged up the steps and around the back to the service doors. Dima pushed one of them open. Inside it was silent and smelled of dust and waxed floors. In a booth by the staircase sat a uniformed girl of about twenty, talking on the phone. She hardly gave them a glance. They skipped downstairs, around a corner, and entered backstage.

An old woman swept the floor. The stagehands wheeled in the lights, shouted up to the electricians. Nobody paid them any mind.

Olesya's heart beat faster. The stage. How she loved it. Her belly ached with a mixture of thrill and terror that never left her, never changed, no matter how many times she danced. It was an addiction—a drug.

"Okay, I looked," she said quickly.

Dima offered her a hand. "One dance?"

"No. No no no no no. I can't. I—"

"There's no one here," he said. "It'll take us just a few minutes."

"I'm not going out there. Forget it." She shook her head.

He came closer. "Just our pas de deux. Second act. That's all I ask for. Please?"

She studied him. "Why?"

"I don't know. For . . . for us."

"For us?"

"Yeah. Would you do it for us?"

She kicked off her boots, slipped out of her coat, and, as she was, in socks, walked onstage. Dima followed her, no longer Dima Rumyantsev, in old jeans and a sweater, but Prince Siegfried. Her Prince. Olesya smiled, thinking of her childhood wish. How she'd always believed her Prince was out there somewhere. How she thought he was the love of her life. How she knew that one day she'd meet him.

And we'd love one another and tell that to each other every day. And we'd never fight. Not once. Never ever ever.

"What?" Dima asked.

"Nothing."

"No, what?"

"It's not important."

They started, and it all left her—her fears, her worries, even her hopes.

There was only music.

It had never felt this easy before. It cost her no effort. *Why did I need to work so hard?* she thought. She didn't need to. All she needed was to trust herself. Her body did the rest.

It wasn't until they finished that Olesya became aware of the silence.

The stagehands and the sweeper stood in a group, watching them, their faces awed.

Dima breathed hard, looking at something over her shoulder.

Olesya spun around.

In the wings stood Alla Borisovna and Natasha. Alla Borisovna brought up her hands and clapped once, twice, three times. The stagehands joined her.

Olesya blushed and bowed to hide it.

When she looked up, a change had come over Alla Borisovna. She was smiling. She was actually smiling.

"Congratulations, Olesya Belaya," she said, "on becoming our new principal."

Olesya choked on her breath.

Natasha gasped. Her face turned gray. She threw a murderous look at Olesya, uttered a wail, and tore past the dancers arriving for the warmup.

Alla Borisovna didn't move a muscle. "You're not refusing my offer," she said. It wasn't a question, and Olesya didn't see anything anymore.

It all blurred.

21:14

The audience was wild.

"Bravo! Bravo!"

My first standing ovation, Olesya thought, and bowed.

She was both aware and unaware of the pain in her feet, and of the sweat streaming down her back, of her bodice itching. She bowed again and again, the applause washing over her in a hot wave.

This was her moment.

She peered into the audience. It was impossible to see a single face, and still, she searched. One face she longed to see. One face that wasn't there. One face—

The lights went on.

Olesya's breath stopped.

There, in the back of the orchestra, the last row. He got up and waved to her.

Her heart leaped. Could it be? Could it be—

A girl got up next to the man. She was about twelve years old. They walked to the stage and stopped at the barrier.

"That's my Lidochka," Yuri said.

"Hello." Lidochka stared up at Olesya with her mouth open.

Olesya's heart dropped. "Hello," she said. "It's very nice to meet you."

Lidochka seemed to have lost her ability to speak.

Dima tapped on Olesya's shoulder.

"Just a minute," she said, and kneeled. "Do you want to be a ballerina?"

Lidochka nodded.

"Do you like to dance?"

Another nod.

"Why?"

She shrugged.

"Why do you like it?"

"I don't know."

"You don't know?"

"It's because . . ." She hesitated and glanced at Yuri.

"Go on, dorogusha. Tell her."

"I guess it's because . . ." She searched for the words. "It's like I'm not there anymore. Like there's only—"

"Music," Olesya finished.

"Only music." The girl smiled.

Olesya smiled back. "Come visit me in Moscow."

Lidochka looked at Yuri.

"Is that what you want?"

She nodded fiercely.

"Well, then. I guess we're coming for a visit. That all right with you?"

"Of course," Olesya said. "Of course it is."

Lidochka lit up. "Can I see you dance in Moscow?"

"She's tired, dorogusha," Yuri said. "Come on. Let's not pester her with questions."

"But, Papa, I want to see her dance on the Bolshoi stage!"

"You can," Olesya said. "You can come see me."

"Really?" Lidochka did a little hop and clapped.

"Olesya!" Dima called.

"Coming!"

"We'll be going then," Yuri said. "Goodbye."

"Goodbye!" Lidochka waved.

They worked their way through the crowd to the exit doors.

Olesya watched them go, father and daughter.

Then the curtain closed.

Dima walked up to her. "You all right?"

"I am. I am."

SIMFEROPOL–MOSCOW

14 February 1989
15:24

Olesya sat in a train compartment, looking out the window. The long apartment blocks slid by in the warm dusk. The snow was gone. Everything was dripping.

Dima walked in and closed the door behind him.

She didn't move.

He sat across from her, put his arms on the table, laced his hands. Olesya studied his fingers—long and slender, his fine skin.

"Hey," he said.

"Hey."

"Happy to go back?"

"I think so."

They sat in silence.

"Must be freezing in Moscow," she said.

"Oh, it'll warm up. Soon as we step off the train. You know how they say. You bring the warm weather with you." He smiled.

She nodded.

The train whistled and jerked. The platform rolled away in the window.

"I'm moving out," Olesya said.

"Really?"

"Yeah."

"Did you tell your mom?"

"Not yet. I will."

They watched the houses slide by, the trees, the cars on the road.

"Can I ask where?" Dima said.

"Don't know yet."

"Well, you could . . ." He passed his hand through his hair. "I mean, if you need a place to crash, there's always, you know . . ."

She looked at him.

He glanced down.

There was a knock on the door. They both jumped.

The door rolled open. A young attendant, no older than twenty, tall and gangly, poked in his head. He held a tray with two steaming tea holders.

"Good afternoon," he said. He looked from Olesya to Dima and back to Olesya. "My name is Grisha—"

"Grisha?" Olesya's breath stopped.

"Yes. Something wrong?" He swallowed nervously.

"No . . . no. Nothing."

"Your order." Grisha set the tray on the table.

Dima looked at Olesya.

She looked at the tea. "I don't think we ordered any, Grisha."

"You didn't?" Grisha hung his head. "Wrong again. My apologies." He turned to go.

"That's not how you serve tea!" came from the passageway. "On a naked tray! No napkins, no sugar. Christ Almighty. What kind of service is that? Let me show you how it's done before you embarrass yourself any more."

Grisha paled.

Olesya got up. "Yuri?"

Yuri's broad face appeared in the door. "Goodness! Would you look who's here." He passed his eyes over Dima as though he weren't there. "Where you off to?"

"Home. Moscow."

"Why, I'm headed there myself."

"What, already?" Olesya looked him over. "Wait, where's your uniform?"

"To hell with my uniform."

Grisha cleared his throat.

Yuri peered at him. "What're you standing there for, flapping your eyes at me? Go do your job. And if I see you serving tea like this, I'll unscrew your pimply head and serve it on this very tray to your superior, got that? Now move your skinny ass."

Grisha's eyes rounded. "Yes, boss."

"Don't you 'boss' me. Go. Go!"

Grisha jumped as though scalded and hurried off, the glasses jingling in the holders.

Olesya coughed to suppress a giggle.

"Young people these days." Yuri shook his head. "What's the world coming to, eh? You tell me. When all of us old-timers retire, who's going to teach them? Grandpa Lenin?"

"Hold on," Olesya said, "hold on a minute. You quit your job, didn't you?"

"Sure did. Right after that"—he glared at Dima—"*hoodlum* of yours nearly made me into a meat cutlet."

Dima shifted uncomfortably.

"That shook me up proper." Yuri glared at him still. "Got me to think some things over. Think real good."

"Why are you taking the train?" Olesya said. "I thought you hated them."

Yuri grinned. "My last ride. No more bone-shakers for me after this, thank God. It's all my Lidochka, bless her heart.

She said to me, she said, 'Papa, I know you're scared. I'm scared too. Remember what you always tell me? You've got to face your fear until it has no grip on you. It's like a scary toy you can put in your pocket.' "

"Like a scary toy you can put in your pocket," Olesya repeated.

"That's what she did. She said, 'We're doing this together, Papa. You ride the train, and I go on the stage. Deal?' Now, what do you say to that, eh?" He chuckled.

"So you're taking her to Moscow? To visit me?"

"No. A visit is not enough."

"Wait, you mean—"

Yuri nodded. "Sold the house and my Starushka both. Finished it all this morning. Should've done it a long time ago. Don't know what was holding me back."

"You're moving to Moscow?"

His face lit up. "That's right. My Lidochka is going to be a ballerina."

Olesya's breath quickened. "Where is she?"

"Sleeping. Got so excited we're going, couldn't sleep all night, poor girl. I tell you what. Let's eat dinner together. We're in the next compartment." He jabbed his thumb behind him. "What do you say?"

Olesya glanced at Dima.

He sat motionless, his hands gripping his knees.

"Can we both come?"

Yuri squinted. "Come on out here, son. Need to talk a minute."

Dima's eyes widened. He looked at Olesya.

She nodded.

Yuri walked out. Dima followed him.

Olesya closed the door. She tried not to listen to the muffled conversation, which seemed to be one-sided: Yuri's short, punchy words.

A few minutes later Dima walked back in, flushed.

Olesya rose. "What did he say?"

"Said he'll kill me with his bare hands if he finds out I hurt you."

"Then why are you smiling?"

"I don't know. I don't think he meant it. I think it was a kind of . . ."

"What?"

"A blessing."

"A blessing?"

"A blessing."

They looked at each other for a long time.

"He said Raisa left him. Said you helped."

"Oh."

"And he said I should . . . said I need to help you."

"Help me with what?"

Dima took Olesya's hand. They sat down.

"About trying again," Dima began. "I don't mind what happens. Whatever you call it, whatever you see. TUBE or anything."

"I won't see it. I left it at Baba Zina's house."

"Well, it doesn't bother me. Whatever works for you."

She thought about it. "Even if it's something new."

"Even if it's something new."

"And unexpected. And startling. And ugly."

"All of those things."

"And you won't call me a doll."

"I won't. Promise."

She sighed. "I remembered, you know? I stashed TUBE under the bunk, when we were on the train, coming back from Baba Zina's funeral. That compartment I was in, it was the same compartment all these years later. Can you believe it? It's crazy. It's just crazy. I guess it was time for me to find it. Do you think it was a coincidence? Or not a coincidence at all?"

"It could be. It worked though, right? It helped you."

"It did."

"Do you regret it?"

"No. No." She hesitated. "I regret one thing. I thought you and Natasha—I was so sure—"

"I get it. It must've looked like that. I was so stupid."

"You're not mad at me?"

"What? Why would I be mad at you?"

"You don't think . . . you don't think I'm crazy?"

Dima shook his head. "No. Not at all."

"Okay."

"Okay."

They fell quiet.

"You're serious," Dima said. "About moving out."

"I am."

"And . . . is the communal kitchen and bathroom okay with you?"

"Sure," she said quickly. "I don't mind at all."

There was a playful light in his eyes. "My bed is squeaky."

"That's fine."

"I smell really bad, too, at the end of the day."

"I can handle it. I don't smell so good myself."

"There's more."

"Oh?"

He moved closer. "You see, there are nosy neighbors. They like listening at night, listening to the noises people make."

"Great. We'll give them a good show. Are you noisy?"

"Not more than usual. I don't think. Are you?"

"I guess we'll find out."

She looked at him.

He traced her face with his fingers and cupped her chin. And then he was kissing her.

Olesya closed her eyes.

EPILOGUE

"He raped me, Mama."

"He didn't rape you."

"Yes, he did. I remembered. I—"

"He didn't rape you! How can you say something like this about your own father?"

"You knew it. You knew and you did nothing . . . *nothing* to stop him."

"Your father was a difficult man. Sometimes he hurt you, but he always meant you well, Olesya. You must understand."

"I must understand."

"Yes. It was his way of disciplining you. You were an incredibly disagreeable child. Very stubborn. But he'd never do something like this. *Never.* I can't imagine . . . I don't understand why all of a sudden you decided to make up this story—"

"Story? It's not a story, Mama, it's the truth."

"Then why didn't you say anything when it happened?"

"What?"

"Why didn't you say anything?"

"Did you . . . did you just say that? You didn't really just say that, did you?"

"Things like that . . . unspeakable things like that. You don't forget them."

"And you'd know."

"That's not how memory works."

"Really. How does it work?"

"I don't know. I'm not an expert. Why are you asking me?"

"All right, you want facts. I understand. I'll give you facts. The first time he did it, I was five. We were in Alupka for Baba Zina's sixtieth birthday. Remember? Remember that day? I remember it very well. He did it before the party. He was 'disciplining' me, as you like to put it. You all went to the market, but he came back. He was mad at you. For having an abortion. That's why he decided to *discipline* me. That's what loving fathers do to their daughters, right? Right, Mama? So . . . can you tell me about it? Why did you have an abortion?"

"I don't know anything about any abortion."

"Mama, please."

"I'm not listening to this."

"Yes, you *are*."

"You're giving me a headache—"

"Oh, I'm giving you a headache. Good. That's very good. It means you're actually listening to me. You don't think I tried telling you? Okay, fine. Maybe I didn't tell you with words, but what about my body? What about my bloody diarrhea? Me not eating? Not sleeping? Wetting the bed? Didn't any of it alert you? Didn't you see it? What was wrong with you, Mama? Were you *blind*?"

"You don't need to yell at me."

"Yes, I do! For once, I do! Because being quiet didn't do *shit* for me! And neither for you! Look at yourself. Look at the life you lead. You're—you're— Remember that drawing I did? At Baba Zina's party. Head, Bodies, and Legs? Remember, Mama?"

"Yes, I remember."

"And?"

"And what? What do you want me to say?"

"Why did you think I drew it?"

"It's impossible. Your father . . . he's quite large, bigger than average. I just can't see how—"

"Neither could I, until it was *in* me."

"How can you—"

"Listen. I want you to listen, Mama, and I want you to know. I want you to know what it felt like. It felt like dying. I really believed it. I really thought I'd die. It was too much for me. So I created this game in my mind. I thought we were playing TUBE. It wasn't Papa, not really. It was TUBE riding through me, like through a tunnel. No big deal. Papa must've caught on to it later. How convenient for him, right? He started calling it that. 'Do you want to play TUBE?' he'd ask me. He asked me in front of you. And you didn't have a clue. It gave him a sick satisfaction doing it. Knowing that you didn't know. That you had no idea. But you suspected. I mean, you're no dummy. You knew something was wrong. So you came back home that one night, remember? When you had a school meeting? You walked in on us. You walked in on Papa raping me. And you did nothing. *Nothing.* Why, Mama? Why? *Why?* Oh, there is no point asking you, is there? I just want you to know one thing. You helped him kill me. That day he did it for the first time, I died. And after that, I wasn't really living, Mama. I was dead. Dead inside me."

"That's a terrible accusation."

"Is it?"

"A terrible accusation to make."

"I see. I'll try one last time. He's dead. Papa is dead. You don't have to keep it secret anymore. You can let go."

"We'll talk tomorrow."

"There won't be a tomorrow. I'm moving out, Mama. Goodbye."

EXTRA PIECES IN THE BOX

SLEEP WELL, PAPA

A SHORT STORY BY
KSENIA ANSKE

But it was in a dream, though, that it happened, and dreams don't count.

— Lyudmila Petrushevskaya,
There Once Lived a Woman Who Tried to Kill Her Neightbor's Baby: Scary Fairy Tales

Papa came to me in a dream. He said the first time he did it was in the bathroom. He was washing me.

"Why?" I asked.

"I don't know," he said. "You were so little, so sweet. You liked it."

The other time I saw him running out of the bedroom, naked.

I said, "Don't do this. Why are you doing this? It's disgusting."

He laughed, said, "What's so disgusting about it? Look."

"I don't want to," I said.

I woke up.

* * *

He came again and he trapped me, wouldn't let me go. Said, "I want to show you." Dragged me with him to the bed. We fought, and I lost.

My alarm started ringing.

I jerked awake and sat and breathed for a long time. There was so much sweat.

That day I didn't go to work.

* * *

That night I set the alarm an hour back.

He showed up the moment I closed my eyes. "You like seeing me. That's why you keep coming."

"Leave me alone," I said. "I need to sleep. I didn't come here to see you. I don't want to see you."

"Tough luck," he said, and he dragged me deeper.

It was an outhouse. It was dark and it stank. He suspended me over the hole and said, "Are you scared?"

"Let go of me."

I thrashed. He was stronger. He pushed me into the hole. I sank in halfway.

"You know what you have to do," he said.

"I don't care."

"Oh yes, you do. How about this?" He pressed on my head.

"Don't."

"Do it."

"No."

"I said, do it!"

I did.

I woke up gagging, fell out of my bed, and retched. The vomit steamed on the carpet.

It was dark, two hours before the alarm.

The next night I didn't go to bed at all.

I drank three cups of coffee around midnight, and by four in the morning I was wide awake and grinning.

I won.

* * *

That day at work I dozed.

He was there right away.

"Did you miss me?" he said.

"Get out! Out!"

"I knew you'd come. It's not like you have a choice."

"I said, out. Get out of my dreams!"

"They're your dreams, aren't they? It means you want me in them."

* * *

I stumbled home that night and fell asleep while eating dinner, my head on the table.

He didn't even talk to me. He stripped me, shoved me in his car. It was freezing. I hugged myself. My teeth chattered like crazy.

"Where are you taking me?"

"You'll see."

There was nothing to see. Only the dark and the white below it. Snow.

"Papa?"

"Be quiet."

"You can't keep me forever, you know."

"You're so naïve."

"It's only a dream."

He smiled. "Is it? Feels plenty real to me."

I pinched myself. "Wake up. Wake up, dammit." Slapped my cheeks. "Come on."

He stopped the car. "We're here."

It was our old house.

He hauled me out of the car, pushed me to the door. "Get in."

I took a step, another, turned, and ran. I could run with my eyes closed. I knew every rock, every tree, every pit in the ground. The snow froze my feet. It didn't matter. I was free.

I'd just keep running until I woke up.

* * *

I never did.

Not that night, not the next, not the week after. He kept me in the house, in the upstairs bedroom, locked. He fed me, let me use the bathroom, let me wash myself, always there, always watching.

After a week I didn't think it a dream anymore. It felt real. There were neighbors. Cars in the street. Stray dogs. Some kids came to the backyard alley, smoked cigarettes, had a snowball fight. I watched them from my window. I wanted to open it, shout.

He stood behind me, his hand on my neck. "You want to go out? Want to join them?"

"No."

"Don't lie to me."

"I'm not."

He tightened his fingers.

"I'm not, Papa, I promise."

"I don't believe you."

"But, Papa—"

"Kneel."

"But—"

"Kneel!"

I did. And in my head, I planned my escape.

If I couldn't leave him, I'd take him with me.

* * *

The next morning he came to my bedroom before I woke up. I felt his breath on my cheek.

"I know you're awake," he said. "No use pretending."

"I'm not sure if I'm awake or not anymore."

"I thought it was your dream."

"I don't think so now."

"And what do you think?"

"I think it's real. I think you're real. I think you and I can live here together like you always wanted to, without Mama. What do you say?"

He looked at me. "I don't like this."

"What?"

"You're playing me."

"Why would I do that?"

"You hate this. I know you, and I know you hate this. I won't let you go until I teach you to love it. Then you'll stay on your own. You'll not want to leave."

The prospect chilled me. "I want to stay."

"Too fast."

I paid for my lie.

* * *

That night I didn't go to sleep after he was done with me. I lay under the covers, still. Then I had it. I crawled out of my bed and crept out of the room and down the stairs. He was in his bed, asleep. I climbed in with him.

"Papa."

"Hmm."

"What are you dreaming about?"

"You."

"What am I doing?"

"Eating dinner."

And so I went into his dream and came back out in my kitchen. I was eating pasta. Papa was sitting across the table, watching me slurp it up and chew.

"You want some?" I said.

"No, thank you. I've already had dinner."

"There's plenty more in the pot."

"I said no."

"Just trying to be hospitable."

"You don't need to be hospitable. It's not your dream, it's mine."

"You sure about that?" I twisted the fork in the pasta and smiled.

He shifted in the seat. "What's there to be sure about?"

"The dream. Whose do you think it is?"

"This is a pointless conversation."

"You're scared."

"Finish your dinner."

"Scared because you're not sure, are you?"

"We're going." He stood up.

"I'm not going anywhere. I'm staying. I kind of like it here. Nice kitchen. Nice food." I scraped the last of the pasta to the edge of the plate and licked it off. "I want seconds."

He understood then and made a dash for the door. I was already on my feet. I sprang after him, leaped on his back like a monkey.

"You're not going anywhere without me," I said.

"Get off."

"Tough luck, Papa."

He rammed his back against the wall. It knocked the breath out of me. I held on.

"Nice try," I said. "It's not real, remember? It's your dream. You want me here, don't you?"

"Get off me."

"You know what you have to do," I said.

"No."

"Suit yourself. I like it here."

"No!"

He ran out the door.

It was like when I was little, riding him piggy-back. I curled my legs around his waist, held on to his neck. He panted hard, ran himself into exhaustion. Tried shaking me off a few times.

In the end he gave up. We ran all the way to my work and past it, to the railway and to the woods behind it, stopped by the dark, slow river.

There he collapsed.

"You got what you wanted," he said.

"Not yet."

"What else."

"It's obvious, isn't it?"

He looked at me.

I looked at my watch.

"No," he said.

I shrugged. "I'm in no hurry."

He was breathing fast. "Let's go back. Just you and me. In the house. Wasn't it nice?"

"I didn't know the dead could dream," I said. "Didn't know their dreams were so boring."

A train went by. We both looked up and watched it disappear in the haze.

He sat up. "The dead don't sleep," he said.

"In my dream they do."

"We talked about this." He got to his feet.

"Did we?"

I was fast.

I hunched my shoulders, tucked in my neck, and ran at him, drove my head into his stomach. He doubled over. I pushed him in the river. It wasn't deep here, but the bank was steep, and he couldn't swim. I watched him struggle, call to me, watched him recognize the look in my eyes.

That's when he sank.

* * *

I woke up in my bathroom.

The water was running over the edge of the tub. It was cold. I stirred it around.

"Sleep well, Papa," I said. "I know I will."

THANK YOU

This book wouldn't be possible without all of you who helped it come out of the dark tunnel—no pun intended. Despite my fears. My doubts. My hesitations. You told me this story had to be told. It's for you that I wrote it.

If I forgot to include your name, please forgive me.

Thank you.

Thank you to Alexander Chee for tweeting, "I wish Amtrak had residencies for writers."

Thank you to Amtrak for making it a reality, for selecting me as one of the winners and for giving me this book idea.

Thank you to my beta readers for heartfelt and honest feedback: Aditya Thakur, Alora Wogsland, Amani AlShaali, Andrew Flynn, Annette Thomas, Annie Pavese, Ayla Ault, Caspar Menke, Catalina Jaramillo, Danielle Caro, Eric Avedissian, Helen Naylor, Gabriel Novo, Glenn Battle, Heather Dannewitz, Jeff Bergstrand, Jennie Richmond, Jenrieshka Aërin, Jonathon Goodfellow, Julian Hill, Katie Lee Cook, Karl J. Folk, Lily Matilda, Myra Ahmad, Nanci Behseresht, Nandi Cook, Lizzie Ward, Prachi Percy Sharma, Regina Roi, Richard Quaal, Samantha Davenport, Sandra Hould, Susan Albrecht, Susan Papas, Thomas Paxton, Valentina Zaitseva.

Thank you to my Patreon patrons for funding this book: Allen Lucas, Amy Frank, Amy L. Sauder, Andrei Podoprigora, Anna Girardini, Anna Shatrova, Anya Milioutina, Asher London, Beth Morey, Brent Chambers, Cat VanBilliard, Catherine W., Charming Cookie Jar, Chris Mahan, Christie Stratos, Christina M. Gregory, Claire Coates, Claudette Colombi, Cookie Arnone, Dani Duck, Deborah Beale, Erin Greene, Eve, Francesca Moroney, Gardening Angel, Gene Trujillo, Hans von Totenland, Iole Alessandrini, Jacques de Villiers, Jaye Tomas, Jennifer Esther Wieland, Jessica Degarmo, John Hays, Joshua Long, Kate Martyniouk, Katherine Stevens, Ken Wallo, Kent Oz, Kevin Lewis, Kim Winey, Kiri Callaghan, Liam Hayes, Lillith Black, Lindsey Rampton, Lizz Dubs, Michael Edlund, Nicolas Lemieux, Nikos Papageorgiou, Paul Casey, Paula Smith, Rachel Barnard, Rhiannon Louve, Roger Bigney, Samantha Davenport, Sara Amundson, Sir Steven Wilkinson, Stephanie Reed, Vera Golosova, Yanick Luechinger.

Thank you to my team for putting it all together: Anya Milioutina, Sarah Grace Liu, Sandeep Likhar, Spencer Borup, Vera Golosova.

Thank you to Ksenia Mineeva, Bolshoi Ballet ballerina, for invaluable input.

Thank you to Pacific Northwest Ballet dancers and teachers for answering my questions.

Thank you to my kids Anya and Peter for letting me disappear for five years to finish this project. I love you so much.

Thank you to my partner Royce for patiently listening to every draft of this book. If not for you, my love, I wouldn't be a writer.

And, lastly, thank you to all the Little Olesyas out there—who are still silent. You have inspired me to give this story a voice. For that, I'm eternally grateful.

BEFORE YOU GO

Dear Reader,

Thank you for reading this book. I hope you enjoyed it. I even hope it gave you a nightmare or two. After all, it was supposed to scare you, didn't it?

If you want more people to read it, please take a minute to review it on Amazon or Goodreads (or both!). It would mean the world to me. And to someone else, who will enjoy this book as much as you did.

BE SURE TO ALSO READ

Rosehead

Misunderstood and overmedicated, twelve-year-old Lilith Bloom finds the prospect of a grand family reunion decidedly dull . . . That is, until she discovers that the rose garden surrounding her grandfather's Berlin mansion is, well, completely and utterly carnivorous. Armed with Panther, her talking pet whippet, and the help of the mute boy next door, Lilith must unravel the secrets behind the mysterious estate, all while her family remains gloriously unaware that they are about to be devoured.

Irkadura

Neglected since birth by her mother, Irina Myshko hasn't spoken a word for most of her short Soviet life. Outcast as a mute idiot and abused by her mother's boyfriends, she escapes into an alternate reality where true natures show and people are revealed as the beasts they are. Pregnant, homeless, and penniless, Irina has to make a choice — learn to live in this splintered world or descend into madness.

The Badlings

Of all of the naughty, mischievous, disrespectful, and downright horrible things that children can be, a badling is perhaps one of the worst. Badlings abandon books without finishing them, leaving their characters sad and lonely—not to mention angry. Meet Bells, Peacock, Rusty, and Grand, four ragtag friends convicted of this monstrous crime. As punishment, they get sucked into a book of unfinished stories, whose patchwork pages they must traverse . . . and read to the end this time.

Siren Suicides

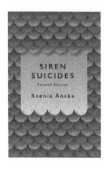

On a rainy September morning 16-year-old Ailen Bright flees her abusive father by jumping off the Seattle Aurora Bridge. Instead of a true death, in the water she finds several silver-skinned sirens who convert her to one of their own. As a newborn siren she is dead, supernaturally strong, and hungry for her new sustenance—human souls. Ailen refuses to kill . . . at first. With time she must face the agony that comes with starvation, while being relentlessly pursued by a siren hunter. An enthralling and dark look into the mind and heart of a suicidal teenager, this urban fantasy follows Ailen's struggle to figure out the meaning of life, her confusing feelings for her best friend Hunter, and her desperate battle for her father's love.

ABOUT THE AUTHOR

Photo by Deanna Teasley

Ksenia Anske was born in Moscow, Russia, and came to the US in 1998. She is the author of dark fantasy short fiction and 7 novels, and the resident writer of the Amtrak Residency Program 2015. Her novel Rosehead won Honorary Mention in the YA Category in the Indie Ebook Award 2016. Ksenia lives in Seattle with her partner Royce Daniel and her son Peter.

CONNECT WITH KSENIA ANSKE

Twitter @kseniaanske
Facebook/kseniaanskeauthor
Instagram @kseniaanske
TikTok @kseniaanske
YouTube/kseniaanske
Pinterest/kseniaanske
Website www.kseniaanske.com